THE ATTENDANT

TONY POWERS

Black Rose Writing | Texas

ISBN: 978-1-68433-922-8
PUBLISHED BY BLACK ROSE WRITING
www.blackrosewriting.com

Printed in the United States of America
Suggested Retail Price (SRP) $19.95

The Attendant is printed in Gentium Book Basic

*As a planet-friendly publisher, Black Rose Writing does its best to eliminate unnecessary waste to reduce paper usage and energy costs, while never compromising the reading experience. As a result, the final word count vs. page count may not meet common expectations.

Cover Design: Howard S. Puris

For my family, blood and chosen.

ONE

Richard Alleroy sat reading his paper as he sipped his second cup of coffee. The geraniums, hollyhocks, and daisies his wife Margaret had planted along the west wall of their large terrace would soon be blooming. As would the periwinkles, lily of the valley and Jacob's ladder over on the shadier side. He folded his Wall Street Journal neatly, stood and looked out over the East River. The sun was still low in the Eastern sky. It would be a pleasant Monday. After a short while he called for his car to be out front in thirty minutes. He walked inside and upstairs to the master where his wife still lay sleeping, her blindfold and earphones ensuring she would not be roused by his daily six-thirty a.m. ablutions. In the bathroom he brushed his teeth, took off his silk dressing gown and carefully stepped into the large glass enclosed shower. He allowed himself to luxuriate for a minute beneath the rain shower and in the generous massaging spray that came from each of the six jets. He showered and shaved, put on deodorant, combed his hair, and dried himself. He went into his large drawer-lined walk-in closet to dress. As he buttoned his shirt his eyes traveled over the two dozen bespoke suits hanging neatly and put on one of the midnight blue single-breasted chalk-striped ones. He put on a dark blue tie with white polka-dots and made a neat four-in-hand knot. He grabbed a crisp white linen handkerchief from another drawer and made his way back downstairs. In his study he grabbed his briefcase and headed down the hall to the front door. He paused in front of the hall mirror to study his reflection. As he straightened the pinch in his tie he decided he would order two of the same style suits as the one he had on. Of late, he'd become partial to the soft-shouldered two-button single-breasted kind believing they made him look younger than his fifty-six years. His measurements hadn't changed, but if they needed him to come in for a fitting he could combine this with a visit to the London office. He shook the handkerchief open, pushed it down into his suit jacket's breast pocket, careful to make sure it showed to his satisfaction, picked up his briefcase and walked out of the front door to take their private elevator down to his idling Mercedes, now double-parked in front of his building - and being watched by his doorman.

•   •   •

At 6:30 A.M. Emanuel Graves 48, now living in The Bronx, fumbled for the remote one of his rickety TV tray tables, this one used as a night table, and turned on his twenty-four-inch TV which was set to one of the news channels. Not the Right leaning one. He stretched, got out of his sofa bed, padded the four steps to his small bathroom and relieved himself. He moved to his kitchenette, turned on the cold water and opened the small refrigerator. He let the water run until it was clear and cold while he poured himself half a glass of orange juice concentrate. Satisfied that the water was cold enough he added it to the juice. He shook his pills from their vials into his palm, popped them into his mouth and washed them down with the watered juice. On TV they were showing some billionaire rocketing into space. *He should try to rocket across town.* He stood watching the news for a minute as he sipped his juice. He took a small pot out of the sink and filled it with enough water to make a cup of instant and set it on the hot plate. He preferred this method of making his morning coffee over using his small microwave for this. While waiting for the water to boil he measured a spoonful of instant coffee into his cup and took a slice of Wonder Bread and the margarine from the fridge and put it the bread into the toaster. On TV the news people were talking about people being blocked from voting. *I'm so glad I fought a war for this.* He stood waiting for the toast to pop up. When it did, he gingerly removed it, placed it on a piece of paper towel and smoothed the margarine over it. He returned the margarine to the fridge door and reached for the container of milk on the shelf, smelled it, and deciding it was still good added some to his coffee. He opened another tray table, placed the toast and coffee on it, sat down on the bed, pulled the tray to him and eyed the TV as he ate his meager breakfast. He finished his breakfast and placed the TV tray back under the bed where it lived. He washed his cup and placed it in the small dish rack next to the sink. He blew his nose in the paper towel, crumpled it and placed it in the plastic shopping bag which hung from one of the kitchen cabinet's knobs. He yawned and stretched mightily. He walked over to the window to check the sky, then walked back to smooth his bedding and closed his sofa-bed. He went back into his bathroom, had his morning evacuation, *gotta get toilet paper*, brushed his teeth at the sink and then stepped into the narrow shower stall which was crammed into the small bathroom. With his elbows hitting the stall shower's plastic curtain and making a thunk as they hit its metal walls he showered quickly. *Have to buy soap too.* He toweled himself off and put on the clean underwear he took from a small three drawer night stand on the other side of what was now his couch. From the cardboard armoire in the corner, next to the stacks of books on the floor, he took out his one pair of neatly shined black shoes and a wire hanger that held jeans and a work shirt. Today he'd wear jeans and a couple of days later he would wear cargo pants. He put his clothes on and placed the shoes in a small athletic bag. He then took his black pants and white shirt off another wire hanger, folded them neatly and place them in the small bag on top of the shoes - one of which held a small combination lock and a black bowtie.

•   •   •

The car phone rang as Alleroy was passing the Thirty-Fourth Street exit ramp on the FDR Drive. He could see it was his daughter Anne. He lowered Chopin's Nocturne, one of the pieces that relaxed him during each morning's drive to the office and answered.

"Hi sweetheart," he said, keeping his eyes on the road as they spoke.

"Daddy, Emily and I just spoken with Tante Amélie and she would love it if we came and spent three weeks with her after graduation."

Anne was one of his eighteen year old twin daughters. Emily was the other. Alleroy was the father of four. The twins and their two younger brothers; Richard Jr. seventeen, and Royce, sixteen.

"And we can join you guys on the Cote in July," she said.

Alleroy turned the suggestion over in his mind and said; "Yes...it'll be good for you both - but you'll speak with your mother about it, yes?"

"Of course," she replied, knowing her mother would agree.

After they said their goodbyes, Alleroy raised the music and continued on down the Drive. He exited at South Street and, as usual, found himself in traffic. He made his stop-and-go way slowly up Broad Street to Wall Street and finally pulled into his garage. As he got out a valet got in and the car disappeared down the ramp. Alleroy then briskly walked the two blocks to his office at 111 Wall and entered the building. He strode through the lobby to the bank of elevators and stood waiting with the others for one of the elevators that would take him up to the offices of Merrill, Harkness, Hirsch, Alleroy, Perlman and Smythe, where he was key man and general partner - the man who managed the money. A tall man approached him.

"Rich, been a while, how's the family?" He held out his hand. Don Crane was a long-time friend and belonged to the Yale chapter of Alleroy's fraternity.

"Don...I know, too long." He shook Don's hand. "Margaret's well thanks, she's still very involved with The Children's Aid Society and Foster Pride. I honestly don't know where she finds the time. And the girls are preparing to enter Harvard in the fall. You're well? The family?"

"Bess is good. The kids too. And I'm still a fourteen handicap. I took a triple bogey the other day." He shook his head. "The boys?"

"Um...Junior and Royce are both leaning towards your alma mater. I guess UChicago isn't to their liking." He let out a short laugh.

Alleroy's twin eighteen year old daughters, Emily and Anne, would be graduating from Phillips Exeter June sixth and entering University in the fall. Alleroy's two sons, Richard Jr. and Royce, also at Exeter, would be entering their senior and junior years, respectively, in the fall. They were fairly bright, motivated, and *very* ambitious. Both twins wanted to practice corporate law, Richard Jr. has his sights set on the Foreign Service Office with a view towards becoming a diplomat and Royce had already displayed a keen interest in investment banking. Their combined tuitions and living expenses when all was said and done would exceed 2 million dollars. An out-of-the-question outrageous sum for anyone who wasn't anywhere near as fabulously wealthy as he was.

"Harvard and Yale...your future thanksgivings oughta be real fun. By the by, you and Meg will be getting an invitation to a dinner we're having for Senator Railler next month," Don said. "Hey, you saw that thing about Jack Loomis in the Times?"

Alleroy had indeed seen that Jack Loomis, a mutual friend and business associate had been killed recently in a hit-and-run accident. "I know," he said, "lousy break huh?"

One of the six elevators arrived and the two men, along with others, shuffled into the car. Don leaned close and whispered in Alleroy's ear.

"I saw him what...two week ago," he said, "hit-and-run? It's crazy. They'll get the son-of-a-bitch."

"I hope so," Alleroy said as he shook his head, "for his family's sake."

People were getting off as the elevator climbed upward.

"Imagine, April first." Don said, "You know his wife laughed it off at first when she got the call? She thought it was someone's dumb idea of an April fool's prank."

The two men grew silent as the elevator moved upward, Don getting off on twelve and Alleroy continuing on up to twenty-one. *April fool's day, Jesus...Some joke.*

Alleroy's office was one of the two prized corner offices on the large floor. Upon entering it his new assistant Georgia gave him his messages along with another cup of coffee. He flipped his computer on and checked a few numbers as he sipped his coffee. He finished his coffee, stretched, rose, and headed off to the executive bathroom which was just a few steps down the hall. Fifteen minutes later he returned to his desk. He returned to the numbers on his computer screen. It was then he noticed the small envelope addressed in typeface to Mr. Alleroy. He opened it, read its contents, got up at once, went out into the offices and scanned the area. Everyone was sitting where they should be. He went into the corridor and looked each way. No one was there. He made his way back to his own office.

"Georgia, did you see anyone go into my office in the last fifteen minutes?"

"Actually, I was in the copy room sir."

"Never mind," he said scanning the trading floor again. "It's nothing." *Only my fucking life.*

He went back into his office, closed the door and stared at the type-written note that had alarmed him;

I know. Detroit City & County Employees' Retirement System, Havermayer Village Affordable Housing, RCD Pension, Breedland Pension, all of it. Meet me this morning 9:30 sharp. I'll be sitting on a bench near the Hayes drinking fountain, Mannahatta Park.

TWO

The blinking garish neon sign read OTEL DE EVAN. The Hotel Delevan, no longer a hotel, now just a low rent rooming house in the South Bronx, was where Emanuel's room was. Emanuel William Graves had a routine, and he didn't appreciate a long train delay cutting into this routine. The announcement said that a train had broken down at Prospect Avenue so this morning he would ultimately lose a precious three quarters of an hour courtesy of the New York subway system. Each morning, weather permitting, before going into work he would sit in Mannahatta Park on Wall Street reading and feeding the birds and squirrels. The park was two blocks long and a half block wide and ended at The East River. It was mostly filled during the day with people who worked in the area, and this was mainly at lunch time. By ten at night it was pretty much deserted save for the occasional dog-walker. Some of the benches in the park were in a covered area but Emanuel preferred a bench near the fountain which was in an uncovered area. He always had a book in his pocket. Today he had his dog-eared copy of Lao Tzu's *The Way of Life*. Along with today's book, and as was his habit, he always had a small baggie of birdseed and nuts. Feeding the park's creatures had a soothing effect on him. In general, all animals did - and he regretted that he couldn't have a pet. A cat. He loved cats and, as far as he was concerned, anyone who didn't love cats, or at least like or admire them, was someone not to be trusted.

Each working day, of which there were six, he walked to the Intervale Avenue el station to catch the number two train to Wall and William Streets. He was glad that he was able to get a seat on the train this morning. Some mornings he had to stand all the way to Times Square before he could get a seat. One morning the conductor refused to open the door for him and the others who were standing at the closed doors - even though the train was standing stock-still for at least a minute. Emanuel became incensed after thirty seconds or so had passed and they had all pleaded for the conductor to open the doors. Finally, he lost it and screamed in rage at the conductor; "YOU FUCKING...YOU STUPID—WE'RE ALL WORKING FOR A LIVING HERE!" And after being held for at least a full minute, when the train pulled away from the station Emanuel yelled after it; "LIFE ISN'T TOUGH ENOUGH YOU FUCKING ROBOT MORON!" He was glad that only happened once, but it brought back home to him the intense anger he still could not shake.

At this time of year it was then a pleasant five minute walk from the Wall Street station to his favorite bench in the small park. And as it turns out, Mannahatta Park was not only a block from where *he* worked but also a block from Richard Alleroy's office. Emanuel liked sitting out in the open air since he spent his working day inside in conditions he rather disliked. *I know I would have made a great firefighter...A damn great firefighter. You have to play the hand you're dealt Manny.* It was this mindset that got him through the first Gulf war almost thirty years prior - and which was again getting him through. This particular day there was a train delay. There were too many of these delays of late. *Lots of our money for the Pentagon though.*

It was a nice morning. Sunny and unseasonably warm for mid-April. Emanuel took notice of the people walking to work. The women were beginning to shed the many warm layers of down that had covered their curves for months, and the men were now without coats, hatless, scarfless and in lighter weight suits. This was Emanuel's favorite part of his day. The part of the day he looked forward to every waking morning of every working day. These two hours now, thanks to the MTA, cut to one-and-a-half, were Emanuel's hours of grace. This morning as he walked, making an effort to take his mind off of the New York subway system, he was thinking about the woman in the elevator. He had just come home from work with his Chinese take-out. *She has to be in her forties. Nice looking...a Latina. Likes Chinese food. She was going to ten.* She had dropped her key as she pressed the elevator button and Emanuel had picked them up for her. She thanked him and asked if the restaurant was nearby because she just moved in and loved Chinese food. *She smiled at me. I don't know...*

He entered the pocket park and headed for the bench near the fountain on which he sat six mornings every week. *And...we have company today.* Richard Alleroy was seated at the very bench that Emanuel Graves called his own. As he approached the bench he noticed the well-dressed man was nervously looking each way. George and Gracie, the two squirrels Emanuel brought nuts to six mornings a week, were gamboling nearby. *They know the routine. Smarter than most people.* He sat down at one end of the bench and Alleroy thought; *there are all these empty benches in this park and this guy has to sit down next to me?* Emanuel took his book and the small plastic bag of peanuts from his pocket and threw two nuts onto the path. The two squirrels immediately hurried over, grabbed the nuts, and scampered away. *Run, the kids are waiting.* As Emanuel watched them scurry off Alleroy looked at his wrist and realized in his panic he'd left his watch on the sink when he washed his hands after going to his office bathroom. He reached into his inside breast pocket for his cell phone and further realized that in his haste to get to this bench he'd left *it* on his desk. *And I'm always on the kids for putting their cells on restaurant tables. Christ.* He took a sideways glance at Emanuel. *Could this be the guy? Or an emissary? Looking like this?* He sat there waiting for Emanuel to make the first move - if he was, indeed, an emissary.

After five minutes of waiting - while Emanuel fed the squirrels and birds - Alleroy finally turned to Emanuel and said, "Excuse me, but do you have the time?"

Emanuel looked up at the clear blue cloudless sky and after a few seconds said; "By the sun...I make it...a little after nine."

Alleroy stared at him, "Why don't you just look at your watch?"

Emanuel heard exasperation in the man's tone. "It isn't set," Emanuel replied calmly.

Alleroy shook his head. *What the...What is this?* "Then why the hell do you wear the damn—never mind."

Emanuel shot him a quick glance. *The hell does this guy care?* Alleroy continued to look up and down the park's path. All the other benches were still mostly unoccupied. He looked at Emanuel. "Um...have you by any chance been...sent here?"

Have I been sent here? Emanuel, in a bit of a pissy mood already because of the train delay cutting into his "fresh air time" - and then this nervous stranger who looked as if the universe had caved in on him sitting on his bench, and who had the nerve to get annoyed that he was wearing a watch that wasn't set - as if it was *his* business - *and* who had just asked him a strangely cryptic question, decided he would offer an equally strange and cryptic answer.

"Haven't we all?"

Haven't we all? We're playing games? Alleroy decided to be more direct. "By who? Who sent you?"

Already annoyed by the interruption in his morning's routine; Emanuel was now moved to fuck with this annoying stranger;

"C'mon...you don't know?"

Already on tilt, Alleroy was getting even more unnerved. "A man or a woman?" Was it Gene? *Jesus, is it that traitor Gene? But...what the hell does he know anyway?*

Gene was Alleroy's long-time former assistant who had recently left for a new position at another company in Boston and who had been replaced by Georgia.

"Yes. It was Gene." Emanuel was amused by this bizarre game.

What is this guy talking about? It can't be Gene. "Why are you...You think this is funny?"

"Judging by the way you look friend I'd say it was anything but."

A squirrel appeared on the path. Emanuel threw a nut. The squirrel picked it up in its paws and juggled it for a few seconds before scurrying away. Emanuel studied this man who was asking him these strange questions.

"*Did* Gene send you? Are you here on behalf of someone who left a note on my desk a few minutes ago?"

"And if I am?"

"How much do they want?"

Emanuel continued to look at him. "If I were to go by that suit, I'd say a lot."

It was now Alleroy's turn to stare at Emanuel.

Emanuel, who played chess at a high level - and made a living at it in the Marines - did the New York Times crossword in ink every day, breezed through the puns and anagram puzzles in the Times *and* the British periodicals, usually correctly answered most of the questions on Jeopardy, and loved word games and puzzles of all sorts, couldn't resist playing along with whatever this thing was. Besides that, he now genuinely wanted to know what this man was talking about. What he was afraid of. If it was one thing he was attuned to it was fear. "Why are you so nervous?"

"A man or a woman?"

"Like I said, could be. So, why are you so on edge?"

If this guy is just an intermediary it stands to reason he doesn't know much more than who sent him here...or who gave him his instructions. Alleroy turned sharply to stare at Emanuel. He watched him as Emanuel threw some birdseed onto the path and in a flash a dozen pigeons were there to feed. *You're real cagey, aren't you?*

"Nice that you do that. Some days I also come out here and feed them." *Filthy things.*

Emanuel remained silent. *Sure you do.*

"So...What? You're...an intermediary?"

"What's a mythical three humped camel?" Emanuel smiled at him. "Look...My name is Emanuel. Emanuel Graves. What's *your* name friend?"

Graves? Friend? Is this guy threatening me? Am I being threatened? Did they send this guy to...to scare me? Harm me? But why would they do that? This has to be about a pay-off.

"So? What's your name?"

Alleroy continued to stare at him. *Wouldn't he already know my name?* He turned away. *They must've just shown him my picture.*

"Yeah...you don't want to tell someone like me your name do you? Well, whatever your name is you got that look on your face.

He doesn't know my—that look? What look?

Emanuel looked up at the sky. "Too bad I don't have much more time to play. So who are you expecting?"

Alleroy, his brow furrowed, again stared at Emanuel. This time for some five seconds "You've no idea what I'm talking about do you?" He continued to stare at Emanuel. "*Do you?*"

Richard Alleroy who prided himself on being the baddest shark in the tank and a great reader of people made a decision; He took the crumpled note from his pocket smoothed it out and showed it to Emanuel. "Do you know anything about this?"

His eyes narrowed as he watched Emanuel read the note. "Well? Do you?"

"I know that *someone* knows something they're not *supposed* to know?"

Alleroy leaned in and stared at Emanuel. "Who?"

Emanuel rose, again looking at the sky. "I have to go. Nice talking to you. Maybe I'll see you again.

Alleroy leaned back again. *Is this a threat?*

Emanuel scattered the rest of the birdseed on the path. Alleroy sat there watching him out of the corner of his eye. *Jesus man...Get a grip! You're imagining something that isn't real. This guy isn't anyone. He's a nobody! A lonely guy who feeds pigeons. He doesn't know anything. What the hell am I doing here? What look on my face? Where is this fucking person - because this guy can't be anyone who knows anything about this...or anything else?* Alleroy got up, and still looking around he walked to the fountain and took a drink. *Calm down, you're right. I'll give whoever this person is another half-hour.* He returned to the bench and sat back down. Emanuel turned to leave.

"I guess a guy's got to keep himself in suits right? Uh, not for nothing but...that look on your face...Trust me pal, I've seen it before."

You've seen what look before? Idiot. Alleroy ignored him as Emanuel picked up his athletic bag and walked away. *Where the hell is this person? I'll give them whatever they want but where are they?*

THREE

He crossed the street hardly bothering to look at the oncoming traffic. *What a strange morning. What the hell was that guy talking about? He looked freaked out about something, that's for sure. You never know about people...they look like they have it all and still...*

Emanuel W. Graves was a veteran of the first Gulf war. A war he saw combat in when he was nineteen years of age. The war that came to be known as the video game war. The war they showed live. The war they put music to. Besides Gulf War Syndrome, his other reward for fighting in that war was a gastrointestinal disorder and, considering his job, the irony was too deliciously cruel. *Maybe the more you have the more problems you have. Yeah Manny, you tell yourself you're just fine without a pot to piss in. More fucking irony? Guy looked like a dead man.* A car backfired. A sudden flash of an all-too-familiar terrifying image shot through his mind's eye. *No, no! Not now! We're under attack!* The explosions and screams... the thud of artillery shells and tank shells...*Oh God! Take cover! Take cover!* He placed himself flat against the wall. A full three minutes passed as he told himself; *it's alright. You're here. In New York.*

Going to work. It's alright. He stood there until the shooting and screaming had subsided. Until his trembling ceased and he had calmed himself. And until his breathing had returned to normal.

He was finally able to continue on down Water Street to The Coach and Crown Restaurant. For almost twenty-two years whenever he left the park to take this walk his mood turned from somewhat buoyant to bitter. *They fucked you man. Fucked you real good.* This feeling was impossible to avoid. All the philosophy in the books on Zen and all the books he continually read on the nature of existence, while they helped to somewhat temporarily ameliorate his bitterness and anger, this daily walk down Water Street re-darkened his mood with each step bringing him closer to The Coach and Crown. *Slowly I turned...Step by step...you hadda laugh. Or try.* Another half a block. *Here we go...another day, another dollar...literally.* A few more steps and he was there.

He took a deep breath and entered the restaurant. Lou, the day bartender was spraying Windex on the large mirror behind the bar as Emanuel walked across the room. The day waiters were setting up their stations. One thing he was thankful for was that the C & C didn't open until eleven so he didn't have to work during a breakfast. He walked up to the bar.

"Manny."

"Morning Louie." Emanuel laid a ten on the bar and made his way to a small corridor in the rear corner of the restaurant and through a door to the lockers to change into his work clothes. A few of the waiters greeted him as he passed. In the small locker room he opened a locker, took off his jeans and denim work shirt, hung them on a hook, sat down on the small bench and opened his athletic bag. He took out his neatly folded white shirt, and put it on. Then he stood and put on his black pants. Then he sat back down and put on his shoes. He reached back down into his bag for his black bowtie, grabbed it and rose. He stood at the mirror and put it on, making sure the bowtie was centered. He took a spray bottle of Clorox from the locker; *Once more unto the bleach, dear friends, once more.* He closed the locker with the combination lock and walked back into the restaurant. Louie had laid a five and five singles on the bar. Emanuel grabbed the bills, thanked him and returned to the rear corridor and went into the men's room. He unzipped his fly, urinated, flushed the urinal, zipped up, washed his hands, and while they were still wet unlocked a small cabinet in the bathroom. From the cabinet he took a fancy paper towel and dried his hands. He then took out about twenty of the towels and placed them at the end of the marble countertop along with facial tissues, mouthwash, a stack of small paper cups, two kinds of cologne, a lime scented one which he was partial to and a bay rum. He filled a glass with water and placed it on the countertop. From the cabinet he took ten combs and placed them in the glass of water. He set a hairbrush and a clothes brush neatly alongside the combs. He took pains to line all these things up symmetrically. He checked the soap dispenser to make sure it was full and checked that the urinal cakes were still useable. He also put out a natural liquid hand soap and a few sprigs of eucalyptus which he supplied himself. He then plugged an air-freshener into one of the two sockets. Next he checked the toilet paper in each of the stalls. *Don't forget; buy toilet paper.* One of the rolls was low and needed replacing. Having meticulously gone through his set-up he then checked his appearance in the mirror, careful to see that his recently graying hair was neatly combed. He glanced down at his shoes which were, as usual, spit-shined. He checked his breath in his hand and, just to be certain, poured some mouthwash into a cup and gargled. He spit the mouthwash into the sink, rinsed it and decided all was almost as it had to be. He placed the five singles Louie gave him on a plate on the counter. All was now in order. Then he sat down on the small stool in the corner of the men's room to wait - while once again reading his worn copy of The Way of Life. If nothing else, Emanuel W. Graves believed in doing a job right. That, or don't bother to do it at all.

FOUR

Back in his office, Richard Alleroy was checking numbers on his screen and trying to act as if nothing out of the ordinary had occurred. His cell phone, now back in his pocket, rang. It was his wife reminding him that besides her charity luncheon and hairdresser's appointment she would be at the organizing committee meeting for the museum's spring gala and she would be home late. There was a soft knock at the door and Georgia peeked in.

"Mr. Merrill asks that you come to his office at eleven sharp."

Alarm bells began to go off in Alleroy's head. *Did whoever it is go to them first?* He took a deep breath in an effort to calm himself. He and Edward Merrill, along with Raymond Smythe, three of the six partners, had been fraternity brothers at the U of Chicago. As well as being business associates they were friends. All the partners and their wives often went out to dinner together, and their families all summered in Sag Harbor where they had homes.

·　　·　　·

"Thus the Master is available to all people and doesn't reject anyone. He is ready to use all situations and doesn't waste anything. This is called embodying the light." Emanuel put his book down and sat thinking on what he had just read. *I should talk to her. The situation has presented itself. Don't waste it. Embody the light, man.* Emanuel had steadfastly refused to allow himself any opportunity in his adult life, if any, to meet women. He had denied himself that contact for all these years out of the insecurity that draped itself around him; his Gulf War souvenirs, PTSD, which left him with feelings of

shame and hopelessness, and which intermittently visited upon him horrible flashbacks, and his gastrointestinal problems, which caused the random incidents of incontinence. These, to him, embarrassments - when they occasionally occurred - contributed mightily to his insecurity. Worse, he had to wear an adult diaper in the beginning and, on occasion in the last few years, had to put one on for fear of an unexpected accident. Before he went off to The Gulf War he had a girlfriend who loved him, whom he loved, and two years in a war and two years in a hospital later it was over. He'd pushed her away. That was twenty-five interminable years ago. Emanuel was quite aware that these afflictions he picked up in the Gulf had kept him from any intimate relationship with a woman. He was aware that he was afraid of exposing what he perceived as his "imperfections" to another. And though he knew that any woman worth loving would love him in spite of these imperfections, his fear of eventual rejection because of these afflictions kept him from even making the effort. He couldn't remember the last time a woman had smiled at him the sweet way she did. *I could just sit in the lobby reading—*

The men's room door opened and a well-dressed portly man entered. Emanuel put his book aside, stood and picked up a towel from the pile. The man removed his suit jacket and entered one of the four stalls. Emanuel went to the small closet, took out the toilet brush and toilet cleaner and placed them behind his stool. Loud, wet flatulence, followed by the near empty squirt bottle sound of diarrhea came from within the stall. *You fucking...why the hell do you even go to a restaurant if you know your stomach is on the fritz?* Emanuel was aware that he disliked this man because he reminded him of his own afflictions. Emanuel had learned very early on that as soon as anyone went into a stall and sat he had to begin breathing through his mouth and keep breathing through his mouth until at least five minutes after the customer had left and he'd cleaned the toilet and sprayed the air. And even then he'd still wait a few minutes until his breathing returned to normal again. This was a hard learned lesson. Now, there were times he didn't breath through his nose for hours. *Jesus man, did you eat shit?*

The men's room door opened again and a well-dressed man made a face and mouthed "wow" as he went to a urinal. Emanuel shrugged in a what-can-you-do gesture. The man smiled, nodded, and proceeded to do his business. More unpleasant noises came from the stall. The second man shook, zipped up and washed his hands. Emanuel handed him a towel and, as he wiped his hands, he checked himself in the mirror that ran the length of the four sinks.

"Brudjh your jagget, sir?"

It was a nasal sounding question followed by a nasal sounding answer. "Id's ogay." Emanuel returned the man's smile.

The man took some bills from his pocket and placed a dollar bill on the tip plate. He paused, shook his head, and added another single to the tip plate.

"Thag you sir."

The man gestured towards the stall shaking his head in sympathy and left. After what seemed like twenty minutes and four or five flushes later the stall door opened and the man emerged holding his jacket and looking exhausted. Emanuel, still breathing through his nose, picked a towel from the pile, took the man's jacket from him, and stood waiting while the man washed his hands. *You know what man, I sympathize. I do.* The thought was sincere. The man finished washing his hands and Emanuel handed him the towel. After the man dried his hands Emanuel held his jacket for the man to slip into.

"Thank you."

"By bleasure sir." *Sure.*

The man checked his appearance in the mirror, picked up the bay rum and slapped some on each chubby cheek.

"Would you like be to brudjh your jagget, sir?"

"Not today, thanks." He reached into his pocket, took out his billfold, carefully removed a dollar and placed it onto Emanuel's tip plate.

"Thag you sir."

After the man left Emanuel waited a few seconds, went to the cabinet, grabbed the air freshener spray and liberally misted the room. He reached over the door of the stall that the man had occupied and sprayed some more freshener downward. He went back to the cabinet and exchanged the air freshener for the Clorox, put on a pair of latex gloves, took the Clorox, a toilet cleanser and a toilet brush and, still afraid to breathe through his nose, he opened the stall and proceeded to clean the wet brown spots and streaks on the seat bottom and the remaining splatter in the bowl of the toilet, *Those fucking bureaucrat motherfuckers...*It was the mantra that ran through his mind at least once every working day. *Those motherfuckers...*And try as he might, no Zen parable could make it okay.

FIVE

Margaret Alleroy nee Bauman, whose friends called her Megs, fifty-five, tall, short silver hair, with the air of a patrician, an alumna of Loyola U in Chicago, finished her second cup of coffee while scrolling through the New York Social News on-line. There they were at the Opera News awards dinner as well as at The Eastside Hospital Benefit dinner. She and Richard were both opera buffs and generous benefactors of the opera world as well as supporting the Eastside Hospital's cancer center. Aware of how wonderful her life was, how privileged she was, she felt her obligation was to give back. Besides giving her time and energy to the Opera Fund and The Eastside Hospital, she worked tirelessly for two children's charities. She had lately given her blessing to her twin's request to go to Paris after graduation and spend three weeks with her husband's sister Amélie with the proviso that they both come down from New Hampshire for a weekend before they went off. She closed her laptop and called the personal chauffeur the Alleroy's had on retainer in order to double-check that he was aware of her schedule. Her husband eschewed the Bentley in favor of driving himself in the Mercedes. *How Richard can endure having to negotiate that horrible traffic himself is beyond me.* She then went upstairs to get ready for the Big Brothers Big Sisters luncheon at two PM, and after that the museum organizing committee meeting, of which she was co-chair. Because of a two-thirty Children's Aid Society meeting on Friday she'd moved up her usual three PM Friday hairdresser appointment to today's eleven AM appointment.

•   •   •

Arthur Merrill's assistant looked up at Richard Alleroy, smiled, and waved him in to Merrill's office. Merrill looked up from his laptop and motioned for him to take a seat. Alleroy sat down and waited.

"Richard, we've been friends a long time. Since University. So it pains me to have to tell you that something has come to our attention that appears both alarming and untoward. I think you know to what I am referring."

Of course he knew. A bolt of fear shot through his body. *I didn't do anything that plenty of other guys had done. Probably still are doing. But I'm the one who's fucked.*

"In lieu of calling the authorities, we're going to ask that you stop trading at once. Leave all your company credit cards and your devices, including your cell phone in your office, and leave the building on your own until we decide what our course of action will be. Any distributions due you will cease to go into your account as of now. And, I have to warn you - as a friend - do *not* attempt to pull any monies out of your off-shore bank accounts. We'll return your cell to you as soon as we've gone through it. Is it locked?" Alleroy nodded. "Write the pin down." He slid a pad and pen across the desk to Alleroy who wrote his pin down. "We'll let you know what we're going to do as soon as we've had a chance to sort the situation out and decided on a course of action."

•   •   •

Alleroy stood waiting for the elevator. The panic surging through his body was overwhelming him. His immediate thoughts were for himself and his reputation. His estate would now be wiped out. In two years of inactivity he would lose his series seven license. His life would be changed for the worse. The lives of his wife and children would also be adversely affected. Curiously, that was his second thought. *I need a drink. You need to calm down Rich. Whoever left that note went to them instead. Fucking idiot. I could have given whoever it is a bundle to keep quiet.* He walked blindly out of 111 Wall, and as luck, fate, or whatever, would have it, walked a half block east on Wall made a left on Water and a few paces later found himself in front of the Coach and Crown which also, as luck, fate, kismet, or whatever, would have it, was the first restaurant he came to. He peered through the large front window. *Good, a nice long bar. Crowded. Shit, I hope there's no one in there who knows me.* He entered and quickly took the last empty stool, which was in the middle of the bar. This kept his back to the almost full restaurant.

Scanning the room behind him in the back bar mirror he didn't see anyone he knew. Louie approached and Alleroy ordered a Blanton's, one cube. Louie flipped a coaster onto the bar and placed an old-fashioned glass on the coaster. As he did this, with the other hand he spooned one ice cube into the glass. He turned to the back bar, plucked the Blanton's bottle from the shelf by its neck, turned back around, and deftly poured a generous shot of the bourbon, starting the pour in the glass, raising the bottle at least a foot-and-a-half above the glass in mid-pour, and bringing the pour to an end a quarter inch into the glass where it began. He smiled at Alleroy and moved away to tend to another patron. Alleroy, far too preoccupied to appreciate Louie's artistry, was still scanning the room behind him in the bar mirror. *No one...only halfway good thing about this whole fucking lousy day.* He downed the generous shot and pushed the glass forward on the bar signaling for a re-fill. Louie, who noticed everything that transpired in his "office" was a bit taken aback. *Guy orders a Blanton's and chugs it?* As he repeated the pour; *is he gonna shoot this one too?* Thankfully, for Louie's sense of the etiquette of drinking, Alleroy took a sip of the second drink and then proceeded to slowly sip the rest. All was now restored to order - in Louie's mind anyway. As far as what Richard *Alleroy* was thinking *all* was totally *all* fucked up. *What the hell do I do now? What are they going to do?* One hour and three-and-a-half Blanton's on three rocks later Alleroy rose from his barstool a bit unsteadily. He got Louie's attention; "The men's?"

"The back left."

A bit tipsy, Alleroy began walking, taking pains to appear steady. *You know, you have to drive home later man.* He walked unsteadily to the end of the bar and then across the rear of the restaurant to the back left corner and into the small corridor. He squinted at the three doors and opened the one marked "Highwaymen." Emanuel, seeing the door being opened again put his book face down on his stool and stood. Alleroy entered and went directly to the nearest urinal. *Holy...that's...it's that guy in the park.* Emanuel was somewhat stunned by this turn of events. He picked a towel from the pile and waited for the man to finish and wash his hands. Alleroy washed his hands perfunctorily and Emanuel handed him the towel. *He doesn't recognize me?* Alleroy dried his hands and threw the paper towel on the countertop. He checked himself in the mirror. Emanuel stood silently watching him. Alleroy suddenly leaned forward placing both hands on the sink top to brace himself. He slowly shook his head his straight greying hair falling forward around his temples.

Emanuel moved to him. "Are you okay sir?"

"I'm fine."

Yeah, you're fine. Like you were in the park. Alleroy straightened himself and smoothed his hair back. Emanuel decided to engage - on the off-chance the man would remember him. "Would you care for some bay rum sir?"

"Nah."

Emanuel looked at Alleroy in the mirror. Alleroy looked at him - then looked back at his reflection.

"Shall I brush sir's jacket?"

"It's alright." And with that, Alleroy proceeded to leave the bathroom without going into his pocket. Emanuel's eyes followed him out. *No recognition - no tip. Wow! Too unreal. Either he's so troubled or I'm invisib—are you kidding? Of course I'm invisible. I'm a fucking ghost in a bathroom. A towel dispenser. I might as well be hanging on the wall.* Emanuel threw the towel in the bin, picked up his book, and sat back down to continue reading. *Motherfucker stared at me in the park too...stared!*

Alleroy, having returned to his stool at the bar was deep in thought. *They have my computers, my cell...*He took a sip of bourbon. *Meg said she'd be home late...I can go home. Better get a cup of coffee.* He ordered a cup of coffee and placed his personal Chase Sapphire Reserve card on the bar. He finished the coffee and absent-mindedly motioned for the check. *They'll call me? When? I'm going to have to look as if I'm going to the office every day. Meg can't know about this. I have to buy another cell.* He added an eighteen per cent tip, exactly, signed the slip and placed it back in the folder. *I have to play this right. I can't go to prison.* He took his copy and left the restaurant - relieved he still hadn't run into anyone he knew. He walked to his garage, where they were surprised he hadn't called for his car and told him it might take a while to retrieve. As he stood waiting for it he felt as if his life was at an end.

•   •   •

At least she can sleep. Alleroy lay awake next to his wife, his mind refusing to stop gaming out scenarios. All of them bad. How much did they know? What were they finding out? When will they call? He'd gone back to his office and waited almost four hours until he could retrieve his cell phone. He then spent the rest of the day sitting in the public library until it was his usual time to drive home. *Now what? I knew I should have eased up...I knew it. But...it was so easy. The kids, Meg...they can't know. Madoff destroyed his family. Disgraced them. His kid hung himself. Jesus...*He had finally given *some* thought to what this would do to his family.

Richard Alleroy had always appreciated the finer things in life. The things his parents never had. He had to have the best wine, the best cars, the rare antiques, the museum quality art, the bespoke suits, the haute couture, the summer homes, the yacht. The Alleroy's *always* had all those things. Would he now have to ask his family to give it all up? Could he ask his kids to leave school - and whatever dreams they had for a future? Could he? How could he face them? The once respected name of Alleroy would be synonymous with stealing. *How do I get out of this? Think...you're a smart guy...If anyone can figure a way out of this mess you can.* And yet, lurking there in the darkness, were his serious misgivings that any clean way out of this bind existed. *"We'll let you know what we're going to do as soon as we've sorted the situation out and decided on a course of action." They could have had me arrested on the spot...couldn't they have? "Do not attempt to pull any monies out of your off-shore bank accounts." If I make restitution...will that get me out of this? But...It's so many millions...Jesus Christ...Who the hell could've found out? This is going to ruin me.* He stared at the ceiling. *Okay...hold it! Don't get ahead of your worry schedule. You haven't learned what they're going to do yet. Wait until you find out.*

SIX

Erratic eye movements search up, down and back and forth, across the walls of the white room. The door to the room opens and an elderly man and a beautiful young woman enter. They wear white coats and carry clipboards. They stand at the foot of the bed looking kindly and caring. Their mouths move but there is no sound. They move off to a corner busily conferring. As they do, the door opens again and an ice-cream vendor wheeling a cart enters the room laughing. The bells of the cart tinkle merrily. The man pulls open the door in the top of the cart, reaches down, and pulls out an electro-shock apparatus. The two doctors off in the corner talk excitedly with their hands covering their mouths. They begin to make frantic notes on their clipboards. The ice-cream man advances holding out the electro-shock paddles. He smiles. The doctors begin to smile and move closer. The ice-cream man—

Emanuel bolted awake, still in his chair in front of the small TV, always tuned to the cable news channel. His body was covered with sweat. He brought his knees up to his body and sat there huddled and shivering. His ever-present mantra reverberated inside his skull; *those fucking motherfuckers. Those lying cock-sucking criminal motherfuckers.*

•　　•　　•

At six-thirty AM Alleroy, who may have fallen asleep for an hour, if even that, picked himself up out of bed and padded to the bathroom. Margaret, her blindfold and headset in place, was sleeping the sleep of the unworried. It was his second day of going through the motions as if all was right with the world. *I can't sit in the damn library again. What the hell do I do with myself today? When will they call?* He brushed his teeth and stood there, his eyes searching his face in the mirror. There was no answer forthcoming. A half-hour later he was showered and dressed and had gone downstairs. At the kitchen island he managed to get a piece of toast down along with his coffee while trying to read the Journal. No terrace garden today. *Maybe never.* Another half-hour later he was getting in his car, still not sure of where he would be going, when his cell phone rang. It was Edward Merrill. "Richard, please be here at ten-fifteen sharp."

A deep breath. "Okay."

*Here we go...*He pulled the Mercedes out of his garage made a right turn to Second Avenue and headed south on Second to Sixty-Third Street which would then take him onto the FDR Drive. He barely remembered doing any of this his mind so filled with all the possible scenarios about to unfold. His cell phone rang again.

"Dad, are you and mom coming up for the game?"

It was his younger son Royce, a pitcher for Exeter's Junior varsity baseball team.

"Of course pal. Do you think we'd miss the opener?"

"The Hilltoppers have a strong team this year."

"C'mon...It's Worcester. You'll be up to it. Listen, I'm driving to the office so I better not talk on the phone. I'll call you later, okay?"

The dash clock read seven forty-five as he ended the call. On a normal day, considering the traffic, which was always bad getting to and from the FDR, he would be in the office by eight forty-five. This was no normal day. Not by a long shot. *I still have to kill about an hour fifteen. Maybe I should try and eat something. I should eat but...I'll get a cup of coffee. I should have brought the Journal with me. I should have...Yeah, I should have done a lot of things...Or maybe not.* In the end he decided he'd buy a New York Times and kill some time reading it over coffee. *Then, I don't know...the park?* If he was thinking about anything but what awaited him in Edward Merrill's office he'd have reflected on the strange man he encountered there only a few days back. Unsurprisingly, there was no room for this thought in his overcrowded mind.

Alleroy entered his garage and left the car with the valet. There was a newsstand on the corner. He stopped and bought the Times. He walked to a nearby luncheonette and killed thirty-five minutes over a cup of coffee and an uneaten cheese Danish. *Another forty minutes to go.* He paid his bill and walked a block to Mannahatta Park. He walked to the end of the park closest to his office which, as it happened, was also near the Hayes drinking fountain and was a few paces from where again, as it happened, Emanuel Graves sat at his usual spot reading and feeding the critters that hurried expectantly to his feet. He'd been there for an hour and a half and he had another half hour or so to relax before going to work. And then, as it *also* happened, Emanuel picked the very moment Alleroy passed him to look up from his reading. And of course, he recognized the smartly dressed man carrying a briefcase who looked straight at him, and then kept walking on past him. *This guy's so deep inside his fear-filled mind, he's incapable of recognizing anything - let alone a garden variety Plebe feeding pigeons.* He then sat down on a bench which was some ten yards from Emanuel. This was the second time that this man who Emanuel clearly recognized, this man with whom he'd had a lengthy, if somewhat occult conversation with, did not recognize him. He watched Alleroy sit, look around, look straight at him, and then open his newspaper, look at it, and then put it down next to him on the bench and stare straight ahead. And then, on this morning filled with cosmic serendipity, they both stood at the same time and walked to the fountain to get a drink of water

"You still look worried."

Alleroy, his brow furrowed, stared at the man who just told him he looked "worried" and finally...*finally*, he recognized Emanuel as the man he *thought* was there to meet him yesterday.

"Oh...You. Jesus Chri—Leave me the fuck alone."

Emanuel smiled. *Oh? You recognize me now?* The smile immediately left his face. Alleroy took a long, slow, drink of water. It was as if this most elemental thing could, would, somehow replenish all the energy that had been drained from his being in the last forty-eight hours. He finished and stood up straight wiping his mouth with the back of his hand. Emanuel, rather than bending to drink right away, watched him. *Ask him.*

"Why?"

Alleroy looked at him. *Why?* He turned and walked back to the bench shaking his head. *That's right. This idiot is here every morning feeding these pests.* Emanuel took a quick drink of water and as he did he decided that besides wanting to give this jerk a hard time he looked like someone who needed someone to talk to. He straightened up and walked directly over to where Alleroy was sitting - on *his* bench.

"I think you need to talk to someone who's been there."

Alleroy opened his Times. *Yeah, you've been where I am.* Emanuel sat down at the other end of the bench. He took The Way of Life from his pocket and held it out for Alleroy to see. "Have you ever read this book?"

"Look, I don't need to talk to anyone - let alone you. *Please,* just leave me the fuck alone?"

Let alone me? Emanuel tried to let that remark slide. The effort didn't take. "Yeah, I know - I heard you. There's a quote in this book that I've pondered; "there is no illusion greater than fear.""

Alleroy rolled his eyes. *I wish it were an illusion, pal.* "Hey..." He shook his head and turned to face Emanuel. "Whatever the fuck you are, please go away."

Whatever I am? Emanuel was now a bit angered by the accumulation of insults. The fact that a day after they'd had a prolonged conversation this man looked directly at him and didn't see him at the C & C, and now this man's uncalled for continued dismissiveness. *Fuck this guy.*

"You know, I have to say; that's another *very* nice suit you have on...I'm so glad I killed a few people so you could dress so well. That expression dressed to kill? Kill to dress is more like it."

Killed people? "Oh, fuck off..." Alleroy rose to walk away.

"I *will* follow you, you know."

Alleroy stopped, turned around and glared at Emanuel who returned his gaze evenly. *Have they sent this guy to frighten me after all?* The events that had transpired in his life in the last forty-eight hours had turned his normal resting wariness into full-blown galloping paranoia.

"What do you mean you've killed people?"

"You want to sit and talk about it? That note?"

The "it" Emanuel was referring to was the whiff of fear he smelled coming from Alleroy. The thing, in the first place, he thought he could help with. Alleroy, on the other hand, stopped hearing anything after the words "kill people." He moved to another bench closely followed by Emanuel and sat. And Emanuel sat. He took the small plastic bag from his pocket, scattered some seed on the ground and a dozen pigeons landed at his and Alleroy's feet. *If these filthy things shit on my shoes...He killed people?*

Emanuel pursed his lips and made a kissing sound and George and Gracie scurried up to grab the two groundnuts he threw to them, tuck them away in their cheeks, and scamper off. Alleroy watched as he did this. *This guy would be doing me a favor to kill me. At least Meg and the kids would get the insurance. Oh! Oh no! The insur*—his sudden terrible realization was interrupted by Emanuel.

"Why do you look so afraid?" Emanuel was now very curious about what he was seeing.

"Look, did my partners send you?

"Never met them."

Alleroy's paranoia was running away with his reasoning. *Cute. Never met them. Of course you've never met them.*

"You know, the *look* is even worse today."

"Why did you say you've killed people?"

"Because I have. It's why I have the job I have."

The job you have? Alleroy felt a strange combination of fear and hope. *He's a contract killer?* Had he been thinking straight, or logically, he would have understood that this was not what was happening here. As it turns out he would later wish it *were* the case - and this man would have shot him dead on the spot. Emanuel looked up at the sky.

"I have to go to work. And yeah...I've killed a pile of people! It's on my résumé!"

The declaration sounded like a punch to Alleroy. "The job you have? What job? Am I your job?"

Fucker never even saw me. "You might say." He laughed. "And I'd sure like to be able to dress like you." Emanuel rose. "I'll see you in the funny papers."

Emanuel put his book in one pocket and the plastic bag of nuts and seeds in another, and walked away. Alleroy watched him go. His thoughts now turned to his insurance. After a while he got up and walked to his office.

SEVEN

"We've decided that it's in everyone's best interest *not* to press charges."
Alleroy, was seated among, but apart, from the other five partners in one
of the large conference rooms. His momentary relief at hearing what his
fellow Alpha Phi Edward Merrill said was swiftly washed away by what
Merrill said next.

"You will tell your staff that for personal reasons you're taking a six
month's leave of absence beginning now. They will sign an NDA regarding
anything they may or may not know about you - under severe penalty. At
the end of the six months you will then announce your retirement. And
that goes for doing any more trading for anyone else. You trade anywhere
and we *will* press charges and say we just discovered this. We have
contacted the entities involved and they have agreed to also waive all
charges providing they are made whole again. No one wants the bad press
and possible ruination this will bring." He slid a piece of paper across the
table to Alleroy who glanced at it.

"We've returned your computers to your office, and during lunch
we're going to go there and you'll transfer your assets to us; all your
retirement Accounts, your stock options, your portfolio, and the funds
from your domestic and offshores. We'll make the reparations. You'll put
your Sag Harbor home, the apartment in Barcelona, and your Cap Ferrat
estate on the market immediately to help pay us back the full amount. We
figure that between the sale of these properties, and the monies from all
your holdings, you can almost cover the amount you...well, stole, and we
won't have to force you to put your residence here up for sale. That's more
of a consideration for Margaret and your children than the consideration
you gave this company. We've decided, after much discussion, the only
account we won't freeze is your Chase account. We've also decided to leave
you your cars, but we *will* sell your Hatteras. And also as a consideration

for Margaret, we'll leave you your art. Whatever of it you wish to sell will cover the maintenance and taxes on your home for as long as you can. This will keep you out of prison. We'll announce you're taking a sabbatical for reasons of health. Are we clear?"

Alleroy nodded. His outward demeanor hiding the tsunami of screaming fear inundating his entire being. Neurons were firing frantically across synapses in his brain. *This is...I don't deserve this. I...What have I...I'm done. It's all done.* The partners rose from the table, Merrill gesturing for Alleroy to get up from the table and go to his office. *It's practically every penny. My portfolio, Barcelona, Sag Harbor, France...The Hatteras... I love that boat. Everyone loves that boat. We're supposed to be in Sag Harbor in two months and France in July. Sell the art? That's my hedge. My Chase account will be exhausted in a year. Any advances I can get on my other cards will barely cover a year of the kid's tuitions. Oh God...the tuitions. They're all due in August.* It felt as if he were just hung upside-down and bled. It was an effort for him to push back from the table. *I have to call the real estate agents and I have to figure out a reason to explain selling these things. She could sell her jewelr—-No, no, she can't know anything about this. Not yet. The tuitions...The kids can't know either. I'm going to have to pretend I'm going to the office while I sort this all out.* He was finally forced to think about what this meant for his wife and children. *I have to sort this out soon.* The irony of him choosing the name Alleroy because it evoked something kingly, and now losing the equivalent of a king's ransom, was too glaring to miss. He got up slowly and went blindly to his office to wait for Merrill or Smythe, or whichever of the partners would be overseeing the carnage.

He was glad that the floor was clear and that everyone was at lunch when both Merrill and Smythe came to his office. Alleroy decided he would just ask. "Did you guys send a man to threaten me?"

"What are you talking about?" It was Merrill.

Of course they'll deny it. Why even bother asking? "Nothing. I'm just...forget it. This thing's left me a little paranoid."

"But why even ask such a question?" It was Smythe.

"Some nut in the park just...I'm...It was a dumb question."

And, wanting to get on with it, that's where the partners left it. He proceeded to make the transfers as his partners had ordered, then cleared out his office and was discreetly escorted out of the building. The sealed box that contained the pictures and personal items that filled his office was sent down to his garage and put in the trunk of his Mercedes. He left the car there and then spent most of the rest of the day walking aimlessly. He purchased a hot dog from a street vendor but couldn't get it down and threw most of it away. He had two bourbons in a bar on William Street - from the well - Blanton's, at forty dollars a shot was now out. At four-thirty he went into a movie theater on Fulton Street. He sat there while extras screamed as they were being mutilated by zombies on the screen and, after an hour, left to make his way back to his garage.

Driving up the FDR, not hearing Mozart's Sonata No. 16 in C Major, he suddenly went back to something that his crammed mind had shunted aside - until that moment. *The insurance. My life insurance. Twenty five millio—No! No! Fuck! You...No! You fucking idiot! You changed companies to get a thirty year term at better rates eight months ago...Why did you do this? They won't pay on suicide now!* And then more crazed thoughts rushed in. *Maybe that guy is a contract killer. If he kills me they pay. Stop it...He's just some nobody...I can't kill myself! I can't even swallow some pills! It's fucked!* He slammed his fist down on the steering wheel. Then, as he was cursing his lousy luck - and not even realizing how insane it was that he was upset that he couldn't even kill himself - as he passed the U.N. he thought; *okay...an accident. If it isn't him then it has to be an accident. Somebody has to kill me.* And, as he was exiting the FDR at Sixty-First Street, he remembered the hit-and-run accident: *April fool! Jack Loomis. Jack-rest-in-pieces-Loomis!*

•   •   •

Emanuel made his way down the metal el stairs among the others in the six PM rush hour crowd; many now on their way home to their wives, husbands, lovers and children. On their way to human contact and whatever problems and/or comforts that came with that contact. This night Emanuel was making his way home to his small room, his books, and the new second-hand twenty-four inch TV that replaced his old second-hand fifteen inch TV which had died three months prior. *Should I just ask Arthur if he's seen her lately?* Arthur was the slight pale elderly night man sitting behind the counter of the small mail room in the small lobby of The Delevan. In exchange for sitting behind that counter from five thirty PM until four AM *every* night he was given a small room in the hotel rent free. Emanuel often wished he could have had such a cushy deal. *At least nobody's taking a shit in his office.*

He opened his door and switched on the harsh overhead light. He set his athletic bag down and switched on the small lamp on the nightstand cum dresser and switched off the overhead light. He turned the TV on to his default station, the food channel, opened the sofa bed, sat down on it and took off his sneakers, his jeans and denim work shirt, got up and went to the cardboard armoire. He placed his sneakers on the armoire floor and hung his jeans and shirt on the same wire hanger they hung from earlier. He took his folded black pants and white shirt from his small athletic bag, carefully unfolded them, smoothed them out on his bed and hung them in the armoire as well - careful to separate the two hangers. He then went to his small sink and thoroughly washed his hands, face and armpits. He dried himself and padded around his open sofa bed to the small nightstand/dresser, opened the bottom drawer, took out his neatly folded sweats and put them on along with his flannel lined slippers which were always on the floor next to it. He went to his small fridge and got a Corona, opened it with the church key hanging from the cabinet knob, tossed the bottle cap into the trash under the sink and took a long pull while watching the news. *What a fucking mess this country's become. Even more than it was when I was a dumb kid. This is what my buddies died for?* It was six-fifteen. In forty-five minutes he would sit in his well-worn easy chair, at his other TV tray table, and watch Jeopardy while eating dinner. Every evening, before eating dinner, he watched food shows and looked longingly at all the wonderful dishes of the world he knew he would never get to eat. He only wished he could afford go to places like San Sebastian, Spain, or Lanzhou, China and eat all the wonderful dishes he saw. He did however, indulge himself nightly in one of his few extravagances he could afford. This evening was no different. He went to his fridge and from the small freezer took out his one ice tray and his jug of cheap vodka - which he was just able to squeeze in there in order to keep it ice cold. He shook out the ice cubes, put enough cubes into his one very tall glass, re-filled the tray with water and placed it back where it belonged. He poured himself a healthy shot and a half of vodka and put the jug back into the freezer on top of the ice tray where it remained until six-fifteen PM the next day. From the refrigerator itself he took out the low sodium V-8 juice, tabasco sauce, Worcestershire sauce, prepared horse radish and the bottled lemon juice. He carefully made himself a Bloody Mary, topping it off with celery salt and black pepper. He took a small sip and, satisfied, he sat down on his easy chair with his drink to watch some news. This was a nightly ritual which he enjoyed and which served to calm him and separate him from his day. And, along with the beer he would finish with dinner, it got him a little buzzed. Took the edge off. A win-win - and a way to make the news bearable. He made the drink last for fifteen to twenty minutes, during which he switched back to the food network. When he had drained the last of his nightly treat he rose, rinsed the glass at the sink, re-filled it with water and placed it on the other night table TV tray that was within a right arm distance of his easy chair. He used the water to take his after dinner pills and to keep hydrated. He glanced at his bedside alarm clock. *Seven minutes to Jeopardy.* From a shelf over the sink took he took a package of Macaroni and Cheese. He took his microwaveable bowl from the shelf opened the box and poured the macaroni into the bowl. He added the two thirds of a cup of water to the bowl as the package directed, dropped a small clove of unpeeled garlic into it, placed it in the microwave and set the timer for four minutes. He loved the faint taste of garlic in the mix and that small bit was just enough to be there while not aggravating his GI problems. While waiting for the timer bell to go off he grabbed a shoe brush from the armoire, took his black shoes from the athletic bag, brushed them and then put them and the brush back into the armoire next to his sneakers. He then grabbed the broom that stood next to his front door and quickly swept the linoleum floor of the small room. He scooped up the sweepings, deposited them in the trash bag, returned the broom to its place and washed his hands. As he dried his hands on a dish towel the timer bell sounded. *Perfect timing, as usual Manny.* He removed the bowl from the microwave, tore open the package of cheese sauce and mixed it into the noodles. *One minute to, "This is Jeopardy!" Maybe there's a good old movie on tonight too.* This was his routine after every working day. *This* is what kept Emanuel Graves grounded. *This!* Striving to be perfect in whatever it was he did, however trivial. *Before enlightenment chop wood, carry water. After enlightenment, chop wood, carry water.* Anything he did, however trivial - *especially* trivial - he did with attention to detail. *This* was Emanuel Graves' umbilical cord to self-respect.

•   •   •

Since she wouldn't be home until well after dinner time, which was promptly at eight every evening, Margaret Alleroy had asked their personal chef, who usually came in three times a week to shop and prepare two days' worth of meals to come in tonight. It was one thing to re-heat a casserole, but she preferred that one of her husband's favorite dinners not be re-heated.

Following her instructions the chef had shopped for, and prepared, mini-timbales of Ossetra caviar, crabmeat, and avocado - she would snack on one later - followed by a lemon sorbet palate cleanser, and then an entrée of baby lamb chops with a classic mustard cream *sauce, Pommes Anna, and a green salad. Paired with a nice Pinot Noir, it was one of Richard Alleroy's favorite dinners. Normally, he looked forward to this meal. Normally. Tonight, Richard Alleroy was far more interested in what he was reading on his computer than he was in caviar and lamb chops. Even his very favorite yummy baby ones. He had managed to find the Times' coverage of the hit-and-run accident that had killed poor Jack Loomis and was now searching for any news about the police having apprehended the driver. There wasn't any. If I do this, how? And who? Who do I get to do this? He stared at the computer screen. That guy! Was that guy kidding? He said he killed people. Was he just fucking with me? Now, he sat back as he tried to digest the crazy thoughts that ran wildly through his mind. That guy can obviously use some money. I'll need cash. Mary Beth...She'll front me the cash. A bridge loan...She'll get it back.*

EIGHT

Emanuel enjoyed Jeopardy. Jeopardy was his way of both learning stuff and shoving the day out of his mind. However, he missed at least a third of the program - and especially final Jeopardy - because his mind had turned to the pretty Latina in the elevator who must have recently moved in. He was shamed by the knowledge that because she was living in The Delevan and therefore, he reasoned, probably as beaten by life as he was, it gave him the courage to approach her. Something he knew he could, would, *never* do if, say, she were a businesswoman in a suit, or she didn't live in The Delevan. But this was the way it was. *She's pleasant looking and her smile was sweet, open. She's...attractive.* However superficial all these judgements were - and however demeaning his entire rationale was for being able to approach her - and he *knew* it was demeaning - it was good enough for him to take the leap. He would go down to the lobby and ask Arthur what he knew about her. He took a pen and a pad from his dresser drawer, thought for a bit, and wrote: I'm the man who picked up your key in the elevator the other night. *Should I ask her to get a drink...or, I don't know, what? I have to write something else.* He thought about it and decided to write; can I buy you an egg roll? *That's good. That's perfect. She said she likes Chinese food.* He wrote his name, room number and phone number on it, folded it neatly and took it, along with a five dollar bill, into the noisy elevator that finally came and took him down to the lobby. Arthur, as usual, was seated behind his counter scanning The Racing Form. Emanuel walked up to the counter and leaned in. "Arthur...any winners in there?"

"I dunno...I ain't been too lucky lately." Arthur was an appalling handicapper of the races. This fact did not stop him from blowing too much of his Social Security check on them.

"Hey listen...you know anything about the lady on ten? Just moved in I think."

Arthur put the racing form down and stood. One thing he *was* good at - he knew when a dollar was forthcoming. "Maybe."

Emanuel smiled and slid the five over to him. "You know her name?"

"She said Estella."

Star. "Got a pen?"

Arthur reached around and grabbed a pen from off the small desk and handed it to Emanuel who then wrote Estella on the folded note and handed it, and the pen, to Arthur. "Will you see that she gets this? Thanks." He handed Arthur the folded note fully expecting that he would read it - which was fine with him. He thanked Arthur and returned to his room to watch a Fred Astaire and Ginger Rogers movie on TCM until it was time to go to sleep.

●　　　●　　　●

Merciful sleep was not coming for Richard Alleroy. *I can't jump. I can't just walk in front of a bus...the possibility exists that the driver might tell them I did it deliberately. Same for a car...The subway. Jumping in front of...or off of...it can't be any of that. It has to be an accident. An accident. A hit and run.* He lay awake thinking of how on earth he could get someone to hit him with a car. *Maybe that guy?* The fact that he was doing this didn't even enter his mind as something crazy. All he could think of was the way out. For himself, and for his family. In the morning, again after having slept fitfully for maybe a couple of hours, he went through the charade of pretending to go to the office. This entire Wednesday he would spend deep in thought in The Public Library.

Richard Alleroy came from a lower middle class Chicago family whose surname was Alyokhin. He had two sisters. He was the middle child. His father, who emigrated from Russia, had a hardware store on the South Side near where young Richard Alyokhin grew up. Before he entered the U. of Chicago Booth School of Business on a scholarship he changed his last name legally to Alleroy. He liked the names' subtle allusion to being a king, a la Roy - in the manner of a king. It sounded right and suited his ambitions perfectly. The only person who ever remarked on this was another scholarship student. A woman he met at a fraternity/sorority dance at Loyola U. He married her five years later. They had much in common. Both middle class children of immigrants who studied hard knowing at an early age that the only entry into the life they aspired to was to go to University. And, coming from families that could not afford to send them there, the only way to go to University was to go on a full ride. They were peas in a pod. She also loved the name Alleroy. He was mad about her and basked in her approval of whatever achievements he managed. Ten years later, they had their first children, twin daughters, followed in short order by two sons. They were a joyful, wonderful family. Now, all that he and Margaret had achieved was about to be taken from them. Their fortune, along with their position in society. Alleroy loved his wife and children. Still, the extent of the damage resulting from what he did, how profoundly it would affect them, wasn't nearly as uppermost in his mind as what he now needed to do save his own face and fortune. *That* was what was percolating in his fevered brain. The line he straddled between egocentricity and narcissism was always blurred.

He was always a belt-and-suspenders type overly anxious about security - to the point of paranoia. Because of this, and although he was enrolled in his company's partner's insurance plan, he still also felt the need to purchase a very large life insurance policy. So, to further protect his considerable assets, he purchased a ten million dollar twenty year term life insurance policy following some sound advice from a friend and financial advisor. He was 36 years old at the time and already very, very successful and very wealthy. Because his age, health, earnings, assets, investments, and capital gains all met the criteria for an insurance company to issue such a large policy this was doable. Now, along with his Merrill, Harkness, Hirsch, Alleroy, Perlman and Smythe key man insurance being cancelled at the end of the month, this twenty year term policy had run out eight months prior and he purchased a new twenty-five million dollar thirty year term policy. Most importantly, he did so with a different insurance company. Once again, he was able to purchase this large a policy because of his considerable assets - and because of the help again provided by the same friend who counselled him on his first term policy. Alleroy, understood that this sort of purchase needed more than just Googling the necessary steps to take in this action. However, the *kicker* was this new policy would *not cover suicide. Not for two years.* Of course, at the time he made this change in his insurance there was no reason to think that something as unthinkable as suicide would *ever* be an issue. Moreover, during this two year waiting period, he would have to face his children as he pulled them from their schools. Margaret would have questions for him he could not answer. He would be broke, disgraced, and broken. Now, suicide *was* very much an issue and, to most, given the circumstances, it would have been an almost insurmountable issue. To most.

•   •   •

Emanuel stared at the watch on his left wrist. His best buddy's watch, forever set to seven forty-two, the time when his Marine buddy Sergeant Joe Mannion stepped on a roadside bomb. *An EFP. An Explosively Formed Penetrator. A penetrator. Explosively formed. How poetic. They sure couldn't call it what it is could they? A fucking tear-a-body-apart-to-nothing weapon.* At least the watch survived. Emanuel felt that wearing his friend Joey's watch was a way of honoring him. Like a monument of a sort. Another person might think he'd have been better off *not* wearing it. Someone else might suggest that he wore the watch to further validate his grievances. But who among us, knowing the story behind the watch, would suggest any of that to Emanuel?

He was sitting in his easy chair trying decide if he was even comfortable with what he had done in writing that note when his telephone rang. It startled him because his phone so rarely rang. At its fourth insistent ring he picked it up. "Hello?"

"Emanuel? It's Estella."

It's her! There was a few seconds of silence while Emanuel considered what to say. *Man, say something.* "That's...You have a lovely name. Star..."

"Your note made me smile—

*I made her smile...*He smiled.

—"Would you want to go with me some time to that Chinese restaurant you told me about?"

"That...that would be great. Estella. Yeah."

"What are you doing tomorrow night?"

NINE

It was another sunny April morning as Alleroy entered Mannahatta Park. Sure enough, some fifty yards away, he could see Emanuel sitting on his favorite bench thumbing through a book while casually tossing nuts and birdseed onto the ground in front of him. As he approached the bench he wondered if the plan he was about to set into motion was a futile one. When he was some ten yards up the path Emanuel, still perusing his book, said; "Did they ever show?"

He saw me? Alleroy continued on to the bench. "You mind?"

Why the change of attitude man? Emanuel gestured for him to sit and Alleroy sat down at the other end of the bench.

"So? Did they?"

"It was someone who wanted to blackmail me and no, they did not. They went to my partners instead and now I'm out of a job."

"So...Get another job. Jesus...Is that why you look like that?"

"There is no "another" job."

"Blackmail you...why?"

"I've been caught committing fraud."

Alleroy threw two nuts to George and Gracie and smiled broadly as he watched them scamper off. "You were in The Coach and Crown a few days ago."

"You followed me?"

"Didn't need to. You were in my men's room the other day. In the Coach and Crown."

"I don't understand."

"I handed you a towel. You didn't recognize me after we'd talked for an hour in Mannahatta Park."

It took Alleroy a few seconds to process what he had just heard; *Holy Christ...Was he...He was that attendant in the bathroom?* Emanuel looked up at the sky.

Rich, cut to the chase. "You said you killed people."

Emanuel, for his part, suddenly felt the urge to unburden himself of some of his grievances. Some of his unyielding guilt. And to who better than this stranger who looked like death?

"I was what you could call a legal killer."

Alleroy looked at him quizzically.

"We stacked bodies up like cordwood...women, children...It's possible we killed thousands. It's what to do when you're nineteen, gung ho and stupid. Ever see trenches with people's arms and legs sticking out of them?" Emanuel rose and went to the fountain. He took a long drink of water, returned and sat back down. "I got a PTSD discharge. Landed in a veteran's hospital. Two years' worth. Then they said I was a head case. A psycho. They said they wouldn't, but they put it on my *fucking discharge record anyway!*"

Alleroy now understood - the man *had* killed. In a *war*. And he could see Emanuel was growing increasingly agitated. *Is he my guy?* Emanuel, who normally kept his temper at bay, now found himself growing increasingly angry.

"I couldn't get a decent job anywhere. Two years I tried. Cops, Fire Department, Post Office, Wal-fucking-Mart...I couldn't even drive a cab, because with PTSD on my discharge record, I couldn't get a driver's license. I still can't. The government wouldn't take the PTSD off my record. What they *did* do was convince The Coach and Crown I wouldn't go berserk and gun people face down into their chicken cacciatore. That they could trust me to clean a Goddamn toilet and hand out a lousy towel. And who in their right mind wanted the job anyway?"

Alleroy barely heard the actual words the tumblers in his mind were spinning so furiously. What he did hear, loudly and clearly, was the extreme anger, the raging resentment in the man's voice. *Whatever this guy's nut is, and it can't be much, he probably barely covers it with what he makes in that shitter. God, he fucking hates it. Pure hatred. Anybody who fought for his country and then was this royally fucked by them into this horrible job would have to. This is as close as I'm going to get to someone who might be willing to do this.*

"Wow, Emanuel...I don't...I don't exactly know what to say, other than I can certainly understand why you would feel the way you do. You get disability, yes?"

"Yeah, I get disability... Twenty lousy per cent disability; a big two hundred eighty four dollars and ninety three cents a month. Thirty four dollars and ninety-three cents more than a quarter of my rent. Too bad I didn't lose a few limbs, huh? And so the hell what? I'm not a charity case. I work."

Emanuel sat silent for a bit. Then, under his breath; "Motherfuckers put me in a fucking diaper."

The two men sat side by side in silence, each to his own thoughts. Emanuel's; *motherfuckers put me in a fucking diaper and a toilet,* and Alleroy's; *can I get this guy to do this?* Just then Beethoven's Fifth cut through the heavy silence. It was Margaret calling to tell her husband she'd be home late and there was dinner in the fridge. "Work is fine, thanks." She said something and Alleroy responded; "Okay sweetheart. See you later." And he disconnected. *In the old days she would have called the office and they'd have told her I was no longer there. Thank God for cell phones.*

Emanuel, who had no interest in Alleroy's conversation, had resumed reading The Way of Life. Now the sun told him it was time for him to leave for the Coach and Crown. He closed his book and got up.

"I guess I'll see you around."

"You'll see me here. I have nowhere else to go. We'll talk."

As he watched Emanuel walk away Alleroy was thinking; *I can get him to do it.* He shouted after him, "I understand man. I do." Alleroy was seeing five moves ahead already. "We have something in common."

Emanuel shook his head as he kept walking. *Sure we do. I have a closet full of those suits too.*

Alleroy yelled after him; "I'm a vet too." And, having said that, he hoped Emanuel kept on walking. *I'll Google it tonight.*

In completely overlooking the fact that he was now plotting to convince someone to commit what was, in the realest sense, murder, Richard Alleroy now considered himself to be noble. Noble, in that he was willing to lay down his life for the sake of his family's preservation. This was the context in which he *still* thought about the damage his actions would do to his family. His "nobility." *He* was noble - even though he'd had no compunctions about stealing from city workers, and their families, and senior citizens' pension funds. This perverse sense of nobility was what would buoy him through the next few weeks until he had done what he had to. In this, he was, to be generous, a case study in self-delusion. His delusion-driven rationale, as far as the commission of his crime went, was that his victims could afford the amounts he skimmed since he'd made them a tidy fortune over the course of the previous decade and a half.

He sat there convincing himself that this man would jump at the money. That this man, who felt so wronged and so trapped in a meaningless existence, would see this as a way out. His *only* way out. *He's my guy. He's angry, bitter, hates what's been done to him...Will certainly go for the money...But it has to be enough cash on the table. And, there can't be any holes in the plan. And, he has to believe there'd be no way to trace any of it back to him.*

●　　　●　　　●

Emanuel had a date. To eat in a restaurant. He hadn't had that sort of a date in some thirty years. In the thirty years that had gone by since the last time he'd been on an actual date with a woman, the girlfriend who he pushed away, he'd only been with hookers. Fifteen minutes here, a half-hour or an hour there. Nothing that anyone would call a date, or meaningful, by any stretch of the imagination. Just a bit less lonely than masturbation. And, like Estella, he met most of those women where he lived, and they exchanged hellos in the lobby whenever they would cross paths coming and going. They were, for the most part, hardened by life. Never once was he moved to want to go on anything like a date in a public place with them. And he was certain they felt the same way. It was business. *This woman Estella, it's different. But...we'll have some Chinese...No big deal. It'll be nice.*

She was not on the rebound. There was nothing to rebound from. Her marriage, when she was thirty-six, was over in month two after he hit her. Though she wanted children she was grateful not to have had a child of his. At the moment she was reading Love in the Time of Cholera, watching - but mostly listening to - cable news, and still in mild shock at her out-of-character boldness in calling Emanuel. She put her book down. *Pero, it'll be a nice to not have dinner alone. He looks sweet...kind.* She was sure the place couldn't be expensive. *Not in this neighborhood.* "Can I buy you an eggroll?" She laughed. *It's a good line. Droll. It speaks of an intelligence. I can't remember the last time someone made me laugh. That's pretty grim girl. He's probably as broke as I am living here...At least he's kept his sense of humor. I'm not going to let him pay for me though.* She switched to the Food Channel and went back to reading about Florentino's love for Fermina. A love she always yearned for.

TEN

For the last twenty-four hours Richard Alleroy had nothing else on his mind other than how he was going to convince this man to pull off this "accident." *I'll need cash. A hundred fifty K ought to do it. But I need to speak with Mary Beth on the phone. I can't do this on-line. She needs to hear my voice.* Now, after twenty-four mostly sleepless hours, he was fairly certain he had formulated a plan that would work. A quick search on his wife's laptop, while she slept, told him he could use a prepaid phone card to call *Zürich* on a pay phone. He just had to follow the instructions on the card as to how to place the call. *She'll take it out of her safety deposit box and get on a plane with it. No other way. One night, a hotel, and right back. I'll write Margaret a letter of explanation, send it to Mary Beth, and ask Mary Beth to send it to Margaret after. I have to instruct Margaret to see that Mary Beth gets her money back from the insurance. It'll also explain to Meg why this had to be done. I'll have to instruct her not to investigate my death in any way lest it cause any problems with the insurance pay-out. And, if it doesn't work I'll tell Mary Beth to destroy the letter.* These were some of the necessary pieces that were a part of the "suicide" plan taking shape in Richard Alleroy's mind. He was careful to go to the Google Web History and delete the search in the browser. *Just in case Meg should stumble on these searches.*

I have to do some research to make this work. If I'm going to convince this Emanuel guy to do this, the plan has to be convincing. It has to sound foolproof or he'll never go for it.

•　　•　　•

As he sat across from Estella, he was aware that this was the first time since he was nineteen that he was on a date. When they met in the lobby he was surprised at what he had failed to notice in the harsh light of the elevator...*She's...so pretty.* She wore no make-up save for a pale shade of red lipstick. *I'm an idiot.*

They shared a shrimp chow fun and a dish of wok fried green beans. The green bean dish had garlic in it. They were each pleased that the other wasn't one of those types that would avoid garlic on a date. Even so, Emanuel tried not to place too many green beans on the end of his chopsticks - while silently hoping his stomach would handle it. They each drank a Corona. And, when they shared a smile because they both asked for a glass, she confided in him that were she at home she would just drink it from the bottle. He confessed he did the same...and they each put their beer glasses aside. She told him her people were from the Dominican Republic and her parents, who worked in one of the luxury resorts, were still there. He liked her voice. He thought it was pleasing to the ear and he could detect in it the slight Dominican trace. *I like her. What do I say when she asks what I do for a living?*

"Tell me about yourself."

And there it is. What do I do?

It was obvious to Emanuel that this woman was special. There is such a thing as knowing that a certain someone is a perfect someone for you. Now, he was afraid of what her reaction would be when, eventually, she would find out where he worked. Apart from his letting his anger and resentments getting the better of him, and telling that nut in the park about his Army experiences, he seldom if ever talked about them. But he needed to let her know about his time in the service and the aftermath of his tour. He had to qualify why he had the job he had; even though circumstances had conspired to place him *in* that job he was nevertheless understandably ashamed of doing it. But he had to tell her. He had to force himself to face himself. To bare himself. He knew that if he was ever to have any hope of a healthy relationship, he would have to confide in someone. And he hoped this sweet woman would understand. This was a moment he had thought about for years. Someone with whom he vibed. Someone he thought he could have something real with. Someone like Estella. Now, he'd finally met her - and now that moment had arrived. *Should I?* He finished chewing the noodles that were in his mouth.

"I work lunches in The Coach and Crown restaurant in the financial district...It's on Water Street. What do you do with your days?"

And that was all he could manage. And she noticed the deflection. Not exactly a lie because it *was* true. Perhaps it wasn't technically a lie but it was a deliberate error of omission and one he hoped would lead her to assume he worked as a waiter...or a bartender. She didn't want to press him to go any deeper into his life. If they were to make something out of this, then before she would let it get any further she would make sure that all would be revealed. He heard her answer that she worked as a check-out person in the Key Foods on Southern Boulevard while he was promising himself he would tell her everything if their friendship blossomed into something deeper. And, because he believed it would, he still wondered if he could bring himself to eventually tell her the truth.

"Emanuel, what's your fortune?" She had broken open a fortune cookie and was looking at it thoughtfully.

"Well...Estella...this is a very interesting fortune. I'm not sure we could call this a fortune but I *may* have to do this. It says; tomorrow morning take a left as soon as you leave home."

Estella laughed. "Do you think they know something?"

I wish I could and not go to work again. Emanuel asked; "What does yours say?"

"The fortune you seek is in another cookie. Lucky numbers; 23, 2, 19, 34, 7, 12." She looked up at him. "That's funny for a number of reasons."

Emanuel laughed. "Yeah, too numeral to mention."

They both laughed.

"Split another Corona?"

•   •   •

The dinner party was a pleasant affair. Eight friends and acquaintances were at the table, including Margaret's museum organizing committee co-chair and her husband. They were working on their third bottle of the 2016 Diviner Cabernet Sauvignon. Before sitting down to dinner, they'd had Pissaladiers paired with a lovely 2017 Mas de Gourgonnier Rosé in the living room. Everyone was enjoying the good company, the delicious food, the wine...except Richard Alleroy, who was authoring a *spectacular* performance as a man who had the world by the balls. The chef had made a glorious standing rack of lamb with a pilaf stuffing and Dijon mustard glazed carrots.

After the entrée plates were cleared they discussed the museum's fall exhibition of the great surrealists. They ate their salad last. Margaret had asked the chef to make Salade de Poire Pochee, mixed greens tossed with port wine honey vin, topped with port wine poached pears, rum soaked raisins, pine nuts, and goat cheese. The evening was a smashing success. And when it came to an end and the last glass had been cleared, and everyone had said their goodbyes, Margaret said she was tired and was going upstairs. "Don't be too long Richard."

All Richard Alleroy could think of was what was on his mind for the entirety of the evening; getting back to the plan he was formulating. *I can use the cash I have left for openers but...I need to call Mary Beth. And get that Times. And I need to call the first precinct. He'll go for it if it sounds like a sure thing.*

• • •

There can be little doubt that the finer things enhance the moment. But there can be *no* doubt that for Emanuel and Estella Corona beer from the bottle was as fine a thing as any 2016 Diviner Cabernet Sauvignon.

ELEVEN

Alleroy was on his wife's laptop again. He had located the back issue of the New York Times which ran the story of Jack Loomis' untimely demise by a hit and run driver. He would call the Times from a public phone tomorrow to order it for pick-up. *What if he asks to see my driver's license? I can't be too careful.* He was shocked to find that when he searched "fake I.D. NYC" there was a glut of services that he could email, and certain areas in Brooklyn, Times Square and Chinatown, where he just could walk around and ask about a fake driver's license. Email was out of the question. Going to one of these neighborhoods could be risky but this was what he had to do. He decided that once he found one of these places he would pay more to get the I.D. in short order. He reasoned that getting a phony I.D. was the prudent thing to do. Just in case. Belt-and-suspenders.

He was now looking up the phone number of the First Precinct. The First was the police precinct which covered the one square mile of the Wall Street/SOHO/Tribeca area. He'd decided that his death had to occur somewhere near Emanuel and on some street that was also fairly deserted late at night. The Wall Street area fit the bill. He would need to scope out the perfect staging ground within this area for it. He also needed to find out the number of prowl cars, if any, or beat cops, if any, that patrolled the area late at night. That, and the frequency of their runs. It was obvious that making this call from a pay phone was impossible considering how it would look against the story he was going to tell them. Google had informed him that using a VOIP app like Magic Jack would allow him to make calls without setting up any sort of service. He would call from a coffee shop using the shop's Wi-Fi network. For this he would need to buy a tablet - using cash. And he'd need to temporarily turn off the tablet's cellular service to make such a call. All these precautions would make the call untraceable. He decided he would call the precinct around ten PM.

Hopefully, at that precinct, at that hour, in that quiet an area at night, he would get a bored desk sergeant on the line and, pretending to be a script writer working on a major movie to be shot in the area, in the interest of accuracy he needed to know a few things. Also hopefully, the cop would like the idea of being in on the planning of a major motion picture. Especially one starring Robert De Niro. The plan to get himself killed was taking shape in his mind. *Mary Beth would come through. She has to.* He closed her computer. *I have to get this done now because the insurance will take months to pay.* With so much on his mind, he just forgot to delete these searches.

•   •   •

On the walk back to The Delavan Estella and Emanuel each discovered they enjoyed reading more than watching TV. And, except for movies and Jeopardy, the TV they watched was food and news. She watched the news because she was worried about the direction the country was taking. And because there were so many politicians of color, especially Latinas, coming on to our political scene lately. He kept up with the news because, as he told her, he longed down to the last drop of marrow in his bones to see these fat, privileged, money-grabbing, political criminals thrown into jail. These people who treated other people as if they didn't matter; who had committed treason in order to ascend to power. He wanted to see them get what he *knew* they rightly deserved. When he told her of these feelings she responded in kind, saying she agreed and that this was why it was so important that more working class people were entering politics. Still, she could feel his deep-seated anger and wondered what else could be behind it.

•   •   •

He'd gone to Times Square and, in a matter of minutes, located someone who would make him a fake NY driver's license. The samples he was shown were very good and upon ordinary inspection would easily fool anyone. The cost was $125. He gave the man his price and told him he would give him another $200 if he could have it ready for him in two days. The man eagerly agreed. Next, he bought an international calling card from a CVS pharmacy with cash and called his sister Mary Beth in Zurich from a public phone booth on the far end of West Twenty-Sixth Street. Alleroy explained his situation to her, told her he was going to commit suicide, and that he needed the bridge loan to make ends meet until the insurance paid off. And, if he needed more it would be covered since Margaret would pay her back from the insurance settlement. He told her he would leave his wife a note explaining everything and instructing her to pay Mary Beth whatever she was owed. His sister tried her best to talk him out of committing suicide, even saying she would organize an intervention. However, after he went into great detail about the dire consequences his fraud would have on his family, she finally grasped the magnitude of what this would do to Margaret and the children. She finally understood that this was his only way out, gave up trying to talk him out of it, and agreed to bring him one hundred fifty thousand undeclared dollars in cash. One hundred and forty thousand dollars more than the U.S. customs cash limit. He told her he probably wouldn't need more than that but, if he did he'd let her know. She knew that the insurance pay-out would cover it. As far as bringing it in, it wasn't as if she'd never carried large amounts of undeclared cash, or diamonds, or whatever, in and out of Switzerland for her somewhat shady husband, so...

Alleroy conveniently left out the part about recently updating his insurance with a new company and, because of that recent change, they wouldn't pay on suicide and that his plan was to have someone kill him in some kind of event. Minor details. She was to fly in on Swiss Air with the cash in a few days and he would meet her at JFK. She would then check into the airport Hilton and leave late the following evening. A funeral would be her reason for the quick turnaround. He didn't have any compunctions about lying to her because the ends, he reasoned, would justify the means. It would be a win-win. The fact that he would be dead never even factored into his plan. In his mind he was dead anyway. He wondered at the time why Bernie Madoff, who didn't kill himself the first time he tried, didn't try again. Had he no shame? How could he just go to jail leaving them to face the frightful stain on his name? Now, he was living that very situation. Alleroy knew he couldn't do the same thing. Unlike Madoff, he couldn't face his family and the overarching shame he felt at ruining everything. He *had* to do this crazy thing he was planning. There was no other way. *He* would also be taking care of his family. Admirable? In his mind, yes, he was. The letter he would leave his wife would tell her how much he loved her, what he did and why he had to end it this way. Alleroy knew Margaret would grieve, be hurt, and be shocked by the whole thing. He was sure she would be angry at him feeling that they *could* live like ordinary people. He also knew she would understand that he couldn't live with the shame and that he also had to do this for their children. That it was the only way. He trusted his sister to tell Margaret about her missing laptop. Still, he thought it necessary to explain in his own words why he had to use her laptop and why he had to get rid of it, and why she had to burn the letter as soon as she read it. Everything had to be covered - even the obvious. Emanuel Graves? Why, he would be making out as well, wouldn't he? Alleroy was certain he could convince Graves to take the money. He would make his plan sound foolproof. It wouldn't only *sound* foolproof, it would *be* foolproof. Alleroy now had to make certain everything went off as he would be gaming it out.

He had set the burner phone to go straight to voicemail with the message; "this is Ron Clark at Tribeca leave a detailed message thank you." Now, with his wife asleep, Alleroy was on his terrace calling the First Precinct from the burner.

"Yes, Officer Travers...this is Ron Clark with Robert De Niro's Tribeca productions. We're about to begin pre-production on Mr. De Niro's next film in which the First Precinct figures in a major way. It's a heist film, and Mr. De Niro, who plays a captain in the First, brings down the perpetrators. I should add that the movie highlights the bravery of the men and women of the First. Some of our producers will be asking to interview a few officers at the Precinct in a few days...perhaps you'd be willing to help us as well?"

That was Alleroy's opening call to the First. In that one call he found out that, at the hour of the evening he was considering, there were eight prowl cars on the street in the Precinct's one hundred square blocks, and that the area itself was considered a low-crime area. Something Officer Travers was quite proud of. He also learned that Monday, Thursday, Friday, and Saturday had the least occurrences of crime, and the crimes in the entire Precinct were mostly robberies and burglaries. He told

Officer Travers that the working title of the film was "The First" and that Tribeca would be in contact with him. He rang off quite satisfied with himself.

•   •   •

The next afternoon at five o'clock Alleroy, in jeans, sneakers and a work shirt, was standing on a corner diagonally across from the Coach and Crown. He had spent a mostly sleepless night gaming out more of his plan and now was waiting for Emanuel Graves to leave work and head for home. He wanted to see where Emanuel lived. *How* he lived. At five-fifteen Emanuel exited the C&C and made his way West on Wall to the Wall Street subway station at William Street. Walking on the other side of Wall Street, Alleroy followed him down into the subway and into the crowded rush-hour. He stood on the platform about fifteen yards away from Emanuel - taking care he was out of Emanuel's sightline. *Jesus, it's hot as a bitch and people do this every day.* The overhead LED sign read that the two train would be arriving at the station in three minutes. He was going to get into the car at the opposite end of where Emanuel would be. That was the plan. He almost didn't make it owing to, among all the others, three very large people getting *out* of the car and two very large people just in front of him getting *into* the car. *Holy shit. This is brutal.* The car's air-conditioning was operating at less than half-power. At the last moment he saw Emanuel realize this car wasn't as comfortable as the one behind it and had hastily gone to it instead. Alleroy, who had fought to enter this uncomfortably warm car, made even warmer by all the human flesh now packed into it, was not as quick - and so was stuck where he was. He knew where Emanuel *was* but had lost sight of him. As the train pulled away from the station Alleroy knew he was going to have to push his way through the crowd at the next stop to get into the car Emanuel was in. The iffy part of this maneuver was that this would place him in the same part of the car as Emanuel. *I don't know if I should. If he sees me...I have to jump two doors to the middle.* That, he decided, was his move. That, or else he would have to bag it. He would have to negotiate the distance of a car-and-a-half through what would be a very crowded financial area rush-hour crowd who were mostly trying to board this already crowded subway train. And who would all be moving perpendicular to the direction he would need to be moving.

The train was now pulling into the Fulton Street station. Alleroy was trying to turn himself around to at least face the door. This put him practically nose to nose with three people, all hopelessly trying not to make eye contact with each other. *He does this every day. It's a cattle car. He's crazy not to take the money.* After what seemed to Alleroy like an eternity in a sauna the train slowed and came to a halt and the crowd that stood on the platform waiting for the doors of the train to open, and intent on shoving their bodies into any car they could, was four deep. Alleroy started to push his way closer to his side of the door. "Excuse me. Excuse me. Getting out. Getting out. Excuse me. Please."

The doors of the train still hadn't opened and this clammy delay allowed him to get closer to the door. Outside, on the platform, at each door of each car, people were anxiously waiting to charge onto the train even though there was hardly any room for them to charge anywhere. After five or so hot, sweaty, seconds the doors opened. Channeling his inner Jim Brown, he bulled his way through the horde now trying to enter the car he was leaving - a horde single-mindedly hell-bent on getting home ASAP. No one seemed to care that he was pushing and shoving his way through them. Or that he was moving sideways and, in effect, was in everybody's way. It was something they seemed used to experiencing. He was fighting his way to the middle doors of the next car. As he passed the first door where Emanuel was standing, his back to the door, Alleroy could feel the cool air coming from inside this car. He managed to reach the middle doors of this car and, with Herculean effort, squeeze himself just past the car's doorframe and inside. People behind him were trying to jam themselves into the car and into him. He just went with the flow and allowed himself to be involuntarily moved a few feet deeper into the packed car. Finally, the doors closed and the train pulled away from the station. He could see Emanuel at the end of the car. *Thank God it's cool in here. Now...Where the hell are we going?*

Where they were going was to the South Bronx. The Intervale Avenue station at Westchester Avenue to be precise. The train rumbled through the tunnel, taking on and disgorging passengers as it went - but the mass of humanity never seemed to thin out. Alleroy kept his eye on Emanuel, who had his back to him, while wondering when the man would get off the train. The stops went by. The train was now at Ninety-Sixth Street and Broadway on the upper West side of Manhattan and the passenger load still showed little signs of thinning. If anything, the car was taking on a few more bodies. *Is everybody going where we're going?* Of course he knew they weren't, but he kept wondering when the car would become just a little less packed. Finally, at One Hundred and Thirty Fifth Street and Lenox Avenue, enough people got off so as to make it possible for Alleroy to be able to move his position. And ten minutes later the train emerged into the fading early evening sun.

Alleroy checked his watch; it was now six fifteen. Now, with fewer people in the car he had to be careful so as not to let Emanuel see him. With that in mind, he took an open seat at the very end of the car shielded by a heavy-set woman seated next to him. When the doors opened at Jackson Avenue he was ready to get off if Emanuel did. But Emanuel still stood where he stood since he got on. *How far up are we going to go?* Now, the train rolled into Prospect Avenue and still Emanuel didn't move. And now Intervale Avenue. Emanuel, lost in thoughts of Estella, suddenly bolted for the door. Alleroy was so surprised by Emanuel's sudden movement out the door that he almost got left on the train. He recovered just in time to slip through the closing doors and onto the platform as Emanuel began walking to the stairs that went down to the street below. He followed Emanuel down the stairs at a discrete distance. On the opposite side of the street Alleroy tailed him as he headed South on Intervale, keeping the same discrete distance diagonal to and behind Emanuel. A block later at One Hundred Sixty Third Street Emanuel made a left and walked one more block and then stepped into a bodega on the corner of One Hundred Sixty Third Street and Kelly. Alleroy pretended to be interested in the sneakers in a shoe store window. *Where the fuck am I?* After a few minutes Emanuel emerged carrying a bunch of flowers. *He bought flowers. He's got a girlfriend? Or a wife?* He continued on three more blocks with Alleroy following on the other side of the street. Just off the corner where One Hundred and Sixty Third Street met Simpson Street Emanuel turned into the Delevan. Across the street Alleroy stood looking at the sign; *otel De evan? Derevan? Denevan? I'll Google it later. This is where you live? Yeah, you'll take the bucks.* He stood there for a while thinking about going into the building, thought better of it, and then thought about flagging a cab and then thought better of that as well. *Too expensive. Jesus...it's come to this Rich. Take the train. At least going downtown at this hour won't be crowded. I'll probably sit all the way.* He was glad it was early evening and still light out, and he'd had the foresight to throw some jeans and denim clothes in a gym bag earlier. Changing in the back seat of his car was a necessary pain in the ass. Besides not having to take that sweaty train ride uptown dressed for the office, he was now equally glad that he didn't have to walk through this neighborhood in a stick-out-like-a-sore-thumb $30K Brioni suit. He suddenly stopped walking; he'd had an insight. He understood that death wasn't what he feared. It was being mugged or being physically hurt - and *not* killed. He stood there with this sudden awareness. A few seconds later he began to walk back to the Intervale Avenue el station. *Probably why the thought of going into a bad neighborhood and insulting someone never even entered my mind.* He continued on to the el station. *It'll be time I can use to think about the next steps.*

TWELVE

Estella Cendy Rosario's people came from The Dominican Republic, a country where child marriage is legal, and where it is common for young girls to move in to the homes of grown men and become their wives. When she was thirteen two of her friends, also thirteen, were raped. All of this made her somewhat wary of men. Twenty-seven years before, Estella came to America to live with her Aunt Valentina, an American citizen, on Manhattan's upper West side. This, so she could eventually go to an American community college. She was then fourteen. As a minor child and family-sponsored immigrant, she obtained a green-card and, as she was already proficient in English, became a citizen when she was eighteen. That same year she graduated with honors from Commerce High School. With the funds her parents sent from the DR, combined with her various menial service sector jobs, she was able to support herself without burdening her aunt. She then enrolled in The Bronx Community College of The City University of New York. Her parents, and her aunt, were understandably proud of her. She graduated with honors at age twenty-one with an Associate in Applied Science Degree in Computer Information Systems. Upon graduating in 2001 she got a job as a computer support specialist with Loehmann's Department stores in Manhattan. She was forced to move back in with her aunt in 2011 after she got out of an abusive marriage with a man who also had a prior secret life of crime. Except for that, things were going well for her - until the last of Loehmann's 39 stores closed in 2014. She was without a paycheck and found it difficult in the economic climate to get another decent-paying corporate job. Or was it that she was a woman? Or a Latina? Or that she was in her mid-thirties? She gave those questions a passing thought and, rather than dwell on this unfortunate turn of events, got on with it. Getting on with it meant taking what she could and looking ahead instead of back. After a few weeks of searching, she got a check-out job in a Key Foods near her aunt's apartment on Amsterdam Avenue on Manhattan's Upper West side. When her dear aunt passed away she could no longer afford to live on *any* side of Manhattan, East or West, Upper or Lower. Still wanting to be close to Manhattan, and the possibility of another job in her field, the South Bronx was her best alternative. The Delevan, with its furnished rooms, was the only place that was both cheap and without the usual rental requirements of most buildings, namely a job and forty times the monthly rent in the bank. Having become a valued employee, her job at Key Foods was transferred with her and this was how she found herself now working at the Key Foods on Southern Boulevard and East One Hundred and Sixty-Seventh Street in The Bronx. She made her parents aware of all of this while leading them to think none of it was a hardship for her. But, in truth, she was struggling - and not happy. Reading Márquez she thought she'd never meet her Florentino. Now, meeting Emanuel, she wondered if, by the grace of kind fate, she had.

•   •   •

Emanuel was also wondering. He liked this woman a lot. It was obvious to him that Estella was a person of quality; intelligent and sympathetic. It was also obvious that she was both strong *and* feminine. He could tell she liked him, but *he* was wondering - even though he sensed that she indeed possessed the qualities he saw in her - would she still want him when she learned what he did to pay the rent? When she learned of his infirmities? To be precise, it was more than wondering - it was fear. He was a bit scared of the possibility that she *wouldn't* still like him. So he was quite a bit more than scared to reveal himself to her completely. He wanted to, he *so* wanted to, but...If he did, *when* he did, would that reduce him in her eyes? He was aware that this questioning of her character was an insult - even *if* it was unspoken. But his fears were so etched into his psyche that he was powerless to override them. At least, at present. He hoped that in time, if they were to continue - and he so hoped they would - that she would show him that his fear that his infirmities would turn her off were unfounded. He longed to be close to a woman again. To that nurturing strength unique to women. He *knew* that a good woman would understand, be accepting...love him, in spite of his wounds. *Knew* it, and yet, it wasn't enough to just know it. He *also* knew that if he didn't love *himself*, a woman, *any* woman, any *person*, would soon tire of it all, be exhausted by the effort to continually strengthen him. He knew that a woman, especially one who chose to give herself to a man, would ultimately be disappointed in his shame, and his inability to be comfortable with who he was - warts and all. So he knew that if there was to be any future for himself and Estella, and he so *badly* wanted the possibility of this future, he would have to be fearless in baring himself to her and unashamed of the hand life had given him to play. He *knew* this, yet...

• • •

Estella finished shaving whatever barely perceptible stubble there was on her legs and underarms, rinsed off, and stepped out of her shower. She dried herself briskly, wrapped the terry bath sheet around her torso, combed her medium-length raven hair, and then brushed her teeth. She paused to look at the TV which, when turned on, was set to a news channel. What caught her attention was that the assembled pundits were commenting on the draconian restrictions being placed on women in Missouri who needed an abortion. She stared in utter dismay. *What are girls supposed to do if they're raped? Self-righteous idiots. What were my friends supposed to do, become mothers at thirteen?* Shaking her head, she reached into the drawer in the nightstand next to the sofa bed and took out her nail care products. She sat down and began to carefully color her toenails with insta-dry nail polish. The mani-pedis of the past were now a luxury she didn't need to spend money on, and besides, she liked doing her own nails. Tonight she chose a bright red. She was five-six, had a medium frame, and weighed one hundred forty to one hundred and forty-five pounds. This number depended on how much she gave in to her love of chocolate which, since meeting Emanuel, she was resisting mightily. Commensurate with her height, her feet were long and slender - size eight and a half. When she was at home she walked around barefoot on her floors which she kept as clean and polished as her nails. As an exercise she occasionally walked on the balls of her feet. She liked that Emanuel was tall - at least six foot - and husky. Tonight, for their second date, she and Emanuel would be going to the Concourse Plaza Multiplex to see Roma. Angry at what she was seeing and hearing about Missouri she was glad it was seven and time to change the channel. Jeopardy was about to begin and she enjoyed watching it and seeing how many questions she could answer correctly. She usually did quite well. Emanuel would be knocking on her door in a half-hour, perfect timing for the eight-twenty showing. It would be a one block walk to the BX6 Bus at Southern Boulevard, a twenty minute bus ride west on One Hundred Sixty-Third Street and then a pleasant five minute walk to the Grand Concourse. Time to talk.

She polished her toenails *and* her fingernails as she watched Single Jeopardy. From her armoire she chose a colorful African print linen/cotton summer dress and began to dress for her date just as Double Jeopardy began.

●   ●   ●

At the same time that Estella and Emanuel were getting ready to go to see Roma, Richard Alleroy, on the pretext of a late business dinner, was walking the streets of the area covered by the First Precinct. This was the third night he had walked these streets. He noticed that on every block there were at least two or three older cars. The kind that had the button door locks that could be jimmied. He had thought McGarrity's, a bar on Nassau and Beaver Streets, would do nicely for the pitch he was formulating in his mind. It was seven-twenty PM and the bar, which was crowded with people when Alleroy entered, was beginning to thin out. That was good. Still, he decided on his way back down to his garage to check out some other locations that might better suit his purpose.

On this third night, he concluded from his thorough reconnaissance of the area that The Pearl Bar on the corner of Pearl and William Streets was a better fit for what he had in mind. This night, at 9 PM, he entered the Pearl, which he knew, from his walk the night before, would be closing at eleven and which was now about a third full. He entered, went to the bar, and ordered a well *bourbon* neat. The barman, an older ruddy faced purveyor of spirits, poured a generous drink. Alleroy laid a twenty on the bar, and took his glass to a small table at the window from where he sat watching the street and sipping his whiskey. He was noting the traffic and the pedestrians. But mostly, if any prowl cars or beat police appeared while he was there.

• • •

Emanuel had thought to stop at the bodega on Kelly and pick out one of the mixed bouquets of colorful flowers outside the store. *I hope she'll like these.* Now, bouquet in hand, as he approached Estella's door his nervousness was palpable. He felt a kind of fear he hadn't felt in years. A fear he hadn't felt at all on their first date in the Chinese restaurant. He had called to ask her if she wanted to see Roma with him the night after they ate Chinese food together. But, now that this second date, this movie night was upon him, it took on some meaning in Emanuel's mind that made him edgy. He felt his nerves getting to him earlier at work thinking about this night and realizing that there might be something happening here that was far more serious than casually splitting some shrimp chow fun and wok fried blistered green beans. Emanuel was palpably nervous. He reached her door and stood there. Stood there afraid to knock. Afraid that this was something more than he was ready to handle. It might have only been a second date, but he was keenly aware that Estella was someone special. Someone deserving of flowers. Someone for the long haul. He felt this from the moment they met, and now he was afraid he might be starting something he couldn't finish – and she would be a casualty. *Do I wanna do this? If...If I do this how far am I willing to go? Can I tell her I work in a toilet? That I've had to wear a diaper and will probably have to do so again...more than a few times?* He stood there turning these scary thoughts over in his mind. Finally, he reached a conclusion. *I...I can't do this. I can't. How can I ever be completely honest with her?* He turned and began walking back to the elevator - then he stopped. *Emanuel, are you sure you want to end this? Because this is what you're doing.* He stood there debating what to do. He felt...He *knew*...his life was at a crossroad. He was keenly aware that this was possibly his last chance at something good. He knew how much what he did next would mean to the rest of his life. He knew how wonderful this woman was. She was a keeper. Not to be trifled with. He sensed she possessed a formidable weight. *Do I take this leap? I'll have to show this woman who I am. All of it. Am I going to chicken out of this and slink away like a coward? The way I did the other night? Am I a coward? Do I deserve what I know I want? Am I a phony?* He stood there questioning himself. *Emanuel! Answer!* Questioning his very being. Knowing what the answers to these questions *had* to be - or he would well and *truly* become invisible. He stood there for what seemed like an eternity. The two paths leading to his future lay clearly before him. Seconds passed before he took a deep breath, and summoning all the courage he *hoped* he possessed, he turned - and with resolve walked back to Estella's door. Without thinking, without pausing, he knocked.

THIRTEEN

Now, convinced that he had found the perfect place to carry out his plan, Alleroy left the Pearl, walked to where he parked his car and drove home. Tomorrow evening, just to make sure, he would again sit in The Pearl and suss out the street traffic, and after that he would meet his sister at the JFK Hilton to get the hundred and fifty thousand dollars in cash she was bringing in. As he had to do for the last few weeks, he had to keep up the charade of being busy with work for his wife. At least his children were out of the house. *I have to get the cash, and then I have to go to that restaurant and convince this guy to do what I need him to do. He'll do it. I'm reading him right...He will.*

At ten-twenty PM he left his Mercedes in his garage, walked two blocks, breezily entered his building while offering his usual perfunctory greeting to the night doorman, and proceeded on up to his penthouse triplex. He was eerily satisfied with the steps he was about to take. Sure in his conviction that his plan was well thought out and would, without a doubt, solve his financial problem and save him from having to live in shame.

Richard Alleroy wasn't known as one of the models for the character of Gordon Gekko in the movie Wall Street for nothing. Before he ever set foot on Wall Street, he had almost a rabid desire and a fanatical commitment to be the best. Better than the best. And he had no qualms about going to any lengths to be *just* that. A world-class manipulator, he possessed a strong analytical foundation coupled with what others perceived to be a cold intensity. As such, he was a huge risk taker. He was almost the perfect thief. Almost. The fate of this man who lived in a penthouse now lay in the hands of a nobody who lived in a dump and cleaned toilets for a pittance. As an avid admirer of Dada, Alleroy had to admit that the whole thing was perfectly surreal.

•   •   •

The bouquet Emanuel gave to Estella has some peonies in it – Emanuel didn't know what most of the flowers were, he knew the daisies and the two red roses but that was it - he just knew they looked pretty. Estella was touched that Emanuel brought her flowers. A man hadn't given her flowers in what seemed like forever. After she cut the bottoms of the stems and put the flowers in a vase, Estella pinned one of the smaller pale pink peonies in her hair above her left ear. The contrast against her jet black hair was striking and as Emanuel watched her do that he recognized that she was so much more than just pretty. He was struck by how graceful and truly beautiful she was. Emanuel told her how pretty the flower looked in her hair and she was clearly pleased that he liked it.

On the walk to the bus that would take them across One Hundred Sixty-Third Street Estella told Emanuel that she had been wanting to see Roma ever since it came to the Multiplex but that she didn't want to go alone. "I'm glad you wanted to see Roma Emanuel. I might have had to wait until it played on TV to see it, and then I don't think it would have been the same experience."

She had taken Emanuel's arm as they walked, and although he was happy at having such a beautiful woman on his arm, his thoughts about having to tell her things about himself that he was ashamed of were still nagging at him. "I haven't been to a movie theater in so long. Now that I think about it I guess I didn't want to go alone either."

She turned to him and smiled. "I like that I can wear heels with you."

Emanuel searched his mind for something clever to say in response to that but nothing came and he fell silent as they continued on to the bus stop. *Jesus, I like this woman. I have to tell her. I have to.* The more he saw how wonderful a life with her could be the more upset with himself he became. However, his outward demeanor didn't reveal the conflict he was experiencing within his soul. *There's only one way to rid myself of this...this feeling, and that's to come clean. Tonight. I have to. It can't be any other way. If I lose her I lose her. It wasn't meant to be.*

Estella had her own thoughts; she was thinking that Emanuel had great strength. *This is a real man. He's decent...and caring. I want to know more about him.* And just the Emanuel broke the silence; "How do you feel about eating at a Dominican restaurant after the movie?"

"I'd love it Emanuel."

"Great. Because there's a good one three blocks from the movie called Alebrescado, I looked it up."

"Wow... I would love some home cooking. Do you know if they have goat?"

"The menu said they did."

"You checked the menu?"

"And the reviews. They're all pretty good."

"Emanuel...You know, I knew you were—" She stopped and turned to him. "Can I please call you Manny?"

"You know...I have to say I haven't heard 'Manny' come out of the mouth of a pretty woman in too many years. Manny sounds nice coming from you. I...I... you know, I really like your voice Estella."

"Stella. Manny and Stella. Yes?"

They stood looking at each other - and Emanuel wanted *so* to kiss her, and Estella *so* wanted him to. Finally, she had to break the tension; "Manny, you know alebrescado in Dominican slang means excited."

They both smiled broadly and continued walking. They reached the bus stop just as the bus came.

"Perfect timing eh...Stella?"

"Perfect...Manny."

•　　•　　•

Alleroy was opening a bottle of wine. Margaret, who insisted on waiting up for him this night, was taking a chicken out of the oven. She had roasted it along with potatoes, carrots and parsnips. She had also put together a simple butter lettuce, avocado and radish salad, showered with some shaved Reggiano and lightly dressed with a vinaigrette. She loved to cook and was quite good at it. Alleroy, once again, was about to go through the motions of someone to whom food had some taste. He had absolutely no appetite, and when Margaret remarked that he looked as if he'd lost weight he told her he was on a new regimen at the gym and his new trainer was making him work very hard. He also told her some business had come up and he would be home quite late tomorrow night also and please not to wait up again. Before his partners busted him his life was a bit of a lie - *now* his life had become a complete and *utter* lie. Curiously, that was the only part of this that didn't bother him. Lie? So *what*. What bothered him was that he had been caught, and his reputation would be in ruins if he wasn't able to carry out his demented plan - which he *knew* was demented, but it was all there was to do.

•   •   •

Her arm in his, they were walking to the restaurant. "Manny, did you like Roma as much as I did?"

"I loved it Stella. Cuarón is a master. I had looked him up tonight also. You know that besides directing it, he wrote it, was the cinematographer, and edited it."

"I am *so* impressed. It is a glorious film. If someone would ask me what it's about I would have to say it's...it's... it's a meditation. On life. It's not about any *one* thing...it's about life. It's about *all* things. And, the cinematography...the cinematography...just *so* beautiful. Manny, *every* frame. And, the fact that it's in black and white...you know, in some strange way, films in black and white always seem even more real."

"I think if I saw this film in color..." He shook his head. "I'm not so sure it would have...you know, touched me as much."

She pressed herself closer to him as they neared the restaurant. "Manny, as much as I love goat, I think maybe it's a bit too late for something so heavy."

Emanuel, with his stomach problems, was glad to hear Estella say that. As they entered the restaurant she said; "I bet they have a nice avocado salad."

"They do. I saw it when I checked the menu. I think you're right about it being kind of late for anything heavy, and an avocado salad sounds just perfect to me."

As they sat down at one of the tables in a corner they both said; "And, a couple of Coronas." And they laughed.

They were enjoying the salads having agreed that the goat would wait for another time.

"Manny, please don't think I am prying but...I've noticed your watch doesn't work. Is there a reason you wear it?"

Emanuel took a pull on his Corona and then sat back. He was relieved to have been given this opening to tell Estella about his Gulf war experience. He saw it as a way for him to slowly tell her all the things he was ashamed of. He told her of his buddy who stepped on that explosive device and that he had set his watch to the time it happened as a reminder to honor his friend who had saved his life by pulling him from a burning vehicle. He told her about his time in the VA hospital and his PTSD. However, that was as far as he could go. He couldn't tell her the rest...it was certainly not the right time - or place. He vowed to himself that he would tell her everything in due time.

She listened to him, and while she sympathized with what he told her, she did not want to appear to be pitying him in any way. She simply reached across the table and held his hand as he related this part of his story. He understood her gesture to mean she sympathized with what he had gone through. They both knew that no sympathetic words were necessary. She wanted to tell him though, that she thought that wearing his dead buddy's watch that way was, perhaps, too much of a daily reminder of the horrors he experienced, but she knew that she shouldn't broach this subject now. In time.

Emanuel, having gotten some of this off his chest felt some relief, but he was aware that there was so much more he had to tell Estella. He also was aware he couldn't wait too long before he told her everything. He also hoped with all his heart that when he did she wouldn't turn away from him.

• • •

The next afternoon at four P.M. Alleroy left the New York Public Library on Fifth Avenue and Forty-Second Street where he had killed the rest of the day after sitting in a movie house for two-and-a-half hours. He couldn't tell you anything about the film - even if you offered him a thousand dollars to do so. He walked west across Forty-Second Street to Eighth Avenue to pick up his new I.D. It was four-fifteen PM and, as promised, it was ready. It was quite a good job of fakery and well worth the agreed on extra $200. He left feeling as if all was going smoothly. Phase one was almost complete. Tonight he would again go to The Pearl until closing just to double check everything; the cops, the traffic, the number of people in the bar and on the street at that hour, and after that drive to the airport to get the cash.

At one fifteen AM Richard Alleroy was driving away from the airport Hilton having just had drinks with his sister Mary Beth, who tried her best to talk him out of committing suicide. In the end, it was quite easy for him to assure her that what he was doing was the only way for his family to avoid suffering for what he'd done. She could see that he meant it when he said he didn't want to live with the ignominy this would otherwise bring to him and to Margaret and the kids. And, after seeing and hearing him, she was convinced and gave him the hundred and fifty thousand dollars in cash with the clear understanding that if he needed more he could have it. Having done what she could to try to dissuade her brother from what she thought he was about to do, they said their goodbyes. As planned, she would be on a plane back to *Zürich* the next afternoon. The cash was now secure in Alleroy's briefcase. *I'll show this to him with the promise of more. It'll be more effective if I use my attaché case. It'll work. It has to work.*

He got home at twelve-thirty. Margaret was asleep upstairs. Rather than stash the money in their safe he went to his study and locked it in one of his desk drawers. Having secured the cash, he then sat down at his wife's computer and Googled; in 1989 what war was the United States in? Alleroy was 20 years old then. This was a crucial part of the story that he knew days ago he would be creating for Emanuel Graves. As he usually did, he went to Google Web History and deleted this particular search in the browser. Tomorrow, he would begin phase two of his plan.

FOURTEEN

Alleroy entered the Coach and Crown. He took a seat at the end of the bar and ordered a Blanton's, one cube. A special, but expensive, treat. Louie, who never forgot a face that ordered a drink from him, or the drink they ordered, already knew what the man at the end of the bar would be wanting. Louie poured his drink; "run a tab?" Alleroy nodded his assent. He took a sip of the Blanton's. *The smooth butterscotch/vanilla warmth took him out of himself for an all too brief instant. He put the glass down, slowly rose from his seat and headed for the men's room.*

As Alleroy opened the men's room door Emanuel put his book aside and stood. Seeing who it was, Emanuel took a deep breath and wondered why this man was in his bathroom and what did he want. Alleroy walked to the sink and stood looking at his reflection in the mirror.

"I wanted you to know that I understand what you've gone through. In 1989 I was in Operation Just Cause in Panama. I saw the things you ended up enduring. I was lucky, and to this day, I feel guilty at having come through that hell in one piece."

Emanuel stood there looking at him, his brow furrowed in thought. His response was halting.

"All...right...and?

Alleroy turned to face Emanuel. "And...I'm sorry we got off on the wrong foot. In the park." He turned to face Emanuel. "Can we please start over?" Emanuel, thrown off balance by this turn of events, slowly nodded his assent.

Alleroy also nodded slowly. "I was in the 319th Military Intelligence Battalion."

Emanuel finally offered, "The Marines. 2nd Battalion 5th Marines."

"The two-five?" Alleroy seemed in awe. "Retreat, hell?" He had done his research well. He had Googled all the major forces in the Gulf war and knew that the legendary 2nd battalion 5th Marines were in the thick of it - and knew their motto. Further, he had gone over all the possible ways this could go. "My God...You...You were a member of the most highly decorated battalion in the Marine Corps?" Emanuel now saw before him someone whose admiration for his sacrifice seemed genuine and heartfelt. He managed; "Did uh...you see any action?"

The bathroom door opened, a man entered and went to a urinal. Out of the corner of his eye Alleroy watched as Emanuel did his job. *And now you work in a toilet.* The man dried his hands on the towel Emanuel gave him, went into his pocket, placed a dollar on the tip plate and left.

Emanuel threw the man's used towel into the linen bin as Alleroy continued; "Like I said, I was lucky. Real lucky. I *didn't* see any action. But, a real good buddy of mine, a guy I genuinely loved like a brother, wasn't so lucky. He was killed at a checkpoint outside PDF headquarters in Panama City. I was in the Jeep with him when it happened. He got shot in the back. First Lieutenant Robert Valencia, he got the Purple Heart. I was just an Army private, but we were tight. I think about him often. I'm not ashamed to say that I've cried over his grave quite a few times.

Emanuel sat down. "Excuse me for sitting, it's just I'm on my feet a lot and...Hey, I'm uh, sorry for your loss. Yeah, you *were* lucky, you came out of that thing a whole lot better than most."

"*Dumb* luck...We were pretty well off, so after I was mustered out my father was able to put me through college. You're sorry? I'm sorry about what they did with your discharge record. That's something to be real pissed about."

The door opened and another man entered and went into a stall. Alleroy thought it was a good time for him to return to the bar, let Emanuel do his job and think about their conversation. "I'll come back in a bit."

Alleroy left the men's room, sat back down at the end of the bar and leisurely sipped his drink. Searching the restaurant's patrons, he was again thankful that there was no one in the place who knew him. *He feels like we have something in common. We don't have the luxury of time here. Still, we have to reel him in slowly. He's a big fish. The biggest. After we see Royce pitch,*

I'll bring the Times to the park. Show him the Loomis story. He finished his drink, signaled Louie for another and rose to go back to the men's room.

He entered the men's room just as another man was leaving. He was met by the off-putting smell of a mixture of Clorox, Lysol Bathroom cleaner and feces. Emanuel was just coming out from one of the stalls. He had on his rubber gloves, and was holding a pail that had in it all his cleaning supplies. *Unbelievable. This is this guy's existence every lousy day. I'd be furious if I were fucked into this.* Seeing Alleroy, Emanuel just shook his head and proceeded to return all his cleaning equipment to the closet. He put the pail on the floor, took his supplies from it, and put them in the bathroom's closet. Alleroy watched him. *Christ, I feel like I'm seeing something this guy would hate anyone to see. It's like I'm seeing him naked.* Emanuel finished arranging the supplies on the closet shelf, closed it, turned to Alleroy and shrugged. "What are you going to do eh?"

Alleroy shook his head and looked at him. "I don't know if I could do it man."

"What else am I going to do?"

"I feel you."

"You *feel* me?"

"I...I didn't mean...It isn't fair. That's all. How the hell could they do this to a guy who served?"

Emanuel had no answer. He was exhausted by the rage he felt at this daily disrespect of his sacrifice. Every day he walked down Water Street to the Coach and Crown, every single time he entered this men's room, the anger he felt at being put in this situation, at not being good enough to be in the Fire Department, or the Police Department, when he had faced real gun fire and conflagration beyond what *anyone* should *ever* have to face, was all-encompassing. All-consuming. Without actually being killed in battle, he had lost his life. And his love. Now, he had another chance and, to add insult to injury, he had to admit to himself that he was terrified to come out from hiding.

"So, Emanuel...you married? Have a girlfriend?"

"A girlfriend."

"You guys live together?"

"Uh, well we just started. But Estella lives two floors above me so..."

"Estella...What a lovely name. Well, soon huh?" He winked.

"Maybe. We'll see."

"You really like her huh?"

"I think I love her."

"Then I know you'll understand. I know you already feel protective of Estella. Emanuel, for my wife's sake - and until I can sort myself out - I have to pretend I'm going into the office every day. Would you mind terribly if I sat with you sometime? Oh...my name is Craig...Craig Wilson. Junior, to be exact." He held his hand out to Emanuel, "to a new start then?" and the two men shook hands.

"Emanuel...I just have to know about your watch. I can't help thinking it signifies something important to you, yes?"

And Emanuel told "Craig" the story about his Marine buddy Sergeant Joe Mannion. When he finished the two men stood silent for a bit. Then Alleroy approached Emanuel and the two men embraced. They had a common bond. In a sense, *they* were buddies. At least, that's what Emanuel felt was the case. As he left the men's room Alleroy was thinking; *this guy and his girlfriend live in that fleabag in The Bronx.*

•   •   •

The Central New England Prep School Baseball League was pretty good as prep school leagues went. It had sent quite a few young men off to college on a free ride to play baseball on an athletic scholarship. Some, up to the show. Unfortunately, young Royce Alleroy would not be one of those players. Rather than having a curveball that fell off the plate, his, more often or not, got served up on a platter. His fast ball was clocked at 72 MPH on the gun. His three year record was four and six with two no-decisions. He was a *nice* player, but college scouts were not impressed by *nice*. Had they *been* impressed, it might have taken a small bit of financial pressure off of his father who was vacantly presiding over a gathering of the family at Amos Alonzo Stagg Field to watch young Royce pitch his heart out against Worcester.

Richard and Meg had flown Spirit to Exeter, and Emily and Anne picked them up at the airport. Richard Jr. met them in the stands. It was a beautiful day for baseball, sunny and mild without a trace of wind. Royce was pitching a pretty good game while his defense helped him out with a couple of sparkling plays. After one strikeout Royce looked up at his dad who, looking but not seeing, managed to give him a thumbs up though he had no clue as to what had just happened. It being a home crowd, Alleroy was reasonably sure his alternate cheering and groaning whenever the spectators cheered or groaned was consistent with rooting for the home team. His children were, of course, quite happy to see them both, and Richard Sr. played the role of the relaxed patriarch quite skillfully.

Exeter won the game on a last inning home run. Royce, however, was taken out in the sixth and got another no decision. They waited outside for him to clean up and after all the happy hugs and congratulations they went for an early dinner at their favorite hamburger and beer joint in town. Richard Jr. and Anne went in Emily's car, and Richard and Margaret went with Royce in his car. Once again, Alleroy was giving an Oscar-worthy performance as the dutiful paterfamilias. In truth, his mind was on being *just* that, the duty to the perfection of the scheme that *had* to save him from their abject disapproval. And, as soon as he got home and Margaret had gone upstairs to bed, he got on her computer, searched how to steal a car, and saw that something called a slide hammer would do the trick. He also found that *anyone* could purchase a slim jim and a slide hammer from Home Depot.

FIFTEEN

"*Being deeply loved by someone gives you strength, while loving someone deeply gives you courage.*"

Eyes closed, Emanuel had been meditating on this quote from The Way of Life for some ten minutes when he heard footsteps approaching and then felt someone quietly sit down on the other end of his bench. In that meditative ten minutes he had resolved to tell Estella everything. He would reveal all his infirmities to her and trust she would see past them to the man he was. She would understand that none of it mattered - and all of it was because he was defending his country. *I was doing something honorable. I was young, and dumb, and a pawn in a war for oil. Manny, man, you don't need to get into that. Just...tell her everything, the when and how of it, and she'll get it. She's smart. And kind. She'll get it. You won't lose her.* "*Loving someone deeply gives you courage,*" *Manny. Courage.*

After a few moments, he opened his eyes to see George and Gracie at his feet waiting for a few more groundnuts. And, he was surprised to also see Alleroy sitting three feet from him. He had an attaché case, which he laid flat on the bench between them, and The New York Times lay in his lap.

"I've interrupted you. I'm sorry but...I was hoping you'd be here this morning."

Emanuel, still with his thoughts as he absently reached into his paper bag and threw the two squirrels their treats - as well as some birdseed for the pigeons managed; "Every morning except Sunday."

He rose, walked to the fountain, took a long drink of water, returned and sat down.

"You okay?"

"I've been better Emanuel. Um...I wanted to show you something." He took the Times from under his arm. It was the back copy Alleroy ordered. He opened it to the page with the Jack Loomis hit-and-run story, slid closer to Emanuel and handed the Times to him. "Did you by any chance see this story about a hit-and run?"

Emanuel took the newspaper, gave the story a perfunctory look, shook his head and handed the paper back to Alleroy. "No."

"They still haven't caught whoever it was who did this. And, this guy Loomis was someone with juice. He had connections. Interesting eh?"

"I don't know...is it?" He briefly scanned the article. "And anyway, it only just happened a couple of weeks ago - they'll get whoever did it." He handed the newspaper back to Alleroy. "I mean, if you say this guy was important, they'll find the driver."

Alleroy raised his attaché case and slid the Times underneath it. "His company was in trouble."

"So?"

"So...it strikes me as curious."

"I'm not followi—Craig, really man. I'm sorry, but I just don't care about whatever this is, you know?"

"He committed fraud and was facing jail time, Emanuel."

"And he probably deserved it."

Emanuel couldn't have known, and, Alleroy suspected, wouldn't care to find out, that Loomis' company was *not* in trouble and Loomis himself hadn't done *anything* to warrant his being thrown in jail. Alleroy scooched over to the other end of the bench. "Could the 'accident' - he made the air quotes gesture - have been on purpose?"

"Umm..." Emanuel shook his head. *What is this guy on about?* "How should I know?"

"Maybe this guy couldn't stand being discredited among his peers, his family...and maybe this guy couldn't collect on suicide. So...maybe this guy worked it out this way."

"By getting himself run over." Emanuel was incredulous..

"It could have been his only way to save his family. He had a wife and three kids."

"You know...alright...Alright, let's say this guy made this insane plan and got himself killed so he could collect. And, by the way, insurance pays on suicide. Okay? The police'll—

—"Insurance doesn't pay if he just changed his policy. Not for two years."

"Look, *if* he did this deranged thing, they'll get whoever drove the car. There are probably paint particles left behind in every high speed hit-and-run. They'll run computerized tests. They'll track down the car, the owner, they'll—"

—"What if the car was stolen?"

"Oh, come on."

"Come on what? What if the car was stolen?"

And, it was just about then that the light went on in Emanuel's head. He said his next words looking straight ahead. "You...committed fraud."

"As I said."

Still looking straight ahead, Emanuel said, "And, you...don't want to go to jail."

"It's more than that. I'm so ashamed. I can't face my wife, my children, colleagues, my friends. I just want to disappear." This was the play. Not that he was most concerned about himself.

Emanuel now had the entire picture. "And you can't collect on suicide. Wow."

"Yes. Wow."

The two men sat silent for a couple of minutes.

"Craig, if your wife and children love y—"

—"Please...Emanuel...There's no way I can tell my wife and children that I stole from pension funds. How can I face them? I can't. I...I'm so ashamed." And he broke down in tears. The enormity of the consequences of being caught out, what his actions could lead to, unless his crazy scheme worked, came down on him like the proverbial ton of bricks. At that moment he was crushed...for *himself.*

Dude stole from pension funds? When Emanuel heard that "Craig" stole from pension funds he found it quite difficult to continue to sympathize with him. Of course, Alleroy said this on purpose - knowing this would engender in Emanuel some animus towards him.

Just then, George and Gracie scampered back to Emanuel. He took a couple of nuts from his wrinkled brown paper bag and held one out in each hand for them to take. He took such pleasure in watching them use their tiny paws to take the nuts from his hands. He put the bag back in his pocket of his cargo pants and sat back. He forced his mind back to Estella. *Loving someone deeply gives you courage. Tell her.* He wanted to be done with yet another strange conversation with Craig. This one, not as much cryptic as it was disturbing. Alleroy's tears made Emanuel angry. *Jeez man, you're crying? You robbed old people. Unreal.*

Alleroy was aware he was crying mostly for what he had done to himself, and *then* what this would do to his family. He felt no remorse about stealing huge amounts of monies from elderly pensioners. He took the crisp white linen handkerchief from his jacket's breast pocket to dry his eyes. "I'm sorry." He dabbed at the corners of his eyes. *Jesus...That just happened.* He finished wiping his eyes and put the handkerchief back in his breast pocket, still obsessively careful to arrange it just right. *The tears may have helped.* He had recovered his equilibrium. "I'm very sorry."

Emanuel, ignored the apology. His thoughts were now squarely on Estella and how to broach the subject of his infirmities, and his insecurities about them. Things about himself he had so far managed to avoid telling her. Things he knew he would have to tell her.

Alleroy was now composed. "You can see what a dreadful dilemma I'm facing."

Emanuel, torn away from his thoughts by this stranger, couldn't keep himself from responding with some annoyance; "Craig...Forgive me but...I have to ask; what, or who, are you sorry for? Exactly."

Alleroy, having gone over the many ways this back and forth could go, now had to choose to go with the way he'd decided to play it; further alienate Emanuel by telling him how he didn't feel one way or another about taking money from pension funds and, at the same time, play for sympathy. He needed to keep Emanuel on his side, and yet he also had to make Emanuel dislike him intensely enough to want to hit him with a speeding car. Want to kill him. It was a delicate balancing act, and one which Alleroy believed he was perfectly suited to perform.

"I'd be lying if I told you I was sorry for taking those funds." He looked at Emanuel trying to gauge the man's response to this admission. Emanuel turned and stared at him. Alleroy could see the animosity on Emanuel's face. "But, I *am* deeply sorry for what this could do to my wife and children." He knew this was what he was supposed to say as he clicked the locks on the attaché case, lifted the top, and swiveled the case around to face Emanuel.

"What the hell are...What is this?"

"*This*...is a down payment."

Emanuel was looking at forty thousand dollars laid out in two layers of twenty neat bundles. Alleroy thought that would be a good number for an opener. He waited a moment until Emanuel had taken in the sight of so much hard cash. Then he swiveled the case around so it faced him, slowly shut it, and left it sitting there on the bench between them.

"It's forty thousand" He stared at Emanuel who was shaking his head in disbelief. "And there's more if you help me."

Emanuel sat there frozen in disbelief at what he had just seen and heard. After some seconds, while Alleroy stared at him, Emanuel opened his mouth as if he was about to speak and then closed it. He sat there shaking his head as exactly what was being asked of him by this man became clear to him. Finally, after some ten long seconds had passed, he spoke.

"I can't help you. I'm sorry."

Alleroy already knew this would be Emanuel's first response. "Fifty thousand then." He kept staring at Emanuel. "You can do a lot for yourself and your girlfriend with this."

It was more than twice as much as Emanuel's life savings. "You're crazy."

Finally, Alleroy looked away. "I'm desperate. It's the only way I can save my reputation and my family. Madoff's son hung himself. His wife had to forfeit everything she had and eventually had to move away. All my kid's dreams and plans will be destroyed if I don't do this." He closed his attaché case.

Emanuel was still shaking his head. *Fifty thousand dollars?* "I sympathize with your problem but, uh...There's no way I can be a part of this." With that Emanuel stood. "You, and your family, ought to maybe learn to live a simpler life. Think about it. I have to go." *Fifty thousand dollars?*

Emanuel had been saving one hundred dollars a month for all the years he'd been at The Coach and Crown. This little bit more than twenty-four thousand dollars in his savings account was his nest egg. Not a lot to retire on. Fifty thousand dollars was a lot of money to him.

Alleroy watched Emanuel walk away. *I can convince this guy.*

SIXTEEN

All the way uptown that early evening Emanuel, try as he might, could not keep from seeing that forty thousand dollars staring up at him from that attaché case. *And then he said fifty.* Emanuel stared blindly out of the train window as it emerged from the tunnel. *What the f—why are you even thinking about this? This guy is crazy, and he's trying to drag you into his craziness.* However, his thoughts were getting more and more fanciful, and he couldn't shut them out. *We could get a place together. Who knows how much he's willing to pay. I could quit. Maybe now I could get another job. They'll give me a very good recommendation.* And then he would haul himself back to reality. *Yeah, just run some guy over. Nothing to it.* And then; *He stole money from hard working senior citizens. The money they needed to live out their lives.* And then; *I wonder how much. Fifty? Seventy-five? A hundred? He's pretty desperate.* So flooded by these thoughts was he that he almost missed his stop. And, walking home he was thinking that before he ever did such a thing - if he ever did such a thing - it would be because there was a life together to be had for him and Estella. So now, before he could even make such a decision, he *had* to tell her everything about himself. Would she still want him the way he wanted her? *And,* if she did, could he then commit premeditated murder? *We all have our price don't we?* He stopped to pick out a bouquet from the flowers lined up in front of the bodega on Kelly Street. *A hundred thousand! It would mean a new life for us. We could go to all those places, see all those historic sites...I could take us to San Sebastian...We could eat all those wonderful dishes.*

Emanuel Graves was, as noted, born in Brooklyn. However, his was far from a normal childhood experience. For one thing, he never met his father. For another, his mother was a nodding-out junkie. Child Protective Services finally took him from her and placed him in a foster group home after receiving more than one complaint about Emanuel being found sitting on the stoop of his apartment building dirty and unfed, and his mother passed out on the stairs of their one room four floor walk-up. He was six years old. In the third year he was there his mother overdosed. He had no living relatives. In New York City, children can stay in foster care until they reach adulthood. At age fifteen, Emanuel got a break and was adopted by a kindly family who lived in The Bronx, and who had a boy his age but could not have any more children. His new brother and he got on well and Emanuel, who was already in high school through CPS, was enrolled in his brother's high school. He graduated high school at age eighteen, took a summer job upstate. Then the unthinkable happened, and his new family lost their lives when a truck sideswiped them as they were on their way upstate to visit him.

Emanuel was distraught and once again, alone. He had nothing, and nowhere to go back to. So, he did the only thing he could think to do - he joined the Marines. He completed his basic training at Parris Island, South Carolina and was sent to the Middle East as a member of the storied, highly decorated 2nd Battalion 5th Marines. He found something in the Marines that he never had before. He was a valued member of a team, and in such life and death situations deep bonds are forged. Deep, almost loving, bonds. And then Joe Mannion stepped on an EFP. And Emanuel ended up in that military hospital with PTSD. Sad, angry, *very* angry, and again very, *very* alone.

So, why shouldn't he take this money? The universe damn well owed him! Whether irrational or not, this was where Emanuel was at. This Craig guy was a piece of shit. He stole from old people. There were a hundred reasons in Emanuel's mind to rationalize what he was thinking about doing. One for every lousy break he had to shrug off in order just to continue. But first he would have to square things with Estella - or, there would be no *real* reason for him to run this Craig guy down.

●   ●   ●

Alleroy called his sister from a pay phone to tell her he was eventually going to get rid of Margaret's laptop and to please explain to her what happened to it, and that he had to do it and why he had to do it. When she asked why he had to do it, he told her that if the insurance company went

into it, the chance was they would negate the pay-out. When she said she
didn't understand why that could be, he further explained that he had to
do some research on it for his plan and, even though he had been careful
to erase his searches, the possibility, however small, existed that it could
compromise all of them and why take the chance. "You want to be certain
you'll get your money back, don't you?" And, that was enough to get her
to drop the subject.

•   •   •

"Stella, how do you feel about some La Bandera Dominicana with goat?"
Emanuel was on the phone with Stella. "Maybe after Jeopardy we go to
Alebrescado?" Estella, of course, said yes right away. Emanuel had made
his mind up, and tonight he was going to tell Estella everything on the bus
ride home from the restaurant. "I'll call for you about a quarter of eight?"

Estella was so glad he called. "I don't know who I'm more excited to
see Manny - you or the goat." They laughed and rang off.

Emanuel showered, shaved, and dressed before Jeopardy. He
answered almost all the questions, including final Jeopardy, and clicked
off the TV. He put on a lightweight windbreaker, grabbed the bouquet
which he managed to squeeze into the refrigerator, left his room, and
headed up two floors to Estella. He felt a little nervous as he waited for the
elevator. *She'll understand. I know she will. But I can't minimize it. I have to give
it to her straight.* The elevator arrived and Emanuel got in and pressed ten.
Here we go Manny. The elevator lurched slowly upward. *I can do this.* And, of
course, it stopped on nine, whereupon old Mrs. Guilfoyle, walker and all,
slowly maneuvered herself into the small car.

"Emanuel...If you don't mind, I'll take a ride with you."

"Of course not. It's always nice to see you. How are you Mrs. G?"

"Old, Emanuel, thank you."

"No, you're not. Come on with your bad self."

She smiled and said what she'd said to him many times before, "My
advice Emanuel...don't grow old." And, as always, he responded; "I'm
trying Mrs. G. I'm trying."

The elevator came to a shuddering stop on ten. Emanuel smooshed
himself between Mrs. Guilfoyle's walker and the wall in order to slide to

the door. "Those are very pretty flowers Emanuel. Some girl is very lucky."
As the elevator door closed Emanuel thanked her - and blew her a kiss. He
walked down the hallway to Estella's door. *It's good to make her smile.*

·   ·   ·

Alleroy had been silently standing in the doorway of the kitchen watching
his wife prepare a perfect salade niçoise for their dinner. He had asked her
if she didn't mind eating something light this evening and straight away
she thought she'd make this favorite of theirs. Now, watching the
attention she paid to composing this simple dish, he was overcome with
emotion. It was everything flooding over him at once; the knowledge that
he would soon be leaving her, the many wonderful moments they had
shared, how truly she loved him, how very kind she was, how supportive,
how beautiful...it was too much. He had to step into the dining room for a
minute to compose himself before walking back into the kitchen. He came
up behind her and kissed the nape of her neck. She pressed herself back
into him and they stood like that for a few seconds. "I love you Meg." She
turned to him. "Maybe I should make a niçoise more often." She kissed
him lightly on the mouth and started to turn back around. Alleroy spun
her back around to him and kissed her passionately. The fork she was
holding in her hand clattered to the floor and her arms went up and
around his neck. He pulled back ever so slightly; "The salad will keep."
There is some truth in the idea that knowing of one's impending death can
be an aphrodisiac. And he took her by the hand towards the stairs.

SEVENTEEN

The goat was delicious. Now, walking to the bus that would take them east to The Delevan, Emanuel was screwing up his courage. How was Estella going to respond to what he was going to tell her about himself? This was the key to everything he was fantasizing. Would he still have a girlfriend? Would he do this thing that would reward him with many thousands of dollars? Would they then live together somewhere in an apartment that was far better than where they now were? They made some small talk about how tasty Alebrescado's version of La Bandera Dominicana was. Estella was quite impressed; "I think my parents would like it too." Emanuel nodded. Estella pulled his arm closer to her. "I would love to get them here. It would be so much better for them to live here." He nodded. *The money would do it.*

The bus arrived. They boarded and Emanuel was glad that there weren't too many other riders. They took one of the double seats and settled in for the twenty minute bus ride from the West Bronx to the East Bronx. This ride, thought Emanuel, this ride...will only determine the rest of my life. She sat looking out of the window as the bus started up. Emanuel knew he had to speak up. Now. "Stella...I need to tell you some things about myself that...things about me that I'm scared to tell you."

She turned to look at him; "You're scared to tell me? I don't...What are you talking about?"

Emanuel felt as if he'd started this whole thing off in the wrong way. "No, it's not...I'm not...I told you I'm a veteran yes? My watch?"

She nodded. "Yes...That had to be so hard for you Manny. I'm so sorry you had to go through all that."

He started to say something and stopped. "What is it, Manny? You can tell me."

He gave what he was about to say some thought. "It's...I'm so embarrassed to have to tell you these things about me Stella. I'm afraid it will change something between us. I can't help it, but it's how I feel."

"Manny, what is it? It can't be that terrible, Manny. It can't."

"You know I love you Stella. You know that, right?"

She looked at him for some seconds. "Manny, I love you too. That means, unless you're going to tell me you're some kind of monster, I am going to keep loving you. Lo entiendes? Do you understand?"

He took a long pause and a deep breath. "I have to wear..." He took another deep breath and jumped..."an adult diaper sometimes. Not tonight, not tonight. But sometimes. Stella...I came out of that war with a real bad gastro-intestinal problem. And I...I'm ashamed of it. I have never ever told anyone about this, and I have been afraid to tell you because..."

Estella was looking at him with her brow furrowed. "Manny, Manny...It's alr—Manny, I once mistakenly married a man who had secrets. Too many secrets. You are a hero. He...he was a coward. Violent. To a woman. I don't know how any self-respecting woman can be with a man who can be violent with her...whatever the excuse. One of the reasons I love you is because you are not like that. You—"

—"Stella, listen to me...there's more. There's more." He had to get it out quickly before he lost his courage. "I'm not a waiter in that restaurant. I'm the men's room attendant. It was the only job I could get when I was discha—"

She put her finger to his lips. He didn't need to justify anything, or make any excuses, or offer any reasons...She understood immediately how much this had caused him to feel diminished, less than. She knew he didn't want her pity, even though that emotion was coursing through her. He just wanted her love. And her love was what she wanted to give to him.

"Manny...So what? It's honest work. So *fucking* what!" This, from a woman who couldn't remember when she last said an off-color word. That it came out of her mouth surprised her. But, that was how vehemently she felt about how little any of this mattered to her. This was a good man. She looked at him with that look you've seen - if you're a fortunate man. It is the look a man gets from a woman which contains a love that cannot be measured. It is a look that can *only* come from the eyes of a woman. A crazy combination of mist and sparkle fills their eyes. It is as if their eyes become shimmering stars. It is born of the millennia of evolutionary experience that resides in *every* female of the species. A look just waiting, hoping, *needing* to be triggered. *This* was what Emanuel was now seeing. He had never before seen this look in a woman's eyes, not even from that girl he pushed away so long ago in another lifetime.

"You still want to be with me? Even though—"

—"Even though you are *one silly man* Emanuel Graves."

She went from stern to smile in the blink of an eye. "Yes! Even though *that* and all the rest of it." She shook him by his shoulders. "I'll tell you a few embarrassing things about myself some time. Another night." She let out a short laugh. "Like you're the only one?" And then she said: "Not tonight - and not most nights.

Right? And you're an honest working man. Right?" And then: "Will you please kiss me already?"

Emanuel didn't need too much prompting other than that. He kissed Estella, and the thrill he felt was unlike anything he ever felt from any other kiss. He was now almost moved to tears. The relief he felt was beyond explainable. He felt all the tension leave his body. Estella could feel it as well. She was comforted by his knowing that he could trust her with his deepest secrets. By his knowing that she wouldn't find him wanting for something that was no fault of his own. Things he thought would matter, and she thought were irrelevant - as far as who he was.

For the rest of the way home they sat very close together. She told him about her Aunt Valentina, and how her Aunt made it possible for her to go to college and get a degree. And how, when her Aunt passed, she had to move to The Bronx, and why she was *so* very glad fate led her to The Delevan. At hearing that, Emanuel fairly glowed - and they kissed again. "You two need to get a room." The man seated behind them laughed. And Manny and Stella laughed too. "An' I gotta get home to my wife." And they all laughed some more. At the next stop the man got off, and Emanuel said; "Have fun." Their new friend was laughing along with them as he stepped off the bus.

Emanuel and Estella were now, in some mystical way, sanctified by this bus ride. He had told Estella everything and was relieved it didn't drive her away. He felt lighter. She, in turn, was relieved that he had unburdened himself. She could bear all the weight he would ever lay on her. They each felt, without being able to articulate the feeling, as if some inextricable bond had been created between them in this last twenty wonderful minutes of their life. It was as if they had both tuned in to the same cosmic wavelength that revealed this truth to them; that the Gods had conspired to place them in this time and space. She had her Florentino. And, he knew the *real* reason he had pushed his first girlfriend away from him so long ago. Love had also managed to make him forget what might lay before him in the next few days.

•   •   •

They lay there having exhausted themselves in remembered pleasures that were now all too infrequent. Alleroy lay there looking at the ceiling, thinking this lust he was experiencing was probably the way one's feelings grew more intense as one was walking towards the electric chair.

•   •   •

Manny and Stella sealed their love that night in his sofa-bed. Since it had been a long, long time for each of them since they had been intimate with someone it *was* somewhat awkward at first. But, Estella slowly led them both from awkward to comfortable. Her passion burned so brightly that Emanuel was guided to his own free expression of pure animal sex. In the end it was everything they could have hoped for; their fantasies of how it could be with each other actualized. At last, after a quiet while Estella spoke;

"Manny, how would you feel about getting an apartment somewhere?"

Emanuel turned to her; "Stella...That would be...I would love it."

She threw her arm over his chest and cuddled closer to him.

"Manny, let's find one with a nice kitchen. I could cook all these wonderful Dominican dishes for you. And not spicy."

He was already half asleep. She smiled, kissed his cheek, and closed her eyes. Manny and Stella were now, for better or for worse, one. And, Emanuel, for better or for worse, was now thinking about an apartment, and what Estella said about wanting to bring her parents here...and checking out studying Spanish on-line for free. And, thinking he now might *have* to hear Craig out.

EIGHTEEN

It was another balmy, beautiful April early morning. As usual, Emanuel was in Mannahatta Park. He had tried to read from The Way of Life but finally gave up because he could think of nothing else but last night and this morning. Estella occupied every corner of his mind as he threw groundnuts to George and Gracie.

Alleroy was leaning on one of the railings that ran along the park's boundary, out of Emanuel's sight line. He had been watching Emanuel for a few minutes from about half a block away. This time, Alleroy had fifty thousand dollars in rubber-banded bundles sitting neatly beneath the push-button flap in his attaché case. After a few minutes of watching Emanuel he decided that it was time to circle around and enter the park on the path that led to where Emanuel was sitting.

Emanuel saw Alleroy entering the park and coming down the path. He was carrying his attaché case. His thoughts of Estella and the flashbacks on their lovemaking were about to be interrupted. Alleroy was carrying his *attaché* case. *He's got the forty thousand in there again.*

This has to mean he's got a very large insurance policy or he wouldn't even be considering this insanity. Alleroy had reached Emanuel's bench.

"Well, well...George, Gracie...look...it's Craig."

Alleroy chuckled as he sat down on the end of the bench. "I see your best friends are all here."

Emanuel tossed a couple of more groundnuts to them and watched as they scuttled off.

"Better than some people."

"Have you given my proposition some thought?"

Emanuel let out a nervous laugh at the question. He gave some thought as to how to respond. Finally, he said; "Craig...you think what you're asking me to do is what...easy?"

"I didn't say it would be easy. Did I?"

Emanuel had indeed given the proposition some thought. "The car has to be stolen."

"That way it can't be traced back to the driver."

"Yes... I *know* that."

"*I* know you can use this money." He softly patted the attaché case which he had laid on his lap.

Emanuel decided to ignore that statement for the time being. "And, of course, you *also* know that I can steal a car."

"An older model, yes. There are at least one or two, sometimes more, parked on almost every street at night on the upper West side. I checked. And anyone can see how to steal a car on the net."

"You Googled it." Another statement said with some amazement.

"Yes. And I've scouted the uptown streets as to the parking, and that's what I've seen." He looked straight ahead as he turned his attaché case so the clasps were facing Emanuel. "I bought the slim jim, slide hammer and large gym bag at Home Depot. And you'll wear gloves. For everything."

Emanuel studied him for a few seconds. "You're pretty cold-blooded cray-cray aren't you?"

Alleroy kept looking straight ahead; "Why? Because I'm trying to save my wife and children from the poorhouse?"

"And what's a slide hammer anyway?"

"It's about two feet long. All you do is screw the slide hammer into the ignition lock then give it a few pulls and the ignition cylinder will pull straight out. Then just shove a flat head screwdriver into the ignition switch and start the car. You can see how easy it is to do on a bunch of videos on You Tube. That's what I did. You carry the tools in a gym bag. I'll buy one big enough and—"

—"All I *do*? I *carry*?" Emanuel shook his head in disbelief. "Okay...Back up! I'm *not* a murderer. I know I may have *said* it but—" He turned to Alleroy. "—believe me, I did *not* mean it that way."

Alleroy turned to look at Emanuel; "I know that, Emanuel. I know that."

They looked at each other for a three or four seconds - and then they both turned back and continued to look straight ahead again. For a short while, the two men sat that way in silence. In this silence, Emanuel kept turning the same question over and over in his mind; *we could use this money for her parents...an apartment...I can't believe I'm really thinking about this.* He didn't want to broach the subject of more money. If he did, it would be a tacit agreement that he was in, and he wasn't as yet. Last night he was open to the possibility that this was his ticket to a better life for himself and Estella. Now, in the clear light of the morning after, when push was pushing hard against shove, he wasn't so sure anymore. What if he got caught? What if he did this thing and this guy wasn't killed? What if he did this, could he live with it? Could he keep it from Stella? Would he have to tell her?

Alleroy could tell Emanuel was turning far too many questions over in his mind. He had to say something. He opened the case. The clicking sound prompted Emanuel to look down and see the neat bundles of money again.

"It's fifty thousand. Emanuel, I've played it out. It's foolproof. It's easy to tell if a car is parked for the next day by the signs on the side of the street it's parked on. Odds are the owner won't know it's missing for at least a whole day and—"

—"*Odds?* That's gambling. That's..." Emanuel was shaking his head. "That's a hell of a ways from foolproof Craig."

Alleroy had to keep talking. "Listen to me. I've sat in this one corner bar - The Pearl -on Pearl and Hanover for three nights now. Three nights! And I haven't seen a single prowl car come by, nor have I seen a single cop. He had to talk fast. So, the car is taken, right? It's driven down here and the driver sits in the car a half block away on Pearl - but in full sight of the entrance to this bar. The street is empty." People were approaching; he closed his attaché case but left it between them.

"How on earth do you know there won't be any prowl cars when whoever does this thing?"

"Emanuel, this precinct is three hundred square blocks. There are eight prowl cars on the street at night because the area is considered a low-crime area. And Monday, Thursday, Friday, and Saturday is the night with the lowest incident of crime. I sat in that bar until closing on a Thursday, Friday, and a Saturday, and no cops, no prowl cars. None.

"How do you know there are only eight prowl cars covering that area?"

"I called them and asked."

"And they told you?"

"I said it was research for a De Niro movie."

Emanuel wasn't sure if he was impressed, or freaked out, by how much planning this guy was doing in order to...to get himself *hit by a speeding car and killed!*

"Listen, Emanuel...The computer says that the probability of any of those prowl cars turning into that four square block area at that time on any of those four nights is one in ninety. That's a variable. If one should turn into the block where the bar is then we call it off and—"

— "*We? We* call it off?"

"And we do it the next night."

"And I steal another car?" Emanuel looked at him in disbelief.

"There won't be any prowl car, and you'll only need to take one car."

"*Take*? What, you don't want to use the word *steal*? Like you don't want me to think I'll be doing anything bad? Check that, not *me*...someone." Emanuel was still shaking his head.

"If the bartender happens to miss seeing the accident, the cops will find the book of matches from the bar in my pocket and they'll question him. I'll make sure he'll remember me. He'll tell him I was a little drunk when I left."

"Yeah...and maybe he'll be able to describe the driver of the car."

"Maybe he will. Yes, officer, I think the guy was wearing glasses and had a beard. It all happened so fast. He hit the guy and - I mean, he never stopped, just drove off and..."

"A disguise."

"Glasses without lenses and a beard. I'll buy them in a costume shop. There's a subway station entrance on Pearl and Wall. Drive down Pearl to William, make a right on William, go a block west, maybe to Beaver, ditch the car, and walk in the same direction up William to the Wall Street IRT entrance. Go down to the subway, take the disguise off on the way down the stairs and put it in your pocket. Take the train home to wherever it is you live, throw the glasses in the trash on the way, and burn the beard in your shower when you're home. Done."

Wherever it is I live? Like you don't know. Emanuel listened to all of this, kind of impressed at how thorough Craig was, while at the same time wondering if he was actually going to agree to this insanity. He still didn't want to ask about the possibility of more money. Didn't want to haggle until he was sure he was going to say yes to this plan to commit murder.

"You need to decide soon." Alleroy had to know if this was his man. *He has to do this. Where the hell am I going to find someone else if he doesn't?* "Fifty thousand is a lot of money."

"I don't know...I...I need time to think about this."

"I don't have too much of that to spare. I need to know in a matter of days or I have to move to plan B." And he rose.

Alleroy was trusting that Emanuel wouldn't call this bluff. Of course, he had no plan B - *and* no one to carry *out* this plan he didn't have. It *had* to be Emanuel - and Alleroy knew that Emanuel knew it, but he had to follow up.

"Emanuel, I'll be here tomorrow. You'll let me know then if I have to go to plan B. Have a good night." And he walked off up the path. Emanuel followed him with his eyes until he turned out of the park - and out of Emanuel's sight. *Yeah right, plan B.*

Alleroy still had to kill the rest of the day. He had walked out of the park, walked around to the spot from which he was watching Emanuel earlier, and watched him leave to go to work. He then went back into the park, sat on a bench and thought about what he had to do next to sell Emanuel on his scheme.

•   •   •

Driving home, hardly hearing Mozart's Sonata No. 16 in C Major, Alleroy's thoughts were now *only* on his wife and children. These thoughts had *finally* pierced his pity party, pushed their way to the surface, and he was suddenly overcome with what he *believed* were his emotions. His breath became short, and he felt his heart racing. This was more than just emotional. He had no idea that he was having either a panic attack or an anxiety attack. Whichever sort of attack it was it frightened him. He managed to exit the drive and pull over on the first side street where he could park. Between the shock of being found out, his feverish scheming and planning, and his promoting Emanuel, he had taken far too little time to stop and think, *really* think, about the many ways in which his crimes would affect his family. Somewhere in his dialogue with Emanuel his bubble of self-interest had finally been pierced, and the magnitude of the damage he'd done to his wife and children now hit him hard. He had burst into tears before when he was with Emanuel, but that was more about feeling sorry for himself. This was no longer about him. This was now about how his crime could, *would* destroy his family. Meg, they had been inseparable for thirty-five years. Always each other's support systems. He was there when she birthed their children. He saw her through the postpartum she experienced after giving birth to the girls. He was *always* there for her whenever she needed him for *anything.* He loved her as much as he was capable of loving. Now, he was deserting her. He fixated on his precious children, and the fact that they would be without a father. He would never again be there to counsel them. He held them all when they were baptized. He taught his daughters how to walk, how to swim. He was there when they had their first dates, and at their side when they came out. He taught his sons how to swim as well, and how to catch a baseball. Talked with them man to man when they started to take an interest in girls. He'd forgotten how proud he was of them. He sat there behind the wheel of his car unseeing and unhearing until his breathing and his heartbeat came back to normal. Until now, he had hardly given a thought to the reason for the acute stress he was under. This stress wasn't caused by the knowledge that he would be dead. He was stressed about something far greater than death. It was his fear of being shamed in the eyes of his colleagues, and his wife and children. It was all about *him.* Until now. Although, being hit by a speeding car wasn't anything *not* to fear. Of course, he was afraid of being hit by a car, of dying *that* way. Or, far worse, *not* dying that way.

The immensity of all of this had finally caught up with him. He was buried under the shame about what he'd done. Shame that he had kept bottled up. *And* by the need for his maniacal plan to get the insurance money to work. Before, when he'd thought about the effect his crime would have on his family those thoughts were intermingled with his frantic scheming on a way out of the mess he'd made. *Then,* his stress was more about his inability to face the unbearable shame that he would be forever shrouded in. *Now,* focusing *solely* on how what he did would impact his dear wife and his innocent children, he finally caved in completely. He looked at his reflection in the rear-view mirror.

"You shit the bed Richie. Here lies Richard Alleroy, the slickest guy on the street. Dishonored. A shark forced to decide to stop moving."

He took the crisp white handkerchief from his breast pocket and wiped the sweat from his face. The sadness in knowing that he now had to desert his family in order to save them hurt his heart. He began to sob again. He sat there until his crying abated and he felt he could continue to drive home safely. The insanity of caring that he got home safely and not get into a fatal auto accident, which could be construed as suicide, wasn't lost on him and caused him to manage a wry laugh. And though he wasn't what anyone would call a religious man, before he started the car, he said a prayer that his plan would work. That this *nothing* Emanuel would decide to take the money and, by doing so, be in a position to help him.

NINETEEN

All the way home, Emanuel debated whether or not to do this thing and make a lot of money. *He'll go to seventy-five, maybe a hundred.* If he did do it he knew he could never tell Estella about it, and he would have to make up a story about where he got his sudden windfall. But, what if he didn't tell her at all about the large sum of money he suddenly had? Could he do what he wanted to do for her and her parents without revealing to her that this money existed? The simple answer was; he couldn't. She would have to know about the money in order for him to spend it on them. *An apartment...We could get an apartment in a nicer neighborhood...Maybe in Riverdale.* He knew that they would have to put up a bunch of money up front...He'd heard of people offering a whole year's rent to get around some of the requirements - like if their salary wasn't so great. He wondered what the rents in Riverdale ran to. *I'll check on-line when I get— No, no, don't. Manny, don't. You don't wanna do this. We'll manage without this money. Could we get a place together anyway? I wonder what her take home is. If we put aside, I don't know, two-hundred a week each we could afford to get an apartment for—It has to be two-fifty a week each. She said she once mistakenly married a man who had secrets.* His head was spinning.

And he was violent. There were too many reasons why he shouldn't do this - aside from the obvious one being that it was murder. *What's more violent?* And, one very *good* reason, at least to him, why he should. *Supposing this Craig would go to a hundred thousand...where would I keep it? I can't walk into a bank and deposit a hundred thousand dollars in cash. Maybe a bunch of banks - and a bunch of accounts. I have to search how much cash I could deposit before any alarms go off.* The train was at Intervale Avenue. Emanuel got out, hit the street and, lost in these thoughts, started to walk home. The obvious answer to what to do with the money had yet to occur to him.

Estella meanwhile, was preparing to cook them a one-pot dinner tonight. It was all the hot plate would allow her to make. She used her Key Food employee discount, even though she now felt somewhat flush, and picked out a nice package of organic chicken thighs and drumsticks, a longaniza, a bag of long-grain rice, a box of chicken stock, and the makings of a nice salad. She was going to make a one-pot chicken, sausage, and rice dish her Aunt had taught her. That dish, a green salad with butter lettuce, onion and avocado, and a couple of cold Coronas would be an inexpensive nourishing meal for two...and there would be leftovers. She usually made the dish with spicy longaniza, but she purposely bought the mild so Emanuel wouldn't have any problems digesting it. Salt, pepper, cumin, cilantro, and a small amount of garlic were the seasonings. She prepped it all, put it up, and while it cooked, she took a shower.

Earlier in the day she had been called into the store manager's office who told her he was being transferred. He told her she was being promoted, and congratulated her on being the new store manager. Among other things, she would be responsible for seeing that the sales targets of the store were met by maximizing sales and gross profit. She would also be reviewing sales performance, controlling expenses, and managing inventory. She would also hire, train, develop, and supervise the staff and coordinate daily schedules. It would mean a great deal of responsibility, and the company was confident she could do the job. She was also. Her eyes lit up when she learned that her salary would now be sixty two thousand dollars a year. She was overjoyed. Five thousand, one hundred and sixty-seven dollars a month! Well, this was before taxes but...She couldn't wait to tell Emanuel. *Emanuel.* She also couldn't stop thinking of how wonderful last night was with him. It took some coaxing, but Emanuel, shy and unsure at first, was all she could desire in a lover. She was, on all counts, a very happy woman indeed.

Emanuel wasn't *so* lost in thought that he forgot to pick out a pretty bouquet of flowers at the Kelly Street bodega. He took care to choose one that had pale pink peonies. Estella had told him she was making dinner for them when he called her as he left work. *I'll bet she's a good cook too.* She also told him she had some good news and she'd tell him all about it when he got there.

•   •   •

Alleroy, now composed, pulled into his garage, got out of his car and began the two block walk to his home. *I need to get a gun. That guy on Forty-Second Street might know someone. I'll go there tomorrow. I wonder how much. Whatever it costs...*As he approached the florist on the corner of York Avenue he decided he wanted to give Margaret a dozen Juliet roses - which she loved. On the card he wrote; Because I love you sweetheart. He continued down the block to his building. In the elevator on his way up to their apartment he was overcome by a desire to be with his entire family. He entered his apartment, immediately went to his study and took the bundles of money from his attaché case and locked them away with the other cash in his desk, and then went looking for his wife. She was in the kitchen - as he knew she would be.

"Rich, I hope you're in the mood for—" She had turned around, and when she saw the bouquet he was holding out to her she was almost speechless. "Juliets! Oh, Richard...Richard, they're beautiful, thank you." He kissed her on the cheek as he handed her the flowers. "I'm glad you like them."

"I *love* them...and I adore you. If I didn't know you any better I'd think you'd been a bad boy."

He laughed. She held the flowers to her nose. "Peach...Citrus...The scent. Rich, will you please bring me the large vase from the sideboard?"

He headed for the dining room. "Meg, why don't we have the kids down for the week-end?"

He returned with the vase and she began unwrapping the flowers. "I would love that. You think they'll want to drive down?"

"I'll bribe them with the promise of a good steak. Gallaghers?" Margaret laughed as she trimmed the stems of the roses. "That should do it."

She filled the vase with some water. "I bet they would love some decent pizza too."

"I'm sure they would. We'll go up to Patsy's."

They decided they'd make a conference call to the kids after dinner.

Alleroy was quite proud of his ability to keep it together. To him, this was the ne plus ultra of his ability to compartmentalize. He was keeping his cool even as the firing squad was loading their rifles. No blindfold for him. Not yet anyway.

They finished dinner, called the kids, and made a plan to all get together on the week-end. They finished the bottle of red they had with dinner while watching an old movie on Turner Classic. When it ended Margaret said goodnight and went upstairs. Alleroy was left to grapple with his thoughts. *I can't drag this out too much longer. The guy has nothing, he has to be thinking seriously about this. Should I show him sixty? Skip the prelims and go to the full hundred?* Tomorrow he would go to the park and convince Emanuel to take the money, then go to the fake I.D. guy and see about getting a gun. His plan was coming into sharper focus.

• • •

"Oh, Manny...Estella kissed him passionately as he handed her the flowers.

When they both caught their breath she told Emanuel her news and he was overjoyed for her. She was certain that this meant they could now get a place together. After she told him of her promotion, he insisted on celebrating and he ran out to buy a bottle of red wine to go with dinner. This promotion, and the huge raise, was truly deserving of something a bit more special than beer. He was elated for her. However, by about halfway to the wine store this elation was being tempered by some misgivings about Estella shouldering the major cost of an apartment. An apartment he was sure she was now going to be looking for. He had already disabused himself of the idea of Riverdale because they both had to live somewhere that would be convenient for them to get to work. Further up the two train line maybe. West Farms, Pelham Parkway, or Allerton. However, the more he thought about the whole deal, the more it didn't sit well with him. Emanuel was not what anyone would call "woke." He was an old-fashioned type who believed that the man should be the hunter/provider. It would be one thing if he could put up even half. Half would be alright. He'd feel good about that, held up his end and all. Except there was no *way* he could manage to give her half, or *any* amount of money that would matter towards what they would have to pay up-front in order to get this apartment. And *then* furnish it? Unless, of course - *unless*, he took the money this Craig character was offering. Only he wasn't even remotely certain he could even *begin* to do what was necessary in order to *get* this money. He was also very unsure as to whether he could even steal a car. Still, he couldn't stop turning the opportunity over in his mind. It would be a life-saving windfall. They could go places. *I could get out of that Goddamn bathroom. Plan B my ass. There is no plan B. This guy is anguished. He'll go to a hundred.*

He took the advice of the guy in the wine store and chose a pretty nice bottle of Syrah. *I still have to search how much cash I can deposit in the bank before the IRS is notified. And I have to Google; if I open up a dozen savings accounts in various banks, is there some kind of alert that goes off? Oh wait...a safety deposit box! Of course! I have to check that out too. There's on-line banks also. And, how to hot-wire a car. I need to check all this stuff out before I can decide anything.*

TWENTY

Emanuel was, as advertised, a man of routine. So, as Alleroy entered the park and began to walk down the path leading to where Emanuel *usually* sat feeding whatever creatures came to feed at his feet, he could see that Emanuel *was*, indeed, at his usual spot in the park, doing his usual thing. He reached Emanuel's bench.

"Good morning Emanuel." He brushed the bench with his folded newspaper and sat down. "How are you today?" He placed his attaché case on the bench between them.

"Good morning Craig." He threw some birdseed to the pigeons. "So, how come you didn't bother watching me from the railing back there today?"

Alleroy was surprised at hearing that Emanuel had seen him all along the other day. *He saw me then? Did he see me follow him home?* Alleroy's paranoia suddenly reared its head. He fought the urge to ask Emanuel if he had indeed seen him on the train the other day.

"Emanuel, why don't you meet me tonight and I'll show you the set-up. How we can do this."

Emanuel kept feeding the pigeons that were landing in front of them. Alleroy tapped his attaché case. "This is a lot of money."

"Yeah, all I have to do is commit murder." Emanuel rose, stretched, walked to the fountain, and took a long drink of water. *I wonder just how much more money he'll go to? Not that I'll do this but...I really wonder. How much insurance does he have? It has to be plenty.* Alleroy watched him. He knew Emanuel was turning his proposition over in his mind. *I wonder if he plays chess, because this is a tempo move. He thinks his silence will force me into making a move...maybe upping the amount of money?* He was right. Emanuel wanted to

hear what Alleroy was going to say next without making any commitments - one way or another.

"So, let's meet tonight...How's about I buy you a drink down here around eight? We can check it out for a few hours and you'll see it'll work."

Emanuel returned and sat back down. "You know Craig, you're sitting here telling me you're ruined and yet you have all this money you're willing to give me if I agree to this." He gestured towards Alleroy's attaché case; "Is this fifty thousand dollars that meaningless to you?"

"It's not my money."

"Somebody else knows about this?"

"It's my sister's. She only knows I need this money for an idea I have. That's it."

Emanuel sat there shaking his head. "Why is this the only thing you can think of to do? You know, I asked you before; why can't you just face up to what you did and live a simpler life?

Alleroy couldn't admit to Emanuel that his shame, his disgrace, was the great driving force behind his inability to do just that. While wanting to keep his wife and children in the manner they had become accustomed to was admirable, it was however a convenient excuse. And, one that Emanuel, or any man, could easily identify with. To admit his crime, his fall from grace, admit he was broke, admit he wasn't all that clever enough to get away with it - and that he had been summarily kicked to the street - This was what was unbearable.

"Craig, just get a job in...I don't know, in a store somewhere. The way you dress...you could work in the men's clothing department in a store like...Macy's...or Saks."

"Meet me tonight...please?"

"Why the hell can't you do that? Is it so beneath you?"

"A hundred thousand."

Emanuel was silent. *Holy...A hundred thousand! I knew it. I knew he'd up the ante. And I bet he'll go way more than tha---Manny, Manny...it's murder. Dude! Why are you humoring this lunatic?* While Emanuel knew how crazy he also was acting - to not just say a flat no to this guy and be done with it - he was, underneath it all, very, very curious as to how much this Craig character was willing to part with in order to collect on his insurance. It was also becoming apparent to him that the insurance money involved had to be quite a considerable sum.

"A hundred thousand, Emanuel, a guy like y---" He stopped himself. *Don't insult him. He'll do it...It'll be too much money to resist. Just stay on his side. There's plenty of time for insults later. Reminds me...I still have to get that gun.*

"A hundred thousand. Cash."

Emanuel had remained outwardly unmoved at hearing this figure. He stared up at the sky. "I have to get to work." He scattered some more seed on the ground and the pigeons swooped down in front of them in a flash.

"Just meet me tonight. If you agree, I'll talk to my person and...I might be able to go higher." Emanuel rose to leave. "Emanuel, listen to me...Please. For thousands of reasons, thousands of people all over the world commit suicide every day. No one could tell them that their reasons are *unfounded*. They simply cannot live under the circumstances that they are faced with. I would go home tonight, if I could, and swallow a vial full of pills. End it - if I could. But, I can't. I can't Emanuel. Someone has to help me." Alleroy stood and picked up his attaché case. Do it. He held the case out to Emanuel. "Emanuel, please...take this as a down payment."

Emanuel turned to him. "Craig...You are asking me to commit murder. I can't take this money, man. Look...I need to think about this. I have to go to work."

Emanuel emptied the last of his birdseed on the ground and began to walk away leaving Alleroy standing there holding his attaché case out towards him. Alleroy was right in suspecting that Emanuel would not take his attaché case from him.

As he walked away Emanuel was still unsure as to what he was going to do. *A hundred thousand. Do I really want to even think about this?* And, he couldn't keep himself from wondering again about the amount of insurance involved that would make Craig do such a thing. The truth was, his curiosity was aroused. He stopped, turned around and walked back to Alleroy.

"How much insurance do you have?"

Alleroy, who had manipulated so many, had so many answers ready, wasn't prepared for this question. *What the fuck...*

Emanuel waited. "I'm curious."

Alleroy stood there turning a number of answers over in his mind. "A lot."

Emanuel smiled. "A lot? What does that mean? How much...in dollars?"

Alleroy knew that there would be a right time to tell Emanuel just how much life insurance his family stood to collect upon his death. This was not that time.

"All anyone needs to know is that it's worth dying for."

Anyone? Emanuel glowered at Alleroy. Alleroy was intensely aware that this moment was very important. This was more of the delicate balancing act he had to keep performing. Push it a little more. "Look...Emanuel, I have no idea if you have someone you want to take care of... someone you love. For all I know you don't. You can't." Alleroy knew exactly what buttons to push.

I can't! They stood facing each other. Emanuel was angry. The assumption that someone like him wouldn't have a 'someone' they loved was like a bullet to his heart. Alleroy thought he might get punched. Pull him back.

"No, no. I'm sorry Emanuel. I'm sure you have someone. And whoever she is she's a lucky woman. You would do anything for her right? Maybe you have children too. I know you would do anything for them too, Emanuel. So, I know you understand why I need to do this. I know you do."

Alleroy was right. Emanuel did understand why he wanted to do this. He would do anything for Estella. Maybe, under the same circumstances, he'd even do something as crazy as what Craig was doing. Emanuel, being a person with the capacity to see many sides of a situation, understood Craig's dilemma. Unfortunately. Someone else might have already dismissed Alleroy immediately. Forcefully disabused him of the notion that he might be open to taking whatever money Alleroy would offer. Perhaps even most would. It really didn't take much for anyone to taste Emanuel's anger at why he was where he was. Alleroy, being the shark that he was, and able to smell blood in the water from miles away, could easily smell Emanuel's desperation. Shark or no...it really didn't take too much for anyone to smell Emanuel's anger. Emanuel wanted out of that men's room bad. Had damn good reasons to be pissed off that he was locked in that men's room. Alleroy was counting on every single one of them; Emanuel's history, his resentments, the money Emanuel would never otherwise have a chance at in his entire life...these things would move him to where Alleroy wanted him.

The two men stood facing each other. Alleroy held out his hand. "No hard feelings?" After a few seconds, Emanuel shook Alleroy's hand. "No hard feelings." But he was thinking, a hundred thousand.

"Look, my children are coming to stay with me for the week-end. I won't be able to see you until Monday. So, please...let me buy you a drink tonight."

"Impossible."

"Why?"

"What do you mean 'why'?" Emanuel was clearly annoyed, and Alleroy could see he had to pull back.

"Emanuel...I'm sorry. I'm...It's none of my business."

"You're damn right it's none of your business." He started backing away. Then; "My girlfriend and I have plans." Emanuel had to take the opportunity to tell this guy that he did have a "someone." That he did have someone to take care of. He needed to answer the accusation that he was a person incapable of having love.

As Emanuel turned to go the thought of a hundred thousand dollars, or more, was on his mind. *What if he'll double it?* "I'll give it some thought and let you know Monday Craig." He walked off. Alleroy watched him as he walked up the path and out of the park.

Alleroy, now having the better part of another day to kill, decided to leave his car in the lot where he parked it and took a bus uptown to Forty-Second Street. Almost an hour later he walked west on Forty-Second to the place where he got his fake I.D. The guy told him that he could get a gun from a private, unlicensed seller, and that it would cost him seven to nine hundred depending on what he chose. The I.D. guy made a phone call and a meeting was set up for Monday at three.

•　　　•　　　•

Why hadn't Emanuel already put it to Alleroy that on *no* account would he take part in this scheme? He was asking himself this question as he was on his way home - and to Estella. Was it perhaps because, aside from meeting this wonderful woman, this was surely the most interesting thing to ever happen to Emanuel in many years? Was it because he was quite curious to know just how *much* money this Craig was eventually going to offer him? *This is worth a lot more than a hundred to him.* Was it that he loved games - of *all* sorts - and was this one much too compelling for him to refuse to play? *He never did answer me about how much insurance he has.* Could it possibly be because he would really *like* to kill this creep who had robbed so many pensioners of their life's savings; elderly people who he would be avenging? It could have been any *one* of these things keeping Emanuel involved with this man Craig. More likely, he decided, it was some part of all of them.

The other thing on Emanuel's mind was that there was no way he could confide in Estella about this matter. And this made him very uneasy. How could he ask her what she thought? He already knew what she would say about the whole affair. This was his decision alone to make. Anyway, she would tell him he was crazy for even *thinking* about what to do. And, if he went ahead and *did* do this, he would be both committing a monstrous crime, and keeping something quite revealing about himself from her. He would have to live with the secret that he killed a man in cold blood. For money. *And,* he would be entering their relationship as a liar. The question was; did *that* matter to him *more* than the money? *Who knows? It could even mean a quarter of a million...or close to it.* However, he kept coming back to this; if he did this thing, took this money, could he lay next to her every night harboring such a terrible secret?

TWENTY-ONE

Margaret had prepared a delicious bouillabaisse; one of the family's favorite dishes. Richard Alleroy, once again, made a more than passable showing as a husband and father who had the world by the balls. He laughed at the right moments, ate just enough to seem as if he had an appetite, drank just enough wine, and managed to speak with his children about their studies, their boyfriends and girlfriends, hearing most of whatever it was they told him. He did this, while beneath his calm exterior he was screaming for every excruciating minute to *not* seem like a damned hour. Monday morning seemed very far away.

Even though, for a while, it was somewhat comforting to be surrounded by a family who loved and valued him, who always respected him, he moved through the two days shadowed by the feeling that he was now unworthy of any of it. It was more than a feeling. He was aware that if they knew what he'd done, knowing the stakes, and knew that he'd been dismissed and drained of his finances in lieu of criminal charges, their love and respect would surely curdle to something approaching loathing. This feeling, this knowing, nagged at him and it was difficult for him to look at his children. He was now sorry he had asked for this family week-end.

•　　•　　•

Emanuel was enjoying a treat he hadn't afforded himself in many, many years. A prime bone-in ribeye steak cooked to a mouthwatering perfect mid-rare. With asparagus and a baked potato. Estella was loving watching him enjoying this meal. There was a Sunday sale where she worked and, coupled with her employee's discount, the two steaks were a bargain. She had done all of it in the new toaster oven she bought herself as a gift upon her promotion.

However, as much as Emanuel was enjoying the steak, Estella sensed there was something troubling him. From the second he greeted her with a bouquet of flowers and a kiss, she could see something in his demeanor and hear something in his responses that alerted her that he was unusually preoccupied. Finally, she had to ask; "Manny, is there something wrong?"

Holy...Am I that transparent? He looked up from his plate as he finished chewing, and tried to mask his surprise at both his inability to hide what was on his mind, and her ability to read him. After some seconds he managed; "I have this job offer and...you know, it's on my mind and...Stella, it's kind of complicated. Will you forgive me if I'd rather not talk about it because I don't want to jinx it?"

"I understand." But her curiosity was piqued. "I suppose you'll tell me at some point."

Emanuel smiled and nodded. He was now on high alert to be aware of whatever signals he was giving off. For the moment he had forgotten how attuned Stella was to him. It was understandable that he'd forget this since they hadn't known each other for very long. Now, he was reminded of just how well and truly matched they were, and thus how sensitive she was to whatever frequency he was operating on.

He knew he couldn't just leave it at "rather not talk about it" As if this "job" thing was none of her business. He didn't want it to sound that way either. He reached across the small table and took her hand. "Sweetheart, I'll tell you all about it when I know more...okay?" He almost said I promise, but caught himself and cut a piece of steak onto his fork. "Stella, this is *really* delicious. Thanks." He smiled at her. To his relief she smiled back and didn't ask him about this job again. But she knew, whatever it was, it was something serious.

Now he was wondering how he was ever going to explain to her what was going on...and what he had done or didn't do. In either case it was bad. He knew just the mere fact that he was turning this over in his mind would be troubling to her - to anyone. He also knew this "job" could end up being worth a couple of hundred thousand. Money that would set them up for life. But, after he *made* this money would there even still *be* a "them?"

She went back to her dinner; "Don't forget to eat the asparagus." She smiled. "There's apple pie and chocolate ice cream too."

•   •   •

The children were now back in New Hampshire. As he had done for both nights of what was a difficult week-end, Alleroy lay next to Margaret staring into the quiet darkness wondering if he could do what was trying to do. He wanted to end it, wanted to not be alive. But could he really pursuade this man to help him commit suicide by stepping in front of a speeding car? Should he just forget about the whole thing and beg his family to forgive him? And *then*, after *that* thought, the thought that even if he *did* ask for their forgiveness, and even if they *did* give it to him, and he *didn't* kill himself, what would his life be? His family's lives would be destroyed. Their faith in him would be shattered. And *if* they forgave him, their forgiveness would doubtless come with some measure of pity which would, in time, turn to bitter resentment. *And* he would have lost all right to occupy *any* high ground. *And* his career was over...so what would he do, work in a clothing store - as that idiot had suggested? *And* he had now ruined everything.

Laying there in the dark, with all these "ands" piled on top of him, reflecting on all he had been laying there thinking, he finally got around to asking himself; is this the way I *really* feel about what this means to my family, or the way I *wish* I felt? He lay there searching himself, and because he *was* what he was, the answer didn't bother him as it should have. He was a monster.

•   •   •

They'd made love. Now, while Estella slept soundly Emanuel was asking himself his own questions. *Would she stay with me if I ever told her about this? Can I keep this from her? If I don't do this, and I tell her I just wanted to see how far it would go...like a game...would she understand? Would it change everything between us? Would she understand why I didn't want to tell her what was going on? And even if I do this, and even if I get this money, then what?* He was bombarding himself with questions. All of them revolving around Estella.

Was it now even too late to tell her *anything* about this crazy rich guy Craig's proposition? Had he let it get too far? The understanding that no matter what he did now, Estella would either change her opinion of him, and surely not for the good, or just shut them down completely. Why had he let this get so far along? *Why did I—*He was about to ask himself; why did I have to meet this wonderful woman? And this thought alone spoke volumes. *You are a real asshole, man.* He turned over and looked at Estella sleeping beside him. *You are the best thing that's ever happened to me.* He turned back. *Why did this motherfucker Craig have to pick me? Yeah, you know why. It's maybe a couple hundred thousand. What if I do this, and I tell her what I did, and beg her on my knees not to leave me, would it be enough? If I tell her that now we can get her parents here? Get them an apartment? Would that be enough?* And no matter how he framed it, how he played it out, he knew that *none* of it would be enough. He knew that he and Estella could be over. A clear choice between Estella and the money existed a ways back. By letting this thing get this far he might have already made it impossible for him and Estella to have a life together. *Do I have a chance if I tell her now? If I do, will she still have me?*

He couldn't believe the mess he'd allowed himself to be sucked into. All the years he tried to better himself to no avail. All the years that he fantasized about having a life with someone, and when he finally had a chance, albeit a crazy one, to get out from under, to have money, his fantasy found him. There she stood, arms opened wide, in the way.

He found himself cursing his bad luck. His life of bad timing. And, as he did, he got that by feeling these things he was also, in a way, cursing Estella's very existence. And this realization led him to ask himself; had Estella not come into his life, would he have even thought twice about murdering this guy Craig for money? The answer came immediately; no. For this kind of money, for the chance to live a better life, and taking into account what a scumbag this guy was to steal from working people's pension funds, he would run him over in a heartbeat. Furthermore, this conclusion didn't bother him in the least.

He closed his eyes and tried to fall asleep. He knew that in the morning he would see Craig in the park. The answers to all the questions he'd asked himself helped him make up his mind as to what he was going to do. He was in too far, and far too afraid, to tell Stella about all this. He was going to let this Craig buy him a drink. He was curious to see Craig's plan, and *very* curious to hear just how much money he was actually prepared to part with.

TWENTY-TWO

Richard Alleroy stood at his dining room window sipping a cup of coffee and looking out at the rain coming down. *He won't be in the park in this. I'll go to the restaurant. They said it'll stop by this afternoon...this evening at the latest. My lousy luck that it would rain today. I have to get this guy to come with me tonight. Except...If it's still raining I don't know if it'll be as effective...It won't be the same as when it's clear. I need this to stop.* He finished his coffee and turned away from the window. *Or I'll have to put it off for another night. More fucking shitty luck!*

•   •   •

He could hear that the rain was coming down pretty hard. Emanuel had put his pajamas on, kissed Estella and left her just before she got out of bed to get ready for work. As he did lately, he wore a bathrobe over his pajamas, and slippers, to go between their rooms. Back in his own room, he made a cup of coffee and relaxed while watching the news before getting ready to go to work. Since he wouldn't be sitting in the park this morning he had plenty of time. *He'll come to the restaurant for sure.* He had told Estella that he would be home late tonight because he was having a meeting about the job – and then they were going for a drink. It was small comfort that *this*, at least, was the truth. *I wonder if we'll do it though it if it's still raining. If not, I'll just tell her it's been postponed.*

As usual, the news was depressing. *We could get away from all of this insanity.* And then he remembered there might not be a "we" after he told her everything. It disturbed him that he was contemplating doing something as unhinged as anything he just saw on the news. Equally disturbing was that it didn't too take much effort to push that thought away. *If I don't tell her anything...maybe it's the only way out. Whatever I decide I just don't tell her anything. And if I do get this money I could put it in a safe deposit box...take it out a little at a time...Or, if I tell her one of the restaurant patrons left me a lot of money...A wealthy man I always took special care of who I befriended...who had no one...There are lots of stories like that...Then, I wouldn't even have to use it sparingly. And the government won't get any of it either. We could use it as we wished. It could be in a bunch of safe deposit boxes wherever.* He didn't as yet understand how the mere thought of all this money was slowly corrupting him. *I'll make up some story about this supposed job.*

•   •   •

In keeping with his pretense of still having a position, Alleroy left for "work" at eight-fifteen. Driving down the FDR, knowing Emanuel didn't go to work until eleven and wouldn't be in the park, he was deciding where to kill a few hours. *I have the gun appointment at three. Too bad I can't go there first.* He had done a search on Margaret's laptop and saw there was a library in Battery Park City. *Another waste of time in a fucking library.*

He parked in a garage on Water Street, bought a bunch of newspapers, walked four blocks south under his golf umbrella to the subway at South Ferry, and took a five minute ride to the library in Battery Park City where he spent two hours slowly reading every word in the New York Times, Wall Street Journal, Daily News, and New York Post. At eleven AM he left the library, took the subway back to South Ferry, made his way in the rain to The Coach and Crown.

Outside the restaurant he peered through the somewhat fogged up window trying to see if anyone who he knew was inside. There didn't appear to be. He could see that there were quite a few empty stools at the bar. He took a deep breath, entered, and took a seat at the end of the bar. The stools next to him were thankfully empty. He was in no mood for small talk.

Louie had seen him from the second he walked through the door and put this large umbrella that said "Titleist" into the stand next to the door. He watched Alleroy sit down at the end of the bar, smiled and nodded hello, and pointed to the Blanton's. Alleroy hesitated...and then nodded yes. In short order the coaster was flipped, the one cube slipped into the glass, and a generous shot poured. It may have been a bit early in the day for it but the sip of bourbon felt warm, smooth and comforting as it hit the back of Alleroy's throat. Louie was pleased and turned his attention to the others seated in his domain.

Now, as he sipped his drink, Alleroy was going over the approach he was going to use on Emanuel to get him to go with him to The Pearl tonight. *His eyes lit up when I offered him a hundred K. I have to be clear...It must look like it'll work.* He watched as a few men went into the men's waiting for the right time to speak with Emanuel. The early lunch crowd was showing up and the restaurant was filling up. *I don't know if he'll ever be without guys in there. I'll just have to sit here and wait for a good time. Maybe eat lunch. Oh no...*Don Crane had just entered the restaurant. He put his umbrella in the rack, looked around, saw Alleroy, and headed straight for him and the empty stool next to him. *Shit! My fucking luck. Just what I needed...*

"Rich, hey. What a nice surprise." Don sat down. "What a day huh? What are you drinking?" *Is that a Blanton's? A bit early eh? I don't know why I've never been in here before.* Had to get out of the rain."

Great Don. Just fucking great! I can't believe this. Louie had already flipped a coaster onto the bar in front of Don.

"Yeah, the barman pours a good drink." Alleroy smiled at Louie who nodded in agreement;

Don smiled, "I think a Campari and soda will do me just fine."

They watched as Louie flamed the citrus peel and then Don looked around; "You've been here before Rich?"

"Yeah, I like this place. Good food. How's things? Bess...the kids?"

Don took a sip. "Yum, this is perfect. Everybody's still well. Doing their thing as it were. I'm still a fourteen. How's Margaret?"

Why did this guy have to walk in here today...Why is this happening? "She's great." He took a quick sip. "Thanks. I'll tell her you asked." More men walked into the men's.

"We needed this rain, eh? How's things at the shop?"

Yeah, I really needed this rain you..."Same. Nothing interesting happening."

"I'm supposed to play a round tomorrow. I sure hope the course will dry out by then."

Who gives a fuck? "I'm sure it'll be fine." Since the last man to use the men's came out no one had gone in. Alleroy took a last sip, caught Louie's eye, and signaled for two more. He rose as Louie started to fix the two drinks. "I have to use the men's."

Don also got up. "Yeah, me too."

*Oh Christ...*There was nothing he could do but go to the men's room with Don Crane in tow.

On this day Emanuel was re-reading Meditations by Marcus Aurelius. Its central theme of cosmic perspective always gave him comfort. He was pondering something he had just read in the book yet again; "Accept the things to which fate binds you, and love the people with whom fate brings you together, but do so with all your heart," when Craig entered. However, as he said under his breath, "here we go," he saw the other man enter behind him. He stood, set his book aside, and waited. The two men stood at adjoining urinals and the one he didn't recognize spoke.

"They say it's going clear up by late afternoon, this evening. I bet they'll have the course dry by tomorrow, we pay them enough, right? Hey, we haven't seen you on the links in a while."

Emanuel took two towels from out of the closet. *They know each other. Damn.*

I guess I'm a little too busy trying to fucking kill myself, Don, old bean. "Yeah, I have to get out there soon."

"Tee time is 6 PM tomorrow. We have room for a fourth. What say you?"

Alleroy zipped up and moved to the sink. Emanuel had already turned on the taps and stood ready with a hand towel. Don moved to the adjacent sink and Emanuel repeated his preparation.

"Thanks Don. I'd love to, but tomorrow is out, I'm taking Meg to dinner. Soon though, I promise.

An alarm sounded in Emanuel's brain triggered by the ease with which Craig lied. *Is this guy bullshitting me too?* Alleroy finished washing his hands and he and Emanuel exchanged a brief conspiratorial glance as he took the towel from Emanuel's outstretched hand. Don also had finished washing his hands and Emanuel handed him a towel as well.

"Rich, you want to get some lunch?"

Oh, no. You fucking moron shut the fuck up. "Sure. Let's do it." *I have to get this idiot out of here.* He made for the door; "Those drinks are getting warm." And, as he hoped he would, Don followed him out.

Emanuel threw the two towels in the bin and sat down. *Rich? He called him Rich. What the hell is going on?*

Back inside the dining room, Alleroy's mind was furiously working overtime as the host showed the two men to a table. *I have to do some serious damage control.*

Alleroy remained standing as Don sat down. "Look Don, I just remembered I have to run an errand for Meg before I go back to the office, so I can't have lunch. I know you'll understand. I'm sorry." He started for the bar then stopped and turned around. "Oh, I'll see you on the course soon Don. It's real good seeing you. Enjoy lunch, the food here is real good." *I recommend the kibble, you fucking...*

He went to the bar hastily, settled up with Louie, grabbed his umbrella, turned and waved a goodbye to Don, and stepped out into the rain. *Still fucking raining. That damn idiot. He would show up today.* He started down the block knowing he just had to turn a corner and step under any awning, or into any door, and think about what he was going to do next. He knew he had to go back to the restaurant and repair whatever damage Don may have done. *He heard fucking Don call me Rich. I can't bring it up. He has to. If I do it'll be fishy. It has to appear to be of no significance to me.* He got to the corner of Water and Hanover Square, made a right and stood under a construction scaffolding half way down the block debating whether or not to wait there for at least an hour while Don ate lunch, or go get a bite himself at one of the many greasy spoons in the neighborhood that catered to the Wall Street area lunch business. He decided on the latter and walked to a place called Harry's diner, sat at the counter, ordered scrambled with bacon and coffee, sipped the coffee and didn't touch the food. All the while keeping an eye on the neon-ringed clock on the wall. It seemed an eternity. *Einstein could have come up with his theory of relativity just by sitting here while needing to be somewhere else.* As he sat there he noticed people entering without umbrellas and looking fairly dry. *It's letting up. At least one thing is going right today.* He ordered a second cup of coffee. *Forty minutes to go. At thirty minutes I'll go to the corner and watch for him to come out. It's almost one and I have the gun thing at three. Damn it!*

Emanuel was busy taking care of a steady flow of clients - as he called them. He was also nervously waiting for Craig to return to the men's. It had been at least a half-hour since they would have begun to eat lunch. *Well, they had to order and wait...so maybe it's only twenty minutes since they started eating.* He wanted to step outside and look into the packed dining room to check but he was much too busy, and anyway, management frowned on him leaving his post. *He called him Rich.* He kept turning this thought over in his mind hoping there was a good reason for it. He was going to find out what this good reason was as soon as Craig returned.

Alleroy was now at the corner watching to see Don leave the restaurant. The rain was just a drizzle on its way to ending completely. *Come on man. Lunch is over...let's go.* And finally Don came out of the restaurant and began walking up Water Street to his office. *Thank goodness.* Alleroy now began walking towards the restaurant. He entered, and saw that the restaurant crowd had thinned. *Good.* He looked around to see if there would be any more complications in the person or persons still there that knew him, and satisfied that there were none, went straight to the bar. Louie saw him sit, gestured to the Blanton's, Alleroy nodded, and his drink was served up in short order. He took a nerve-calming sip and watched to see when the men's would be empty – or close to it. After a minute a man came out, and after some minutes more when no one else came out or went in, Alleroy rose and headed for Emanuel.

TWENTY-THREE

Estella was worried. There was something troubling her man. He wasn't sleeping well and she wanted to know what it was that was keeping him awake at night. She was resolved to find out what it was and if there was anything she could do to help. It was obvious to her that the anxiety he was experiencing had everything to do with this new job. This job that was a secret. She had already divorced a husband who kept secrets from her. And worse. She didn't buy the "jinx" excuse he gave her for not telling her what this new job was. While she wanted to know what he was keeping from her, at the same time, she didn't want to grill him...to pry...to hound him about it. At work this afternoon, while managing to hold interviews and place orders, she was giving some serious thought to how to go about asking him what was bothering him and decided that the best way to approach the matter was to tell him she was wondering about his sudden inability to get a good night's sleep. Granted, they'd only been sleeping together for a few weeks, but in the last three or four days she noticed a marked decline in the quality of his sleep.

•　　　•　　　•

Eight miles due South, in another universe, another woman was worried about another man. Margaret Alleroy had also noticed that *her* husband was having difficulty lately getting a good night's sleep. Even more worrisome, when she went to check her browser history for the date of a charity event she had registered for, and had forgotten to enter in her calendar, she came upon some searches she knew she hadn't made. One search read; back copy The New York Times - Jack Loomis, there was one for fake I.D. NYC, and another for First Police Precinct NYC. When she checked on the man named Jack Loomis, she saw he was killed in a hit-

and-run accident. This was very strange. The dates showed that the searches couldn't have been done by any of the kids on the recent weekend they visited, and the times were all late at night. The only other person who could have done these searches was her husband. *Why did he search a hit-and-run accident? A fake I.D.? The first Precinct? What on earth is he up to?* She was very curious as to the reasons he'd made these searches. She was also curious as to *why* he made them, and why on her computer and not his own. All of it was odd, and was causing her to wonder what was going on with him. *He said he'd be home late. That's been happening a lot lately too. I think I'll wait up tonight...There's that movie on Netflix I've been wanting to see.*

•   •   •

Emanuel looked up as he heard the door open. Seeing it was Craig, he slowly put his book down and rose.

"Rich?"

Alleroy stared at him as if he had no idea what Emanuel was referring to. "Come again?"

"Come again? What do you mean come again? Why did that guy call you Rich?"

"What are you talking ab—Oh...Yeah...he did call me Rich. Emanuel, all my friends call me Rich, sometimes Richie Rich, or just plain Rich, because I am...And I made them all rich as well." He stared at himself in the mirror and then turned to face Emanuel. "And I'll do the same for you. So, will you let me buy you a drink tonight so I can show you that I've planned this out perfectly?"

Emanuel stood there turning Alleroy's explanation over in his head. Finally, he let it go. "Craig, let me ask you this; don't you feel the least bit...I don't know, insane...that you're calmly going about planning to be run over by a speeding car?"

"No...not exactly speeding. A car traveling at forty miles per hour will kill a pedestrian ninety percent of the time. So, let's say you do fifty just to make sure."

"Because you don't want to end up a live cripple."

"Exactly."

"And you looked that up too?"

Alleroy nodded yes. Emanuel looked at Craig in amazement that he could stand there so calmly talking about something so utterly macabre. And then he reminded himself that he was going along with this macabre plan, and being just as *macabre in that* he was curious as to just how much money would eventually be involved.

"I asked you how much insurance you had. You never answered."

And at that moment another man entered the men's with a small boy of about seven or eight in tow. The boy was furiously running his fingers over a cell phone. Suddenly, the sound of gunfire came over the phone's speaker. Immediately, Emanuel threw himself into a corner of the men's room covering his head and screaming; "Duck! Duck! Get down! Oh, God! No! No! Medic! MEDIC! He lay there trembling and covered in sweat.

The two men had no idea what was taking place. The boy was frightened and began to cry. Then Alleroy remembered that Emanuel told him of his discharge because of PTSD.

"He's got PTSD. The gunfire triggered an attack. Turn that thing off! Please!" He swiftly moved to Emanuel and began trying to soothe him. The man took the phone from his son, shut it off and put it in his pocket. The boy was still crying and his father was hugging him close and trying to comfort him as well. Alleroy rushed to the closet for a towel, soaked it in cold water and began pressing it to Emanuel's forehead and the back of his neck. *That sound of gunfire was enough to set him off.* "It's alright Emanuel. You're safe. You're in The Coach and Crown. Breathe. Breathe deeply. That's it. Deep breaths." He had no idea of how to deal with Emanuel's episode but what he was doing came naturally and seemed to calm Emanuel down. He continued to apply the cold compress to Emanuel's head, neck and to his wrists. While he was saying these things to Emanuel he was trying to slowly get Emanuel to his feet. The boy had stopped crying and his father stood holding him close and wondering if he should now do what he came in there to do. Alleroy now had Emanuel up and sitting on his stool. His breathing had returned to normal and he was wiping his face with another cold wet towel Alleroy had grabbed, soaked under the tap, and given to him. He sat there looking at the three others in the room feeling embarrassed and quite sheepish at what he felt was a display of weakness.

Alleroy took a knee in front of him. "Why don't you sit a bit longer."

Emanuel's head had now cleared. "I'm okay now." The episode had passed. He slowly stood and gestured to the man to go about his business. Alleroy rose. The man made sure his son was alright and took him into a stall to urinate. Alleroy and Emanuel stood silently as the man helped his boy pee, finish, close his fly and go to a sink to wash his hands. He went to a urinal himself and did his own business as the boy washed his hands. Emanuel had taken two hand towels from the closet and handed one to the small boy who dried his hands as his father began to wash his own hands. Emanuel stood waiting with the other towel as the man, still somewhat unnerved by what he had just witnessed, finished washing and dried his hands. He spoke to Emanuel very quietly so that his son couldn't hear; "I'm sorry that my boy's phone did that to you. Please forgive us." From his billfold he took out a five dollar bill and placed it on Emanuel's tip plate. "Be well." And he and his son left.

Emanuel was now fully back in the present. He began wiping the water from the counter.

"Jesus, Emanuel...How often does that happen?"

"Sometimes I go for months. Sometimes not."

"I'm sorry man."

Emanuel threw the towels in the bin. "Yeah." He looked at himself in the mirror. "'What a mess you are dude."

"You're not a mess...The money'll take care of a lot."

Emanuel stared at Alleroy's reflection in the mirror. "Craig, I need to know how much insurance you have."

"You keep asking me this. Why do you *need* to know?"

"Why do I—I want to know if what you're offering for this is a fair percentage of the pay-off, that's why."

"Emanuel, I assure you it's enough to make you the offer I've made."

"What's the number?"

Just then another man entered and went to one of the urinals. Emanuel took a towel from the closet and waited for the man to finish. When he did Emanuel turned on the tap and the man washed his hands. As the man washed his hands, behind his back Emanuel caught Alleroy's eye in the mirror and mouthed the words "how much?" Alleroy, who'd taken one of the combs on the counter and was leisurely combing his hair, nodded, and gave Emanuel a look that read "wait." The man finished washing and took the towel from Emanuel's hand.

The man dried his hands and scanned the counter top. "Is that Bay Rum?"

"Yes." *Will you please splash yourself and get out of here.*

The man doused himself liberally with Bay Rum, checked himself in the mirror for any signs of food in his teeth, and satisfied that no wayward creamed spinach lingered therein, took his billfold from inside his jacket pocket - *will you please get on with it!* - and carefully searched for, and removed from it, a single dollar bill which he was equally careful to place just *so* on Emanuel's tip plate. *Jesus Christ already!* He smiled at each of the two men and left.

Alleroy knew he had to speak fast. Knew he had to control the situation. "Do you know The Pearl Bar down here?"

And *Emanuel* knew Craig was trying to steer the subject away from the amount of life insurance he was carrying. "I asked you how much life insurance you have."

"If you agree to meet me I'll tell you. I promise. And tonight I'll prove to you that you'll be able to make the money I'm offering you to do this."

Emanuel stood there looking at Alleroy. "How much is it again?"

Alleroy took a few seconds to respond. "I said a hundred thou. Meet me tonight at eight. The Pearl, on the corner of Pearl and William Streets.

One hundred thousand dollars. He'll go more. There's a lot of money involved here. A lot of money. Don't answer. Let him talk.

The two men stood looking at one another. Alleroy understood Emanuel's play. *He wants me to make it even more worth his while. Okay, why not?* And he finally broke the heavy silence. "One hundred twenty-five thousand dollars. But, only if I see you at the Pearl at eight."

One hundred twenty-five thousand dollars. The words ricocheted off the walls of Emanuel's prefrontal cortex. *One hundred twenty-five thousand dollars. And, he'll go more. I know it. He must have a shitload of insurance. So what if he never says what it is. What's the difference, as long as I get the money?* He was now on the precipice of being completely drawn in to Alleroy's madness. The thought of all this money, and being able to leave this job was now tempting him beyond his will to resist.

"Will I see you at The Pearl tonight?"

I told Stella I would be home late tonight. I knew my curiosity had already gotten the better of me and I was going to end up meeting this guy.

Just as Emanuel was about to speak, the door opened and a man entered in a great hurry to get to a urinal opening his fly as he did. "Oh man, you know what I'm sayin'."

He was speaking to no one really, *and* to the two other men of a certain age in the room who knew *exactly* what he was saying. Those two other men stood there silently looking at each other. Then, Emanuel reached into the closet for a hand towel while Alleroy went into a stall, closed the door, and stood there waiting for the intruder to finish and leave. Emanuel stood there, towel in hand, watching the man wash his hands. *I have a chance here to wash my own hands of this whole crazy thing. This interruption...is it a sign? Is fate giving me another chance to walk away from this?*

To most people, this lunacy would have never gotten to this point. *Most* people would have emphatically walked away at the first mention of such a scheme. *Most* people would have never entertained this bizarre version of criminal insanity for a second. Never for even a nanosecond would they ever *consider* committing murder for *anything.* Or care to run the risk of getting caught, having committed this crime, and then spending the rest of their life in a federal penitentiary. *Most* people would sneer at doing anything like this for a *million* dollars, let alone one hundred and twenty-five thousands of them. Be that as it may, *most* people did not grow to adulthood bearing Emanuel's specific childhood scars, the traumas he had to deal with, the resentments he felt - and the impoverishment that he experienced as an adult on a daily basis. And it is certain, that *most* people do not have to spend their working days where he did...and have to live with *why* he had to spend them this way. So, Emanuel William Graves was not "most people." Emanuel Graves *was* the one in a million perfect person who *would* entertain such a chance to get out of what he felt was the unjust prison in which life had conspired to trap him.

"One hundred and twenty-five thousand dollars. Will I see you tonight Emanuel?"

The man was gone and "Craig" stood there awaiting an answer to his question. *Come on...You want to know how much, don't you? Hurry up man, I have to be at forty-second by three.*

Emanuel was again wiping his counter. *He'll go more. How much more? Can I get him to a quarter of a million? Will I really do this for a quarter of a million dollars?* He finished, threw the towel in the bin and turned to Alleroy. "Eight o'clock at the Pearl Craig."

TWENTY-FOUR

It was eight forty-five. Estella had gotten home a few minutes earlier having gone to see two apartments in the Pelham Parkway section of the East Bronx after work. Pelham Parkway was a working-class neighborhood of mixed ethnicity. The people who lived there took pride in their neighborhood and took care to keep it clean and well maintained. It was a mix of low-rise apartment buildings and private homes to the north and east, bordered on two sides by parks to the west and the south. It was a twenty minute walk to The New York Botanical Gardens and The Bronx Zoo. In her eyes it was ideal, *and* it had an el train stop on White Plains Road eight stops from where she worked. It *would* be a little longer ride for Manny, but she was thinking, hoping, maybe he wouldn't be working there after this meeting. It was a pleasant neighborhood with good schools and very good shopping - and most importantly, the rents were still reasonable. She had seen one apartment she really liked. A sixth floor two bedroom corner apartment in an elevator building on Holland Avenue with an eat-in kitchen. The apartment had wonderful light being as it was on the top floor and the living room faced the south. The rent was a very reasonable two thousand, four hundred dollars a month, heat and hot water included. There was a laundry room in the basement. And, since she was dealing directly with the landlord, there was no broker fee. And to help matters along even more the landlord's wife was Dominican and, because he liked her immediately and knew she would be a good tenant, he waived half of the security fee. Between her and Emanuel they could certainly afford it. They already paid one thousand dollars a month each in The Delevan, and this apartment, with the approximate three hundred a month more for utilities, would be thirteen fifty each. Only three hundred fifty more for each of them. Furnishing it would, of course, take some money but she was sure they would be able to do it slowly and affordably, their bedroom and the living room and kitchen first. She called Emanuel and told him all about the apartment and that she thought it was perfect and he would really like it. He trusted her judgment, and though he felt some pressure, agreed that she should take it immediately. She knew she didn't have enough in her checking account to pay the two months plus the twelve hundred security required. But the landlord took into account how long she had been with Key foods, and that she was now a store manager. So, wanting a desirable tenant, he agreed to take a post-dated check that she would make good by end of business tomorrow. She knew she could get an advance on her salary to do this. Estella was overjoyed as she signed the papers and wrote out the check making the apartment theirs. They would be moving in at the end of the month. At eight o'clock, before getting the train back to The Delevan, she called Emanuel to tell him the good news that they had an apartment. They made a plan to see the apartment together tomorrow night.

Back at The Delevan she put together a lovely green salad and put it in the small fridge to keep cold, salted and peppered two chicken breasts and put them in the toaster oven. *This'll be good cold. He'll be hungry when he gets home. Please let his meeting go well. He hates this job he has...Whatever this thing is I hope it leads to something better for him.*

•   •   •

Earlier in the day Richard Alleroy left Emanuel in The Coach and Crown, walked to the garage where he parked his car for the day, and took his briefcase from the trunk. He then walked hurriedly down Water Street to the subway at South Ferry. To his great relief, the rain had finally stopped. He made his way uptown to Forty-Second Street and walked to the fake I.D. joint where he had a three o'clock appointment to buy a gun. He had used his wife's laptop to research the types of guns and when he did he was shocked to see how easy it was to buy an illegal firearm. He certainly was not going to buy a gun online and was glad when the I.D. guy said that he "knew a guy who knew a guy" and could hook him up. Now, he was hoping that the gun "salesman" would have at least one of the guns he had decided he wanted. He was thinking it would be like the movies. The guy would open a case and these guns would be laid out from which he could choose.

It was five to three and in a few minutes he would have a gun. He'd taken five hundred dollars in cash from his safe which still had almost ten thousand dollars in it. He arrived at the door of the I.D. guy's narrow building and climbed the one flight to his shabby office. He entered and the I.D. guy motioned for him to take a seat. He picked up his phone, dialed, and said a few words to the person on the other end, hung up and some two minutes later a man toting a fairly large back pack entered the office. The I.D. guy stood, gestured to the man with the duffle that Alleroy was the buyer and led them both into a small back room and left them alone. Without a word, the man took off the back pack, opened it and removed from it a large polyethylene case. He placed the case on a small table and flipped it open. Inside were six handguns and twenty-four magazines. "I got Two Glocks, Ruger, Smith and Wesson, and Sig Sauer. All nine millimeter. Do you know what you want?"

Alleroy stared at the handguns. "How much is the Ruger?"

"I can do five."

"And the Smith and Wesson?"

"Three eighty."

"With the mag?"

"Four."

Alleroy gestured toward the guns; "May I? The Smith and Wesson?"

The man took the gun from the case and handed it to Alleroy. "It'll do what you want every time."

Alleroy hefted the gun. "Do you have a silencer for it?"

"A suppressor? Another two hundred."

"Is there a shoulder holster that will hold this with the sil—with the suppressor attached?"

"For that piece? Only a belt holster. For another hundred fifty."

It was the first time Alleroy ever had a gun in his hand - and it felt *good*. He debated whether or not to admit to the man that this was so. He decided "why not?" since he was sure he'd never see the guy again. "I need you to show me how to load it, how to put the safety on and off and put the sil—the suppressor on it. I'm new to this."

The dealer smiled tiredly and took the gun that Alleroy was holding out to him and proceeded to give Alleroy a tutorial on the Smith and Wesson 9MM. When he was done, Alleroy gave the dealer seven hundred and fifty dollars and put the gun, the clip and what to him was still a silencer, in his briefcase. He would return the next day for the holster. It was three forty-five when he walked down the stairs and onto Forty-Second Street. He had to go back downtown to his car and stash his briefcase in the trunk. On the bus going downtown he wished he could just go somewhere, put the gun to his head, kill himself then and there and be done with it. As it was, the *only* thing he could kill was the four plus long hours until he could meet Emanuel at The Pearl.

•   •   •

At six Emanuel left work. He had two hours before he was meeting Craig. He had thought of going to get a bite but since the rain had stopped and it was still light out and becoming sunny, he decided to go to the park, try to relax and read Meditations. He figured his bench would probably still be wet, so he went back into the restaurant to borrow a couple of hand towels to wipe it dry. On his way to the park he felt inside his pocket and saw that he had nothing for George and Gracie. He knew they would be expecting something from him so he stopped in a small deli and bought a bag of peanuts. He got to the park and no sooner had he sat down then the two squirrels appeared. He tore open the bag of peanuts, tossed a few to them, and watched as each of them sprinted off with their prize. He sat very still for a moment reflecting on what had happened to him earlier. *A kid with a cell phone.* This was a terribly embarrassing episode and it re-kindled his enduring anger at what the military had done to him. *I have to get out of there.* He watched Gracie bury her peanut. *I wonder if I can get a job where Stella works.* And then he remembered that she'd found them what sounded like a terrific apartment, and they'd be moving in a couple of weeks. *I guess I can afford the extra money. What am I talking about, if I do this thing I can afford a whole lot more. We could afford a whole—*And *then* he remembered that he'd have to tell her a story, a lie, about where he got the money. *Not a good way to start off a marriage Manny. And would she even believe it? When it comes to men, there's a lie detector in every woman. It's part* *of their original equipment. Christ.* He opened his book and tried to read. *This guy has to be insured for plenty. Who knows, it could even mean a quarter of a million. Wait a minute...*He closed his book, took out his cell phone and Googled "largest life insurance plans." *Why haven't I done this already? I don't know, you're slipping Manny.* What came up was that the two largest life insurance plans ever taken out were for two hundred and twelve million dollars and two hundred and one million dollars. *What the...*A further search showed a lot of other policies written in the ten to twenty-five million dollar range. *This guy has to have one of these. He wouldn't want to do this unless the pay-out was really big. I have to watch videos...*He put his cell phone away and sat there deep in thought.

He sat for a few minutes thinking about how his choosing to take part in this scheme would impact his relationship with Estella, the new apartment, his job, and his very life. He was keenly aware that whatever he did he'd already done some damage to his relationship. He re-opened Meditations, flipped to one of the many dog-eared pages in it, and his eyes were drawn to a sentence of special interest to him. One that he'd read many times before; "Whatever happens to you has been waiting to happen since the beginning of time." Each and every time in the past when he contemplated this all too familiar quote he cursed his rotten luck. Hurled oaths at the malefic stars that had fated him to live out such an unsatisfactory existence. What had he done that his fate would amount to having come to the aid of his country - and his country would then turn its back on him? What had his *forbearers* done to have predetermined this life for him? These were *always* the things he thought when he read this quote. Until now. *Now,* he looked at this sentence and immediately thought of Stella. She had come into his life, and in the short space of a few weeks had re-made it. Re-made him. Where before he had nothing to look forward to, he now had a life with this wonderful woman to look forward to. Had Stella been waiting to happen to him since the beginning of time? Had he been waiting to happen for her? Was this also predetermined? Was this fate at work? He sat there turning these questions over in his mind.

Emanuel believed that question is the answer. However, to all the questions he had ever asked about why his life had gone the way it had, fate was the only answer that ever made sense to him. He was trapped from birth by it. Fate, he'd come to believe, had left him no room for choice. All the same, he did not deserve this existence. He was a good person. Ever since he began to question, to ponder the universe and his place in it, to wonder if man has free will and ask all the endless other questions that pertained to existence - to the *why* of *his*, Emanuel William Graves' existence - fate was still the *only* comforting answer to that question. He *couldn't* have changed any of it. And now he was asking if he was fated to do this cold blooded thing. *Has it already been written across time? Is this also my fate? Is this guy and his plot to get himself run over for money just been waiting to happen to me?*

George and Gracie were back. "What do you think guys? Has it?"

He tossed a couple of peanuts onto the pavement and watched them scurry off, each clutching a peanut in their paws.

"No answer, guys? The two squirrels ran up a tree. Emanuel raised his voice a bit; "That's the thanks I get?"

He stared at the quote. He closed the book and sat back. For a long while he sat there thinking about the way his life had gone. Now, when he finally focused outward, the sun had dipped low in the sky in-between the tall buildings. *Who knows...Maybe I have been fated for this. Maybe.*

He sat there a few minutes more pondering whether or not he *ever* had any control over his life and finally told himself that if fate led him here, his destiny was still yet to happen. He could tell by the fading light of the sun that it was close to eight. He rose and began walking. *You have a choice Manny. Finally. Your fate is not your destiny.*

TWENTY-FIVE

At twenty minutes to eleven, The Pearl had less than a dozen customers. The two men had been sitting at a small table by the Pearl's window for close to three hours. Alleroy was finishing his third vodka neat and Emanuel was finishing his third draft beer.

"So, I'm right. No cop cars, no cops...barely any pedestrians. Did I tell you? And a great disguise. We can do this."

Emanuel was staring out the window at the empty street. "Again with the 'we'?"

"I sit here, get good and drunk, and starting about a half-hour before closing I wait for the street to be just like it is now. You're parked on the end of the block with a good view of this place. The end of the block so you don't have to deal with the traffic light on Pearl and Pine. You'll see—

—"In the car that I've just stolen." It wasn't a question. Emanuel was expressionless...still staring out the window to the street.

Alleroy kept talking. "You'll see me leave and pause on the curb. When the light on this corner turns yellow you'll gun the car and start coming, and I'll step off—"

—"And what if by some chance a cop car happens to turn the corner just then?"

"One in ninety. Emanuel." He rose. "One in ninety." He went to the bar and ordered two more drinks.

Emanuel was thinking of calling Estella to tell her he would be home even later than he thought. He reached for his phone but decided it was already too late to call and that she was probably already asleep since she had to get up very early. He sat there waiting on Craig, and wondering how what he'd been doing for the last week would impact his relationship with her. This was now the most salient factor in his decision. Holding on to Estella's love was more important to him than the fact that the money would get him out of this job he hated. She was the most important person in his life. Ever. How could he tell her about this strange last few days? Could he tell her *anything* about this? How on earth could he explain to her that he was even *contemplating* killing a man for money? Right or wrong, Emanuel was now convinced Estella would leave him if he even tried. So, if he *did* do what Craig was after him to do, he was painfully aware he could never tell her. Alleroy returned and set Emanuel's draft down in front of him.

"Thanks. Craig, listen to me." He took a sip of the cold beer. "I have had a lifetime of lousy luck. You *must* know that by now. It—

—"Your luck is about to change."

—"No, man! It would be my lousy luck that a cop car would turn that corner at that very moment and see me do this thing."

"Emanuel, have you seen a patrol car tonight?"

"That's tonight Craig. I can almost guarantee that if I did this there'll be a cop car on my ass as I drive away. Guaranteed."

"I told you that I sat here for a few nights. No cop cars. You *really* think you're *that* snake-bit? Come on Emanuel. *Come on.* This is a chance for you to start a new life. You'll have money. You'll be able to quit that job. Hey, I saw what happened to you today. I'll bet that's happened to you before, trapped in that small room all day. And, if it hasn't happened in there before so what...you are trapped all day every day in a room where guys come to take a shit. What kind of life is that? I know how much you must want to get out of there. I know it, and I also know you can't, not unless you come into a windfall, and I'm offering you a windfall now."

Alleroy's words were like a white-hot branding iron. Emanuel knew that what he was hearing was the terrible truth. He was painfully aware that because of what the military cavalierly put in his record he might never get out of that place. Hadn't he tried and been refused so many times before? Oh, he knew what the money meant alright. He now felt cursed by this whole affair. It was further proof to him that fate continued to be unkind to him and that his destiny was to lose his love no matter what he decided. He sipped his beer silently and continued to stare out the window into the street, fairly wishing that a cop would walk through the door, or a prowl car would appear and finally force him into getting up and giving Craig a definitive "no" to this whole insane thing as he said goodbye and walked out the door.

Richard Alleroy was also thinking. He was thinking that it was time to stop the cat and mouse game they were playing. *I have to offer this guy more than a hundred twenty-five to get him to agree to do what needs to be done here. The question is; how much?* Suddenly Emanuel slammed his mug down on the table and leaned in close to Alleroy. His voice was a rasp.

"You think you're doing me a big favor don't you? You and your fucking 'suicide' have pretty much fucked my life. I finally found someone who I love, who I respect, who makes me happy, and this crazy scheme of yours that I've stupidly gone along with is going to cost me her love. I could have been perfectly fine staying where I am as long as I had this woman in my life...and now it's fucked thanks to you. You really are a piece of shit."

Reel him back in! Now! Alleroy, although surprised by Emanuel's sudden outburst, reacted immediately. "Emanuel, I understand how you feel...And yes, I agree, I'm not a very nice person. But, aside from my shortcomings - which, I grant you, are extensive - why does she have to know anything about thi—?"

—"Because, Craig...Because it's about lying. Secrets. Respect for someone you love. Forget killing you...you don't matter to me even a *little* bit. Man, what a...Just by letting myself be sucked in by the thought of all this money you've dangled in front of me, I've made it impossible to have the only thing I think I've ever wanted. And believe me, I don't blame you I blame myself. I told you Craig - I have lousy luck, and this is just more proof of it." He took a long drink of his beer and rose to leave. He took a long drink of his beer and rose to leave.

Alleroy had to act fast. "Wait man...wait. Listen to me. Sit down...for a minute. Just sit down...Please."

"Why? Huh...why? You gonna dangle some more money in front of me?"

"Okay...Let's forget the money...for now. Yes?" Emanuel stands there. "Look, whatever you think of me I like you. Really. I like you a lot. I know what you've been through in your life. Me? I was born with a silver spoon in my mouth. I've had it real easy. I was a big shot shark on the street. And I went ahead and stole from people anyway. I'm not a good person! My wife and kids are, you are. And it *isn't* fair. Life is *not* fair. Please sit down...just for another minute. Please."

Shaking his head Emanuel slowly sat back down.

"Emanuel...allow me to tell you something about yourself. Please. And understand; I like you. I really like and admire you for how you've conducted your life despite the hand you had to play. *But*...having said that, you seem to think that none of what's happened to you is your fault. I sympathize with your not being able to get a job somewhere else. But, when that was happening to you, why didn't you become your own boss? Buy something and sell it for a small profit. And do it again. And then again and again. People do that. That's how small businesses are built. You didn't have to settle for the job you have no matter what you think."

Emanuel was listening.

"I'm sorry if that's an uncomfortable idea, Emanuel...but I had to say it."

"You don't believe in fate?"

"Sure, I believe in fate but...Let's talk about the hand you had to play. Let's look at life like poker. Six people are playing five card draw. Two of them are dealt the same hand. They each have a deuce, trey, five, six and a ten. Only two of the cards have the same suit. Not a great hand, yes?" Emanuel listened with some interest, especially as he had been recently contemplating this concept of fate and he was curious to hear Craig's take on it. "They each need to draw a four for an inside straight. Four outs to make a gutshot straight, one of the weakest draws in *poker*. And, maybe one or two of those fours are in the other player's hands. And, it's a crappy straight to begin with. Long odds of winning the pot. One of our guys folds and our other guy draws a card. A four. He scoops a big pot. Fate dealt them both the same hand, right? Except, they each played the same hand they were dealt differently." Emanuel sat there wondering if there was something he could have done other than what he did twenty years ago. "I don't know...maybe somewhere along the way, you could have played your hand differently. Taken a slim to none chance instead of folding."

Aside from what Alleroy had just said, Emanuel was also thinking about what he was going to do relative to the quote he was pondering earlier. *Has this been waiting to happen to me since the beginning of time? How do I play this? I know my fate is not my destiny.*

Alleroy could see Emanuel was deep in thought. "More importantly though, why do you think you've lost this wonderful woman? You've done nothing but listen to—to a proposition. You—"

"A proposition?" Emanuel was snapped back out of thought.

"Yes, I've made you a proposition. Okay, you don't wish to accept. Just tell her you received a proposition and you turned it down, that's all." Through all of the past three hours Alleroy appeared to be calm, in control. While beneath the outward cool there lurked a very nervous schemer thinking he was on the verge of losing his mark. Never more so than in the last fifteen minutes. He took a sip of vodka. "Right? You'll tell her it was a proposition."

"And when she asks me what kind of proposition? What? Do I tell her some guy wanted me to kill him for money?"

Alleroy seized the moment. "Tell her it was for two hundred and fifty thousand dollars, and you didn't feel comfortable about it and turned it down."

Alleroy saw Emanuel's frosted mug hesitate almost imperceptibly as it was halfway to his mouth. He knew he had Emanuel's full attention and had to keep talking. "Or, let's see...Tell her that a very old wealthy regular at The Coach and Crown, whom you befriended, and always took special care of, left you a small fortune in his will. Things like that happen all the time. Alleroy was certain that this explanation had to have already crossed Emanuel's mind."

Though Emanuel was somewhat surprised that he had thought of the very same explanation for his sudden windfall as this white-collar criminal Craig just conjured up, his train of thought braked to a halt at the words two hundred and fifty thousand dollars. *A quarter of a million?*

Alleroy knew he now had Emanuel's full attention. "I know you don't like me...Not even a little bit. But...Emanuel, This is life-changing money. You'll tell her that some lonely old man left it to you and that'll be that."

"Okay, except you're forgetting one minor detail Craig."

"No, I'm not. Look, I know I'm asking a lot of you, but it's also a lot of money. Emanuel...You'll have a quarter of a million dollars. Cash."

They sat there staring at each other for a minute. Then Alleroy diverted his eyes and took a drink. Emanuel took a long drink of his beer as well.

"You still haven't seen a cop or a cop car right? This bar is almost empty and the street is empty too."

Emanuel carefully placed the mug down on the table in front of him, picked up the paper napkin, wiped his mouth, slowly wiped the condensation on the table and looked at Alleroy.

"Craig...If...*If*...I should decide to do this, when and where do I get the two hundred and fifty thousand dollars?"

TWENTY-SIX

In the same moment as Richard Alleroy was answering Emanuel Grave's question, there were many, many women in New York City worried about the men in their life. Two of them, Margaret Alleroy and Estella Rosario, were both wide awake and wondering where on earth their men were at this late hour. Of greater concern, they were also wondering what exactly was going on with them. Margaret had never known her husband to be unable to sleep soundly, and Estella was wondering what kind of business meeting could take this long...and be taking place at night?

Margaret had been sleeping in the same bed as her husband ever since they'd been married thirty-one years ago, and for two-and-a-half years before that. She knew he always slept in the royal position, face up and flat on his back, and would fall asleep shortly after he lay down. Now, she could feel his restlessness throughout the night. Moreover, in the wee hours of the morning, when she would have to get up to use the bathroom, she would see him finally asleep and curled up in the fetal position. This was a sleep position she hardly ever saw him in. She suspected something very serious was troubling him and was quite distressed about his physical and mental health. She needed to find out what was troubling him, because something surely was.

• • •

Estella Rosario was debating for the umpteenth time whether or not to call Emanuel, or go to sleep and leave it alone rather than question him as to why this meeting had lasted so late. An hour before, when she first thought about calling him, she dismissed the idea as looking as if she were keeping tabs on him. It was now twelve thirty-five AM and Emanuel still wasn't home. She finally rang his cell phone which immediately went to voicemail. She simply said "hi Manny...it's just that it's so late and I'm hoping you're okay. I love you." Now, she wondered if maybe he was down in his own room and decided to go downstairs to see if he was there. She put on a robe, grabbed his spare key and left her room. While waiting for the elevator she was asking herself if she was overreacting. She told herself that he was a grown man and if he wanted to hang out and have a drink or two with a prospective employer what was the big worry. She knew she shouldn't press him on this business since he had said he'd tell her about it in due time. Most of all, she did not wish to be like a nagging wife. Except it wasn't like him not to call, and she *was* worried that he still wasn't home - unless he *was* downstairs asleep. If so, she reasoned, it would only be because he didn't want to wake her by calling or coming in so late - not knowing that she was still up and wondering where he was. She reached his door, knocked softly and waited listening for any movement, any sound that would tell her all was okay. There was none. She knocked softly again. Nothing. She put the key in the lock, turned it, and slowly opened the door. The room was dark and she tip-toed in. She quietly stood there and when her eyes became accustomed to the dark she could see that Emanuel was not in bed - as she was hoping he would be. She turned, walked out, locked the door and returned to her room while hoping nothing was wrong, he was okay and also hoping she was worrying about nothing. She thought about getting into her bed and decided she would wait up for Emanuel a while longer. And then the phone rang.

•   •   •

Emanuel was on the two train heading home and never heard his ringtone or Estella's message. He had spent an hour since The Pearl closed walking the area with Alleroy as Alleroy showed him where he would park the car and the route he would take to leave the scene, abandon the car and walk to the two train at Wall and William Streets. The very subway station Emanuel had used twice a day, six days a week, for the last twenty-two years. *The bar is on William, the train is on William, my middle name is William...is all this a sign? Is the universe telling me to do this? If this is my fate, if it was always going to happen this way, and if I do this what will my destiny be? I'll have a quarter of a million dollars but will I still have Estella? Can I be with her and have such a terrible secret?* He still hadn't committed to Craig's plan. But now, the idea of having a quarter of a million dollars was sorely tempting him. *Clear. No tax. Serves them right what they did.* He almost forgot what he would have to do to get this money. Almost. *I have to run a man over.*

He'd left Alleroy at the subway station at Wall and William with the promise that he would give him an answer in one or two days at the latest. The way they left it was that Alleroy would meet him in the park tomorrow evening after work, and the day after that, and within that time frame Emanuel would give him a yes or no. If Emanuel agreed then the money, the tools and the disguise would be handed over in Alleroy's car that same night, and the "accident" would take place the night after. At first Alleroy balked at the exchange taking place at night, but Emanuel was adamant about not taking all that money into work. He didn't much like the idea of taking all that stuff home with him even for one night either. He immediately added *if* he agreed. When Alleroy added, on purpose, that he was trusting that Emanuel wouldn't decide to run with the money and not do what he'd agreed to do, Emanuel got very angry at the insinuation. He would honor his obligation should he agree. This seemed to satisfy Alleroy and they shook on it and went their separate ways. What Alleroy was actually satisfied with was that he made Emanuel angry.

As soon as the train came out of the tunnel and into the cool night air Emanuel finally heard his cell phone alerting him that he had a voicemail message. *Shit...I should have called her. Now she's worried. We talked, hung out, had too many drinks and...It looks good but...I still don't want to count any chickens so...*He was going over the story he would have to tell her because she *was* going to ask. *I knew it, she sounded worried.* He knew she had every *right* to ask why he was so long because he didn't call to tell her he'd be later than he thought, and so his thoughtlessness caused her to be worried. *Dummy...if you'd have called you wouldn't need any bullshit story. Should I call her now?* He thought about it for a few seconds. *So what if I wake her, she'll be glad to know I'm not lying dead somewhere.* He pressed call.

•   •   •

Margaret Alleroy was sitting at the kitchen table wondering if this wasn't the only night her husband had come home this late. She was usually asleep by eleven, and for the last week or so when she went to bed he still wasn't home. She had a meeting at nine in the morning with The Children's Aid Society board but, more than sleep, she needed to know what was going on with her husband. Just then she heard his key in the front door. She glanced at the clock on the stove. *Twelve thirty-five.* She heard the door open and then softly close.

She raised her voice so he was sure to hear her. "I'm in the kitchen, Rich."

Just inside the foyer Alleroy stood stock still. *Shit! Christ Meg, what are you doing up?* "I'll be right there." He went to his study, took the gun, the suppressor and the clip from briefcase and stashed them in one of his desk drawers. He locked the drawer, took a deep breath, composed himself as best he could, and went to join his wife in the kitchen.

Margaret was sitting there with a glass of red wine on the table in front of her. An open bottle of 2010 Château La Gravette de Certan was also on the table. Alleroy, already surprised that his wife was up at this hour, entered the kitchen and was further surprised to see her...drinking wine? *Something's wrong.*

"Sweetheart, are you alright?" He sat down opposite her. There was an empty wine glass already at that spot on the table.

She nudged the bottle towards him. "I'm fine Rich. Not to worry. But I am concerned that you're not sleeping and ...I don't know...You've been acting different lately. What's going on?"

Alleroy, who thought he was doing a bang up job of hiding all the pressure he was under, used the time it took to pour himself a glass of wine to think exactly how he was going to respond. Margaret sat waiting as he did this. She knew her husband so well and could see the wheels turning in his head. In all the years of their marriage this was the first time she sensed that there was something terribly wrong. Her husband had never appeared distracted to the point of sleeplessness. She wondered if it might be something to do with his health. That was her biggest worry.

"Rich, when was the last time you saw Doctor Whitlock?"

She thinks it's something to do with my health. I can't. I...I have to.

"I've been having sporadic pain in my left arm lately. I'll make an appointment with him tomorrow. It's just that it comes and goes and I guess I push it out of my mind and forget about it. But, I can see I've caused you some distress and for that I'm sorry honey. I should have called him days ago. I promise you I'll call him."

"Rich...why have you just let this go? *I'll* call him first thing tomorrow. I've never before known you to be unable to get to sleep. I love you, but honestly, we're at an age where we can't be this lackadaisical about our health. It's probably nothing serious, but better safe than sorry."

I guess I'm going to the doctor.

"I'm also going to get you some melatonin. You can't be lying awake all night worrying."

She took a sip of wine. "You have me drinking at one in the morning here. Honestly, Richard." She took another sip of wine. "I think I'm going to need this to get to sleep myself. I wonder, maybe you should cut back on work. Have you given any thought to that?"

"You know, I have." He took a sip. "This is very good, isn't it?"

"Because we have more than enough to spend the rest of our lives in comfort. I mean, how much more do we need? Why should you kill yourself working?"

"You're right sweetheart. I should think about slowing down."

"Well, I think more than slow down. Why don't we travel? Start really enjoying what you've worked so hard for all your life. We've always wanted to take a transatlantic trip on the QE2. And how many times have we talked about the Venice Simplon-Orient-Express? We could travel from London to Venice on the Express. And...we could go back to Istanbul from Venice. Huh? What do you think?"

"I think it's a great idea."

"How about a compromise? If the doctor clears you—Never mind *if*, of course, he will. Or, worst case, you need a stent, we get it done, and when you're back at full strength in a month, you take a year off, and we travel."

"I would love that." Truer words had never come out of Richard Alleroy's mouth. "You have a deal."

Margaret held out her hand. "Let's shake on it."

He held out his hand and they shook on it. Margaret was pleased as she poured a little more wine into each of their glasses. She raised her glass to him and he raised his glass as well. They both smiled and toasted the future. Half of him was screaming to tell her everything, and half of him knew he couldn't. Knew she'd talk him out of it. Knew he couldn't live with everyone's revulsion at what he'd done. Knew that without him she would be better off, and the kids would be better off. However, uppermost in his mind; he believed with every fiber of his being that *he,* Richard Alleroy, would be better off.

When Margaret went up to bed Alleroy said he'd be right up. He went to her computer and searched current moon phases. Then he went upstairs and pretended to sleep until he actually did.

•   •   •

Estella bolted upright in her chair when her phone rang. Before she knew who it was she had a breathless moment of panic. When the phone said "Emanuel" she finally exhaled. At last. He was safe - and she knew she didn't want to question him at all.

TWENTY-SEVEN

It was another pleasant evening in New York City. He had called Estella and begged off seeing their new apartment promising her he would see it with her as soon as he could. It was "this business," he said. She wished him luck but was disappointed because she was looking forward to seeing his face light up when he saw their new place. And their new neighborhood.

It was now six o'clock. A few people sat at benches in Mannahatta Park drinking take-out coffee, or eating a slice of pizza, and chatting before they went on their various ways home. Emanuel had once again come from another day at work that he just wanted to forget as soon as possible. He was seated at his favorite bench awaiting Craig's impending arrival while trying to concentrate on today's chosen book; The Way of Life. He was finding this a bit difficult as his attention was spread thin between Estella, the decision he needed to make, taking care of George and Gracie, and his contemplation of one particular quote on one of the many dog-eared pages in the book; "Your own positive future begins in this moment. All you have is right now. Every goal is possible from here." He had flipped the book open randomly and, of all the seventy-six pages in the book, it had opened to this one. He wasn't sure whether to take this as a sign to agree to Craig's plan - or not. He *was* sure that his positive future was Estella. But it had to also be in the decision he'd made, and changed, at least a dozen times since leaving Craig at the subway station at Wall and William late last night. And he knew that either way he decided, this decision was going to impact his relationship - and *not* in a good way.

He was grateful that Estella hadn't asked him anything about where he was, why he was so late, what his meeting was about...not a thing. She greeted him with open arms, a passionate kiss, and nothing but relief, love and comfort. And she still didn't question him when he told her he might be coming home later than usual for the next few nights. Then they went to bed. In spite of all he had endured in his life, as of this evening, he now allowed himself to *consider* that he might, *might*, in fact, be a very lucky man.

George and Gracie were back, and he dug into the bag of peanuts he bought and threw them each another one. As he watched them rush off, the call of a bird triggered his remembrance of some pieces of a dream he had after they'd made love and he had fallen asleep. He closed his eyes and forced himself to concentrate on it. They were flying, Estella and he, arms spread wide, fingers splayed like the tips of eagle's wings with their fingertips touching. The land was stretched out below them and the sun was bright above them and warm on their backs. And then they were gliding high over the ocean. They could see rolling whitecaps far below. He tried to remember the rest of the dream, if there *was* more, and couldn't. But, just remembering what he did of the dream, seeing it in his mind's eye once again, made him feel good, positive and hopeful. He was thinking that he had never had a flying dream before, and that he had read somewhere that such a dream represented freedom and an escape from the "real" world. He told himself that he had a chance, however risky and criminal, to make this escape here and now. He sat there contemplating the possibility. For the last week he'd heard about Craig's plan and last night he saw that Craig had carefully worked out the physical logistics. Still, after turning the decision over in his mind for some time he reasoned that all the money in the world couldn't possibly buy what he had now - *and* what he stood to soon lose. But, he reminded himself, it *was* a quarter of a million dollars, *with* the possibility of more because, to see and hear him explain the bind he was in, Craig had no other option. At this point he felt damned if he did and damned if he didn't. The lightness of his mood darkened. *I should kill this guy just because of how he's complicated everything for me.* The messy fact then dawned on him that he was in this bind because he went along with this insanity in the first place. Never in his life would he ever think he could, or would, be swayed by the sin of avarice. And now he was, and that darkened his mood even more. *You're a damned idiot! But it's so much money.* He stared at the quote; "*Your own positive future begins in this moment. All you have is right now. Every goal is possible from here.*" He sat there lost in thought. It was now nearing seven, and he began to wonder where this Craig guy was.

For his part, Alleroy had decided to make Emanuel wait *and* meet him empty-handed. Get him angry and off-balance. While he was waiting, Emanuel decided to try and calm his nerves by trying to summon up some more of last night's dream. He sat back and closed his eyes, trying to conjure up some more of his dream, but try as he might nothing else came to him. Another fifteen minutes went by and Emanuel was now beginning to worry that Craig wasn't going to show up. *I have no idea where this guy lives either...or, how to find him if I wanted to.* After a few minutes of trying in vain to remember more of the wonderful flying dream he finally gave up, sat back, kept his eyes closed, and tried to relax.

When he finally did open his eyes he was relieved to see Alleroy enter the park and begin to walk toward him. Emanuel's initial positive reaction at seeing him turned at once to wondering why Alleroy wasn't carrying his attaché case, or any kind of a bag which would contain the tools he would need if he was to do this. Alleroy had decided purposely to leave his attaché case in the trunk of his car. He was banking on Emanuel noticing its absence immediately. He was convinced his attaché case was now imprinted on Emanuel's mind as representing money, and not having it with him, or the tools he said he bought, would have to trouble Emanuel. Furthermore, he suspected that the sight of him without these things, without the "money," would no doubt set off an alarm in Emanuel's mind. Alleroy was counting on this move causing Emanuel to wonder if he had come to his senses and decided to call this whole thing off and, in doing so, had snatched from him his one and only shot he'd ever have at getting a quarter of a million dollars. Which was *exactly* Emanuel's reaction, and *exactly* what he thought. *Is he calling it off? After all this?* Moreover, it was a thought that was accompanied by a sense of loss so great as to send a shudder through Emanuel's entire body. However imagined this "loss" of something he never *had* was, it seemed as real as a heart attack to him. *I can't believe this.* It was as if a sumptuous feast had been set before him, tantalizing him, and then been unceremoniously whisked away without a word as to why. Emanuel was so fixated on the absent attaché case, and tools, that it never even occurred to him to think that *if* Craig *was* calling it off he just wouldn't bother showing up at all.

Emanuel's anxiety mounted as Alleroy, who, except for when he picked up the holster he'd purchased, had killed most of the day sleeping fitfully in his car on the lower East side, and was now taking his good sweet time, drew closer to Emanuel. And as he did he saw Emanuel's furrowed brow. He had also counted correctly on Emanuel's attention being solely drawn to the missing case which signified money, and the missing tools signifying the job, and would be clearly troubled by their absence. Curiously, in this moment of sinking disappointment at the imagined end of the *possibility* of coming into so much life-changing money, Emanuel had forgotten what he would have to *do* in order to *get* this money, so befogged was he by the thought of losing it. This was how completely crazy this whole episode had made him. And then, as Alleroy drew even closer, it finally *did* occur to him that this Craig lunatic wouldn't be here at *all* if he *was* calling it off. He let out a noticeable sigh of relief at this realization. *It has to still be on.* And, the fact that this was a relief to him further confused Emanuel. *Do I want to do this so much?*

Alleroy, who had his eyes glued on Emanuel as he approached him, saw Emanuel let out this sigh, saw him sit back, and saw his shoulders drop as the tension he was feeling left him. Emanuel's body language told Alleroy all he needed to know. His ploy had produced the result he hoped it would. He had made Emanuel *feel*, not just *think*, but viscerally *feel*, what it meant to lose his only chance at ever possessing a quarter of a million dollars. At ever getting out of that bathroom. At ever being unashamed to answer the question, "what do you do?"

But Alleroy had more in mind; he also wanted to again make Emanuel angry. So, he stopped about fifteen feet from Emanuel and bent down to pretend to tie a shoelace that hadn't come loose in one of his British tan Testoni wing-tips. He *wanted* Emanuel to see this fakery. This flagrant pretense did anger Emanuel, who now understood what was happening. He was already annoyed by whatever it was that Craig was pulling and the shoelace thing pushed him over the edge. He rose.

"I'm done." He began to walk off shaking his head and, as Emanuel passed him, Alleroy grabbed him by the arm.

"Get your fucking hands off me Craig." And he yanked his arm from Alleroy's grasp.

"Okay, okay. But, listen to me, Emanuel. Listen to me. I was just trying to get you to see how it felt to lose the opportunity to make a quarter of a million dollars because I want you to do this. I need you to do this. And I want you to hate me so you'll want to see me dead."

Alleroy, who believed in his version of von Bismarck's axiom; tell the truth and fool the world, was gambling that he could make Emanuel dislike him even more than he already did by telling him exactly *what* he was doing and *why* he was doing it, while still getting him to stay with the plan. He had a calculated method to his madness, and one which he was sure would get him to his desired objective which, of course, was to be killed.

"I must be crazy to have let this get this far. You're out of your mind Craig."

"You don't want the two hundred fifty thou?"

"Of course I *want* it. But I can't do what you're asking in order to get it."

"What if I made it three hundred thousand? Three hundred thousand dollars. Almost a third of a million."

Emanuel took a few steps towards leaving. *Three hundred thousand...*He stopped and turned around. "I...Craig, I'm not sure I can do what you want. Or, if I want to do what you're asking me to do here."

As they stood there some ten feet apart looking at each other for some thirty seconds, Alleroy could see that Emanuel wasn't *really* ready to walk away just yet. Emanuel stood there not really sure why he *wasn't* just walking away. *What am I waiting for? Why can't I just kiss this whole thing goodbye?* And then he got his answers.

"Emanuel, what can I do to get you to do this?"

Emanuel knew that just by answering this question he would be prolonging this insanity he'd become involved in. Yet, curiosity was tugging at him. He heard himself say; "I asked you a bunch of times; how much life insurance do you have?" And, as he said it, was both eager to know, and afraid he was digging a hole he wasn't going to climb out from.

"And I told you that if you agree to this I'll tell you. But, I'm going to amend that; I'll tell you when I hand you the money." He looked at Emanuel. "So...how much will it take?"

Emanuel returned Alleroy's stare. An eternity went by before he said; "I'll do it for a million." *She'll understand. I know she will.* The two men stood there looking at each other. *I hope she will.*

The moon was waning, and darkness was swiftly descending on the park. As the park was mainly used by people who worked on the block, took breaks in it, ate lunch in it, and had now gone home, they were now the only two people there. As Alleroy was turning this request over in his mind, Emanuel was wondering if he'd just done something utterly deranged. *Manny, walk. Walk now.* Emanuel stood there shaking his head as if to signal his disappointment in himself. "A million, Craig. One million." Half of him wanted Craig to turn him down. Maybe Craig would do for him what he couldn't do for himself.

"That's a lot of money Emanuel."

"You're asking me to do a lot *for* it."

As Alleroy stood there debating what he wanted to do, Emanuel went to the fountain, bent over and took a long drink of water. *What if he agrees? Jesus.* He straightened up and walked back to where Alleroy was standing.

"I'll have to call my sister. Look, Emanuel, until then there's two hundred and fifty thousand dollars in my attaché in the trunk of my car. Say yes, and we'll walk there and I'll give it to you as a down payment. I'll give my sister a call later and get her to fly the rest in as soon as possible."

Emanuel's eyes narrowed as he stared at Alleroy. "A million." Alleroy slowly nodded yes. Now, it was Emanuel's turn to think. He was a man of his word. It was the one badge of honor in his life he could point to with deserved pride. If he agreed right now at this moment, and took the two hundred and fifty thousand in good faith money, he would be irrevocably committing himself. And committing to commit murder.

A minute, which felt like forever to Alleroy, went by as Emanuel argued with himself. During this time, though he tried to suppress it, his breathing had become deeper and faster. Alleroy could see this. Emanuel was acutely aware that this very moment was probably the single most pivotal moment of his life. Alleroy knew he had to keep quiet and let Emanuel decide on his own, but inside he was praying feverishly that Emanuel would do what he wanted him to do. React the way he hoped he would to his generous offer of a down payment. If he didn't, Alleroy knew he was done. At the same time that Emanuel was struggling with his decision, Alleroy was trying to come up with something that would make sense should Emanuel give him the answer he did not want. He was hoping that the way he had played it would lead Emanuel to the only response that would satisfy both of them.

"Craig...I appreciate the fact that you'd trust me with two hundred and fifty thousand dollars. That level of trust means a lot to me. But...*you* have to appreciate that this is far too big a decision to make on the spot. I mean, a million...that's a whole new ballgame and if I take this down payment, as you put it, then I'm all in. And...I don't know if I am. Not yet anyway. It's very tempting but...I need to sleep on it."

Alleroy, who had listened patiently to Emanuel's response, now mulled what he heard over in his mind. He finally said, "For how long, Emanuel? I need to get this done."

"I'm not sure." Emanuel looked around him at the deserted park. It looked so different to him now. Lonely. And, even though it was a late spring night, cold. The moon was a crescent sliver. Two of the park's streetlamps were out. Large dark pools lay beneath them. His hand felt for the book in his pocket. His fingers touched it as they would a talisman. It was as if he was hoping this book he cherished for its wisdom would reveal something to him. "Can you wait a couple of days? This is a lot to think about."

It'll probably take two days before my sister can get here with the money anyway. *It'll be this dark for the next two days and then there's a new moon.* "Buddy...it's one *million* dollars. Of all people you deserve it. One million dollars Emanuel."

And that's where the two men left it for the short while that each of them would use to weigh the balance of the rest of their lives.

TWENTY-EIGHT

While Estella had honored Emanuel's wish and hadn't asked him what was going on with all the late night meetings, she *was* feeling a bit left out. If he believed that talking about it could jinx it, so be it. She just hoped that whatever these meetings were about that they were going well for him. He did seem unusually preoccupied though, so she knew that whatever this business *was* about it had to be important. She was keenly aware of how very much he wanted out of the job he'd been at for so many years, and which he disliked intensely. The fact that she didn't want to ask him about something he didn't wish to talk about hung heavily in the air though. She was hoping that whatever it was it would be over soon and he could tell her all about it - whatever the outcome. Her own curiosity was itching her like crazy. Still, she vowed she would abide by his fear of "jinxing" whatever it was he was up to.

Estella was *also* coming home later than usual as she was shopping for furniture for their new apartment. That was another thing; he still hadn't found the time to see their new place. She *had* asked him about *that* though, and he couldn't say when he would be able to see it with her. Soon, he said, and she let it go. She tried to shrug it off by chalking it up to how important his meetings had to be, that he was very preoccupied by them, and assuring herself that he would certainly come see the place with her as soon as he could. No matter what, she was set on remaining understanding of whatever it was he was doing until he decided on his own to tell her what was going on. She did appreciate that he said he "trusted her good taste" and was sure the furnishings she bought would be perfect. He had only one request, which he made right after they got into her sofa bed that night. Smack in the middle of a passionate kiss, when their lips parted for a second, he said in a breathy voice; "get a king-size bed with a firm mattress Stella...please." That brought a knowing smile, a giggle, silence...and then the sounds of ardent love-making.

While Emanuel Graves and Estella Rosario were making love, a worried and anxious Richard Alleroy began two days of thinking about what he was doing. And, much later that same night, an exhausted, but momentarily happy, Emanuel Graves began two days of thinking about what he was *going* to do.

True to her word, Margaret Alleroy had purchased some melatonin for her husband. In the kitchen she watched him swallow two 2mg capsules and made him promise he'd come upstairs to bed shortly. Five minutes after she went upstairs he went to her computer to make certain he had the phases of the moon correct. Five minutes after satisfying himself that all was in order he made his way upstairs, undressed, and forgetting to brush his teeth, got into bed next to his wife. Hours passed as he pretended that the melatonin had worked. He made his breathing mimic that of a person who was fast asleep. However hard he tried, however hopefully, even prayerfully that he shut his eyes, he could not doze off. Richard Alleroy's mind was a whirring uncontrollable mess. He was playing and replaying his demise again and again in his mind's eye. And, even worse, picturing his life if this loser Emanuel should, God forbid, finally refuse the money. After hours had passed, and after he was sure that Meg was asleep, he slowly got out of bed, tip-toed downstairs and poured himself a stiff drink of bourbon. The whiskey felt warm going down, and he wished he could drink himself to death right then and there. He wanted the alcohol to muddle his thoughts. To stop him from thinking about what was to come. Yet, the same sentence stubbornly insisted on repeating over and over in his head; "he can't refuse a million dollars." It was as if he was hypnotizing himself, so deeply had he retreated into this mantra. The fact that he couldn't take his own life was torturous, and the thought of having to live a life of disgrace, of being one of the ordinary poor, was repugnant. Here was a man who was thought of by *many* men as being the most persuasive man in the boardroom now reduced to hoping he was good enough to persuade just *one* man who worked in a men's room. It might have been funny if it wasn't so painful. He sat there with his head in his hands. It was now four-twenty in the morning. He never heard Margaret come down the stairs and pad into the dining room where he sat in the dark, head bowed, with a bottle of bourbon in front of him.

"Richard...are you alright?"

The light she had switched on combined with the sound of her voice jolted him upright. "Yes...I...I don't know Meg, I just couldn't get to sleep, and I thought maybe a drink would help. I'm fine. Not to worry."

Margaret sat down and put her arm around him. "Did you sleep at all, sweetheart?"

"I think for a little while, but then I woke and couldn't fall asleep again. I'm sorry Meg, I don't mean to worry you."

"Are you still having that pain?"

"Meg, I'm okay. I'm just experiencing a bit of insomnia. It's nothing. It'll pass."

"Is everything okay at work? Richard, I'm worried about you."

"Work is fine, Meg."

"Are you still having that pain in your left arm?"

Alleroy wanted to say yes, but thought better of it. "No. Please don't worry honey. That hasn't happened again."

"Rich, I've never known you not to be able to sleep. Something is bothering you. Tell me what it is. Maybe I can help."

At that moment, all Richard Alleroy wanted to do was unburden himself. The weight of his predicament was crushing him. He was dangerously close to telling his wife everything. Get it all out in the open. Stop the craziness he had started with the guy in the bathroom. Give his sister back her money. Confess what he did to Meg and to his children. All this was now swirling around in his brain. These thoughts were so insistent, so compelling, that he knew he had to keep himself from even opening his mouth to speak lest he doom himself, and his wife and children, to a life *he* viewed as being without hope. A life of counting every penny. He knew what Margaret would say. She would tell him they could be happy living in a one bedroom apartment in Queens, or some such nonsense. They would live simply, the way they did when they were starting out. He could get a job driving a cab. It's honest work. They would be fine. They'd make new friends. The kids were smart, they'd land on their feet. Not everyone needs a college degree to be successful. They'd work it out. She would be fine. They would still have each other.

These thoughts reminded him of things that he always knew and, from time to time, *when* he reflected on them, he'd successfully brushed off; that she was a far better person than he. That she was, hands down, the stronger of the two. Less attached, if even attached at all, to the many trappings he needed in order to prove his worth as a man. The penthouse, the Mercedes, the bespoke suits, they were his measurement of himself. He *knew* he couldn't live with the dishonor he'd brought to his name, and without his toys. He *needed* all those trappings. She only needed him and her children.

"Richard, did you hear me? I asked you what the matter is. Something is going on with you. What is it? Maybe I can help."

There was no getting around it now, he had to offer Margaret something by way of an explanation of why she found him sitting here in the dark at four-twenty in the morning drinking bourbon. He could only think of one thing that would fly. *Tell the truth and fool the world.* Well, maybe not the whole truth anyway. He would count on Margaret being somewhat unfamiliar with the workings of his business.

"Because of a mistake I made, I stand to lose twenty-five million dollars, and my position, if my attempt at correcting the error isn't approved."

"Oh, honey...Wait, are you saying you think you might lose your job over this?"

Alleroy nodded yes. Still with her arm around him, Margaret leaned in very close to him.

"I am so sorry you're going through this. But really..." She nudged him gently. "Rich, really, it hasn't happened yet...and you don't even know if it *will* happen. This is *not* the end of the world."

Oh Meg, if you only knew.

"And even if it *should* happen, Rich, with your reputation, you can work in any company on the street. They'd be lucky to get you. You're the best Rich...You know you are."

Her heartfelt attempts at comforting him felt to him like punches to his gut. Sitting in sullen silence, he wondered if she would be saying any of this if she knew what he'd done.

"Come on, let's go upstairs. You have to try to get a few hours of sleep before you have to go in."

She rose and held out her hand for him to take. He rose, downed the last bit of bourbon remaining in his glass, took his wife's hand, and together they walked upstairs to their bedroom.

TWENTY-NINE

Emanuel was at his bench absently tossing peanuts to George and Gracie, aware that he would not be seeing Craig this morning and barely able to concentrate on today's book. He knew that Craig was waiting for his sister to deliver the balance of the money he would be offering to him. He still couldn't decide if he was going to accept it. If he was going to do this thing. He was thoroughly preoccupied by this decision almost every waking moment since he'd been offered the million dollars, and he had changed his mind about what he was going to do a few dozen times since.

Being held in Estella's arms at night offered him some sweet respite from his continually obsessing about this intrusion on his equilibrium. Before this he would have never thought of himself as being a good lover, or even a considerate one. But, Estella gently led him to places he'd never before been. She saw his surprise at this as it was happening. And shortly after, when he replayed their lovemaking in his mind, did he understand that she, *she* made him into...well...a lover. There was no other way he could think about it. Didn't he hear her moan, purr with delight, feel her shudder? It filled him with a sense of manhood he had no idea he ever possessed. To have this marvelous woman in his life, to have her love, would have easily been enough to make living a paradise - were it not for what had lately taken up too much of the available space in his mind.

Ever since Estella had come into his life, his job, and what it reminded him of, ceased to be a constant raging source of malcontent. He wasn't aware of how little like a "man" he felt until Estella took him to her bed. To be the source of the pleasure she was experiencing, which was the result of a potency that had gone untapped in him for so long, made him feel not just like a *man*, but like a *super*man. *She* did this. *She* re-made him. Very few things in life can make a man feel unbothered by life's iniquities as being able to satisfy his woman in bed. Emanuel now knew this.

"My sister's flying in tomorrow night."

With those six words which snapped Emanuel back to the present, Richard Alleroy sat down. He only had a newspaper with him. No attaché case. Not only was Emanuel surprised to see him, he was annoyed at being so rudely brought back to Craig's world and his own dilemma.

No one aside from a sociopath would have a problem in deciding whether or not to commit murder. Did the promise of receiving a million dollars for doing so make the act any less than the act of a sociopath? Of course not. Did even considering such an act make him such a person? He wasn't ready to debate the point. Was he one of many who would consider committing murder for a million dollars? He wondered about this, and in this wondering he *also* wondered if this was his way of rationalizing such an act. A way of letting himself off the hook as it were - *if* he decided to take the money. Others would, why shouldn't he? And were there *really* many who would? He thought there were.

When the offer was forty, and then fifty thousand dollars, it did maybe engender fantasies of how much more this Craig guy was willing to offer, and what he, Emanuel, could do with the money. But in all seriousness, he didn't consider the decision to kill this Craig guy for *that* amount to be such a difficult one. Murder someone for forty thousand dollars? Risk being sent to prison for life for fifty thousand dollars? He could fantasize, but when it came down to it, no. No. And then, before he had a chance to walk away, the offer then became one hundred thousand dollars and Emanuel was starting to wonder if *he* was one of those people who *would* do such a thing for a lot of money. And now, at one million dollars, a lottery sized *lot* of money, he was seriously, *seriously* grappling with these questions. Seriously thinking about whether or not he was going to do this and then lie to Estella about the source of his new-found wealth. And, the curious thing of it was that he was more upset about the prospect of having to lie to Estella than he was about killing this custom-tailored crook who stole monies rightfully due old people who *had* to have these funds *just* to house and feed themselves. *She once mistakenly married a man who had secrets...who was violent.*

Emanuel threw some seeds on the ground for the pigeons. "Two more days then, huh?"

Alleroy was now trying unsuccessfully to shoo away the pigeons at his feet. "A million bucks tax-free cash."

"And what'll you do if I say no?"

Alleroy was still trying unsuccessfully to shoo away pigeons. "I go to plan B."

Emanuel threw some more seed on the ground, bringing down even more pigeons. "Who are you kidding?"

Annoyed by the pigeons - and this remark from *such* an inferior - Alleroy rose. He walked a few feet away from the gaggle of feasting pigeons. "What do you mean who am I kidding?"

"Plan B?" Emanuel, on the spur of the moment, decided just for fun he wanted to hear how Craig was going to answer his next question. "What's your plan B?"

Alleroy, who was still standing a few feet away from where the pigeons were feeding, smiled. *Tell the truth and...* "Okay Emanuel, there is no plan B. You got me."

"You know what, Craig?" He threw some more birdseed on the ground. "I'm thinking that it's way too risky." Even as he said this Emanuel wasn't sure he meant it. What he *was* sure of was that he would enjoy seeing Craig's reaction to hearing him say it.

This was not what Alleroy wanted, or expected, to hear. How could a guy who works in a bathroom and lives in a "dump" even *contemplate* turning down a million dollars? This was beyond his way of thinking. If the shoe were on the other foot, he was *certain* he could do what he was asking of Emanuel. For a million? If he was stuck working in a bathroom with no other prospects? If he had this guy's life? What he didn't know enough about, and hadn't added to the equation, was Estella. Sure, he knew Emanuel had a girlfriend, and yes, she lived in the same "dump" two floors above him. What he *couldn't* know was the *extent* of what she gave him. How *much* she made up for everything that had been denied him in his life. Alleroy couldn't come close to conceiving how exciting to both of them their plans for their future were. No idea that Emanuel now even *had* a future to look forward to. As far as he was concerned he was Emanuel's savior...as well as his own.

Emanuel, who was watching Craig closely, could see a look of pure disgust on Craig's face at what he perceived as insolence, *and* at hearing that Emanuel was thinking it was too risky. Alleroy was okay with Emanuel seeing this. *Yes, hate me.* At the same time, he had to admit to a begrudging respect for this "nobody" to even *think* of turning down his "generous" offer.

"I showed you that there was no chance of getting caught, didn't I? You saw that there weren't any cops, right?"

Emanuel continued to feed the pigeons. Now George and Gracie appeared, and the pigeons scattered. Alleroy stood there still looking disgusted at what he was witnessing. *This stupid motherfucker is running a fucking zoo here.* As he reached into his pocket for his bag of peanuts, Emanuel was aware that all this was annoying Craig no end.

"I'll have the money tomorrow night."

"I heard you before."

"Two nights from now I'll meet you here around nine. I'll give you five hundred thousand dollars, the tools and the disguise. And you'll get the other five hundred K the next night when we go. Emanuel, I'm under a time constraint here. My children's tuitions are due in August. It'll take at least two months for the insurance company to pay up. And that's with any luck. You must understand."

"I must? Must I? Hmm...Which one of those do you think is the more proper English Craig?" Emanuel threw two peanuts on the ground and watched as George and Gracie scooted off with them and the pigeons returned to feeding.

"Aren't George and Gracie cute, Craig?"

"How do you know which is which?"

"I don't."

Alleroy was growing more visibly annoyed by Emanuel's teasing.

"Craig...why do you think I can commit murder?"

"Emanuel, I know you're not a killer - as you so quaintly put it. I just know I want—scratch that, I *need*...to commit suicide" He looked at Emanuel. "And you can use the money."

"Yes, but, I asked you; why do you think I can commit murder? What is it about me that leads you to think that such an act is in me? Do you believe that *anyone* will do *anything* for enough money?"

"I believe most would. I'm surprised you don't."

"Maybe I do too. But that doesn't mean *I* would, does it?"

Had Richard Alleroy come to Emanuel Graves with this scheme a month before, he might have had a far easier time getting Emanuel to take the money. Emanuel might have then been unreservedly open to doing what Alleroy wanted - and, for far less money to boot. But, of course that's not the way it turned out and, as any comedian worth their salt will tell you; timing *is* everything.

And now, Alleroy was left with asking flat out if Emanuel was going to do this, or pretending this exchange never happened and plowing straight ahead. The pigeons were busy pecking at the birdseed. Alleroy walked to the fountain in order to give himself time to think about how he was going to play this next beat. As he took a drink he concluded his best move was to plow straight ahead as if this dialogue never happened.

Alleroy slowly walked back, trying to scatter the pigeons as he did, and sat back down. He seemed exhausted. "I was too clever for my own good. Took too many risks."

They were both silent as Emanuel threw some more seed on the ground in front of them and immediately even more pigeons reappeared at their feet.

"If you're doing that to annoy me let me assure you it does."

"Why?"

"Why?" Alleroy bent towards the pigeons and waved his arms to shoo them away. "Because they shit on everything. That's why." The pigeons, quite used to being among people, of course just flapped their wings, jumped a little, went back to pecking and mainly paid him no mind. He gave up trying and sat up straight.

"So did you."

"Very funny."

"Not funny. You did, didn't you? Shit on the old pensioners, shit on your family...shit all over your fancy suit there, right?"

In truth, Alleroy didn't care one way or the other if there were pigeons on the ground in front of them or not. What he did care about was that Emanuel should keep remembering how much he disliked him.

"Those pensioners are fine, believe me. They have a lot more money than you do. The only person who's been hurt here is me."

Emanuel threw some peanuts down and George and Gracie ran up to snatch them. They scattered the pigeons as they did and, as swiftly as the two squirrels arrived, they ran off. He looked up at the sky, got up, and emptied the bag of birdseed on the ground in front of them. Emanuel watched as even more pigeons than before flew down and landed at their feet. There was now a multitude of pigeons in front of Emanuel's bench, and at the feet of the two men. Alleroy couldn't keep from smiling at this obvious "fuck you."

"I have to go to work. I'll see you in a couple of days." And, as Emanuel walked off, Alleroy's smile turned to something dark.

THIRTY

Two nights had now come and gone since Emanuel left Craig sitting there pissed off amongst the pigeons in Mannahatta Park. During this time Manny and Stella had gone to work, seen the new apartment together which they would be moving into in a week - and which Manny *loved - and* where they smiled as they read each other's minds before they broke in the new California king bed. They'd taken in a movie at the Concourse Plaza Multiplex, gone to eat Pollo Guisado at the Dominican restaurant they liked, made love, watched Jeopardy together as they ate a lovely vegetarian Sancocho that Stella cooked, and made love again. Throughout all of it Emanuel was debating his million dollar decision. *And,* to his great chagrin, even for a few moments after they made love, as he lay in Stella's arms, he found himself arguing both sides as to whether or not he was going to steal a car and run this Craig asshole over for a million dollars.

Two days earlier, as Emanuel walked out of Mannahatta Park, a worried Alleroy rose, disgustedly walked around the pigeons to another bench and sat there thinking of what he had come to, and where he was going. *Why the fuck can't it be as easy for me to kill myself as it was for those four people connected to Madoff? Why do I have to depend on this idiot who works in a fucking bathroom? Why don't I know any mobsters...any hit men? They'd do it for a lousy couple of grand.* He was sitting there hosting a grand pity party for himself.

He opened his newspaper, looked at it briefly...and then put it down. *I'd love to know who the fuck it was who blew the whistle on me. Motherfucker. I would have given them plenty to keep their stupid mouth shut. Probably some dumb do-gooder who wouldn't take it anyway. I better remember to get rid of Meg's computer. I'll take it with me and ditch it before I meet him. He has to say yes. He never did ask to see my I.D. either. I also have to remember to put my real license back in my billfold. The sooner they know who I am the better. He's angry.*

He'll do it, it's a million bucks. I can't just let it sit for two days though, I have to be here tomorrow. Prime the pump.

He picked up his newspaper again and tried to read the sports pages. *No use in checking the market.* Unable to concentrate, he put the paper down again. *What am I going to do with the rest of this lousy day? I have nothing to do and all day to do it. What a mess. Why didn't that snitch meet me in the park like they said they would? None of this would be happening if they did what they said they would. Meet me in the park by the Hayes fountain you wrote? Well, I was here asshole, where the fuck were you? You bastard! You cunt! You fucked me good. You could've had a bundle from me, but you couldn't let it go, could you? Fucking goody two-shoes motherfucker.*

He sat there simmering in the sour juices of self-pity and blame. *None* of this would be happening if *only* that person would have come to the park at nine-thirty like they said they would. *This* was why he was in the predicament he now found himself in. *Not* because he ripped off so many thousands of pensioners, but because he *wasn't even given a fair chance* to grease his accuser's palm.

He opened his newspaper again. And...put it down in his lap again. *These retirees have plenty of money. They have beachfront homes in Florida for Chrissakes, I also made them plenty. Oh...and Harkness, Hirsch...Perlman...what, your hands are so squeaky clean? Give me a fucking break.*

He sat there alternating between picking up his newspaper and trying to read it, and putting it down in order to bemoan his fate. Margaret called to tell him she would be leaving at seven to go to a board meeting of Chefs for Seniors Food Delivery. He told her it was very busy but he'd probably be home about then. Finally, after an hour of this he left the park and went to a movie where he had no idea what was on the screen in front of him.

As he was in no mood to talk, he timed it to get home just as Margaret was getting ready to leave for her meeting. Still, she made him a martini, reminded him that he had to forego his lunch hour tomorrow as he had a one PM appointment with their cardiologist, that she would be meeting him there, and went upstairs to finish dressing. When she came back downstairs she told him that his dinner was ready whenever he wanted to eat. The roasted potatoes and asparagus were already cooked and ready to be warmed in the oven, and all he had to do was grill the steak that was already salted and on a rack in the fridge. She kissed him goodbye, said she'd be back in a couple of hours, and as he left she said she wanted to talk with him when she got back. She then left for her meeting.

He had no appetite. He grilled the steak anyway and plated it along with the potatoes and asparagus, sat down and tried to eat as much as he could, which was maybe a quarter of what was in front of him. He didn't want Meg to know that he couldn't eat so he cut what was left into very small pieces and flushed it all down the maid's toilet. He rinsed the plate and put it in the dishwasher. Then he went into the dining room, poured himself three fingers of Blanton's Gold, and sat there going over the way he had to approach what he had to get done. His mind turned to thinking about how such a thing would feel. Picturing it. The impact on the body. *I have to be killed.* He wished he could just swallow a bunch of pills and go to sleep. He wasn't afraid of dying, he was afraid of *not* dying. He took a sip.

Keeping up this charade was wearing him out. At least the bourbon felt good going down. He wished he *did* have heart trouble. A massive heart attack would solve everything. Natural causes. Clean as a whistle. This way was so iffy, but he had to see it through. He just had to convince this guy to show, and *then* - and this was a *big* then - *then*, he *had* to convince this guy, who had *nothing* going for him, less than nothing, to finally say yes and agree to meet to take the five hundred K as a partial payment. The rest would go as planned. If he could just get it to that point he was sure everything would work out. He took another sip.

Has anyone ever worked so hard to be dead he wondered? The past few weeks again brought home to him that it wasn't dying he feared, it was dying in pain. Dying slowly, poorly. Everybody and everything dies. But, some people die in their sleep never knowing they're drawing their last breath, and some people burn to death in a fire. Or drown. *I love these people who say these glib things when everything sucks really bad; "Well...It's better than the alternative." Really? My life will be better? My life will be a living death. Real death will be a welcome relief. That's why there's such a thing as assisted suicide.* As he finished his drink he managed a wan smile realizing that an assisted suicide was exactly what he was seeking now. *What does she want to talk about?* He poured himself three more fingers of bourbon and waited with no small measure of dread for Margaret to return home.

THIRTY-ONE

The rain was coming down in buckets. *Shit, I have to go to that fucking bathroom again.* Alleroy, having already called for his car, was standing at his kitchen window drinking his second cup of coffee after another almost sleepless night.

Last night Margaret had returned from her meeting, poured herself a glass of Pinot Grigio, sat down with him, and said she was very worried about him. When he told her he was fine and not to worry she said she knew he was okay but, she *was* curious as to why he had searched the first precinct on her computer. And a VOIP phone, whatever that was. And, of greater concern; why he was searching their acquaintance Jack Loomis' death in a hit and run accident? All he could think of as he was hearing the words coming from her mouth was; Oh, God...did I not delete those searches? He sat there in well-disguised shock. And the first thing that popped into his mind was; "I didn't want to tell you...or anyone, because I figured you'd only laugh. I mean...*anyone* would laugh, but...I've been researching an idea for a film script...about a murder."

She listened to him and, to his great relief, didn't laugh. And to his greater relief she said she loved crime films. Good for him that he was doing this, and thought it sounded as if those elements might make for a very interesting movie, and could he tell her more about it? He knew that once he did what he had to do to get the insurance money she would figure the whole thing out immediately. He would need to make it crystal clear to her in the letter he was going to leave her that she could *never* say anything to anyone about his scheme. If she did, it could impact the children forever.

And then she said; "But, why on my computer?"

"Well, I've been doing it on mine, but I did that particular search the second it hit me, and I was in the kitchen and there was your laptop so..."

The "aha, I see," expression on her face conveyed the message that she thought his explanation was quite plausible. "Screenplay by Richard Alleroy. It has a nice ring to it. So...can you tell me more, or is it a secret?" She was hoping he *would* tell her a little more about this "film script."

He took a sip of bourbon while he formulated what he would say next. "Thank you for understanding sweetheart...and for not laughing at me but...Wait just a little while. I've been thinking about it constantly and working on it, and I'd love for you to read it when I've finished it. Will you wait?"

"No wonder you've been pre-occupied."

"Yeah, it's...it's intricate. Actually, I've been working on the treatment."

"It sounds good." She finished her wine, rose, kissed him on the cheek and went to the kitchen. As she did she said; "I'll see you at the doctor's at one, don't stay up too late." And she went upstairs to bed.

•　　•　　•

And now it was the morning and he was standing at the window looking at the rain. *That was close last night. How did I not delete those searches? I have to be more careful. What a lousy day out. I can't not go. I have to go. I have to stay on it. And he's not there until eleven also. Shit...I have to sit in that fucking library again for two hours. And the doctor is at one.* He took another sip of coffee. *I could just sit in the car somewhere.* He'd had another night where he found it difficult to fall asleep. He finished his coffee, put the cup in the sink, and got ready to leave. *I'm just going to sit in the car.* He went to the study to get the packs of money from his desk drawer and transfer it to his attaché case. Case in hand, he grabbed his raincoat from the hall closet, and went down to his waiting car.

•　　•　　•

Since it was raining, and she knew that sitting in the park was out, Stella quietly got ready, set the alarm for nine forty-five, and left for work. She also left Manny a pot of coffee on the hot plate, and in bed with the luxury of a couple of more hours of sleep.

At the sound of the alarm, Manny rolled over and got out of bed. His immediate thought was of Craig and what he was going to do. It was all he could think of as he dressed, had coffee, walked to the train, and rode downtown to work.

Emanuel, who hadn't been at work more than fifteen minutes, was sitting and reading Critique of Pure Reason. He had read this book many times before and was staring at a passage he'd highlighted in his yellow marker on one of the books' many dog-eared pages; "To know what questions may reasonably be asked is already a great and necessary proof of sagacity and insight. For if a question is absurd in itself and calls for unnecessary answers, it not only brings disgrace to the person raising it, but may prompt an incautious listener to give absurd answers, thus presenting, as the ancients said, the laughable spectacle of one person milking a he-goat, and another holding the sieve underneath."

He'd read and re-read this quote a few times when the door opened and in walked Craig. He was wearing his wet raincoat and carrying his attaché case and his umbrella. He had gestured to Louie that he really had to go as he passed him and walked straight to the men's room. They were the only two men in the room. Alleroy laid his attaché case down on the counter.

"My sister's in tonight." He flipped the lid of the case open. "That's two hundred and fifty K and the rest is coming in with her later. Do we have a deal?" He closed the case and stood there staring at Emanuel who had put his book aside and was looking at him somewhat incredulously.

"Take it." Alleroy said, pointing to the case. This was the last thing Emanuel expected to happen this morning. For one thing, he had not yet come to a decision as to whether or not he was going to do what Craig wanted. For another, there was no way he could even think of stashing two hundred and fifty thousand dollars the bathroom's closet. Not even if he was always in its presence. Not for a minute, and *certainly* not for six more hours. Anything could happen. Another episode - who knows what? Nope, it was definitely out of the question.

Emanuel calmly replied; "Craig, look...I'm sorry man, but...I'm still thinking it over. This is far from an easy decision. I mean, maybe it's not to you but..." He shook his head slowly.

Just then the door opened and a man entered and went to a urinal. As he did, Alleroy snatched his attaché case off of the counter and disappeared into one of the stalls. *Again I'm in a stall. I can't fucking believe I'm having a fucking meeting in a fucking public bathroom. Please don't anybody take a crap. Please.* Then another man entered and went to another urinal. While the two men did their business Emanuel turned on the sink faucets and stood waiting with two hand towels while they washed their hands. Alleroy was sitting on the closed toilet waiting for them to leave. *This motherfucker has to do this every damn day. And he's having a hard time deciding whether or not to take a million bucks? Come on guys, let's go.* After a couple of minutes the two men left and Alleroy stepped out of the stall.

"Emanuel, I'm certain you'll agree that it's a bit difficult to talk in this...in this place. It's supposed to be nice tomorrow. I think we should continue talking in the park tomorrow morning before you come here."

"I hope you won't mind the pigeons."

Alleroy smiled. "Oh, and about tomorrow night; there's something I must do with my wife until a little after ten, so, assuming you want the million, let's make it in the park at eleven tomorrow night. I'm counting on you to be there. I'll have the five hundred K, the tools, and the disguise with me. I'm hoping you'll come to your senses and do the smart thing; take the money and quit this lousy fucking job. You'll be set for life. Emanuel, you have to go forward with your life. You have to live the motto of the two-five Emanuel; 'retreat, hell.'" Alleroy turned to leave. He opened the door and turned towards Emanuel. "Retreat, hell buddy. Retreat, hell!" And he left.

Emanuel just stood there looking at Craig as the door closed behind him. He knew he'd be in Mannahatta Park tomorrow morning, but he still wasn't sure if he'd be there tomorrow night.

•   •   •

Margaret stood to the side nervously watching as the nurse attached the last of the ten ECG leads to her husband's left leg just above his ankle. Ten seconds later she tore the print-out from the machine, told them that the doctor would be right with them, and left to take the print-out to him.

Alleroy sat up and swiveled around to face Margaret. "I've come home from here, got ready to step into the shower, and discovered two of these pads still on my body."

"We'll make sure she takes all of them off this time." She took a deep breath.

Alleroy noticed this. "Meg, I'm fine. Please don't worry."

They fell silent for a bit as they waited for the doctor. Then;

"How's the film idea coming along?"

"Um...You know...I'm making real good progress on the treatment. I have a feeling I'll have it buttoned up in a few days." He smiled at her. "And, I really hope you'll like it."

Again, they fell silent. After about two minutes, which seemed more like ten to both of them, there was a light knocking on the door and the doctor walked into the room holding the ECG print-out.

Alleroy looked up. "So, Michael? Am I going to live?" *I hope not.*

His doctor walked directly to his computer to briefly study the numbers on the screen and then he turned to them. "I'm afraid you're going to have to put up with him a lot of years more Margaret. Rich...your heart is fine. Strong. No skipped beats. Margaret said you'd been experiencing some pain in your left arm. Has that pain occurred lately?"

"No." *I only wish I could have a heart attack.*

"Are you anxious about something?"

"I uh...I guess I am. I have an issue at work. So, yes,"

Margaret was wiping the gel off of her husband as the nurse removed the leads and pads on his skin. "He's been having trouble sleeping."

"Do you take any sleeping pills?"

"No...Um, I'd rather not take anything Michael. It's this work thing. It'll sort itself out."

"I'd rather schedule you for some tests with a sleep specialist."

The nurse removed the last of the pads and Margaret stepped aside so the doctor could listen to Alleroy's lungs and breathing. "Your lungs are clear and I can't see any problem, but let's be absolutely certain, okay? I'm going to schedule you for a troponin test. And, if this trouble sleeping doesn't improve in a few weeks you're also going for some tests with a sleep specialist. Margaret, you'll let me know?"

As Margaret gathered up her husband's clothes; "Of course. What's a troponin test?"

"We need to see if any silent heart attacks have occurred in the past."

She handed him his shirt. "Silent heart attacks?"

"We want to be thorough."

Alleroy buttoned his shirt. "Thanks Michael." *At least this was better than killing time in the library.*

The doctor opened the door. "From what I can see I don't think you should worry. The nurse will call you about the test. Meanwhile, be well. Nice to see you Margaret." And he left.

● ● ●

While Richard Alleroy was getting the terrible news that he wouldn't be dying from a heart attack any time soon, nor, if things went as he was hoping, would he be able to appear at *whatever* that test was that he was being scheduled to take, Emanuel Graves was sending a thumbs-up text to Estella Rosario in response to her texted picture to him of the couch she liked at So-Fa So Good.

She had already made what to her were the most important purchases of all; her kitchen equipment, pots, pans, dishes, flatware, glasses etc. They would all be delivered to their new apartment with instructions to the store and the building's super to let them in if she wasn't there.

Now, she was bargaining with the furniture store to give her a better price on the couch, easy chairs, kitchen table, coffee table, end tables, dresser, and night tables she'd picked out. She had texted Emanuel pictures of everything for his approval. The store gave her a fair discount, set up a delivery with the same instructions as she gave to the kitchen equipment people, and she walked out of the store satisfied. Her next stop was a linen store where she purchased all their towels and linens. She had furnished their new apartment in one half a day and headed back to work with the plan to stock their pantry with her Key Food discount.

Emanuel was overjoyed. Not only did Estella possess an inner and outer beauty, not only was she *more* than a match for his intelligence, but he was once again amazed at how efficient she was, and *so* glad she was taking care of the job of picking out all of the furnishings for their new place. Shopping was not his thing. As far as the costs were concerned, he would have to go into his savings to put up half. Or, quite possibly, he would be able to pay for everything, forever, with his "inheritance."

•   •   •

Margaret Alleroy poured herself a cup of coffee. It was a relief to know her husband's sleeping problem had nothing to do with his heart. She'd decided that if his difficulty getting to sleep persisted, even *after* he corrected that error he told her about, she would insist he see a sleep specialist and take those tests Doctor Whitlock suggested. She knew her husband had yet another restless night with only a few hours of sleep and hoped he would be able to correct the error. *Twenty-five million dollars. He'd better correct it.* She debated whether or not to ask him how everything was proceeding when he got home from the office. She finished her coffee and went upstairs to get ready for her mani-pedi appointment.

THIRTY-TWO

George and Gracie had run up to Emanuel as soon as the first peanut hit the ground. He'd been sitting at one end of his bench for some fifteen minutes now, anxiously waiting for Craig to show. He scattered some birdseed on the ground and a dozen pigeons swooped down to feast. He'd brought Critique of Pure Reason with him again today and was staring at the yellowed line; "For if a question is absurd in itself and calls for unnecessary answers, it not only brings disgrace to the person raising it, but may prompt an incautious listener to give absurd answers..." when Craig appeared and sat down at the other end of the bench.

"Good morning Emanuel."

Without a word, Emanuel passed the book over to Craig. It was open to the page with this highlighted quote.

"What's this?"

"The quote that's highlighted in yellow...read the second line of it."

Alleroy did. "So?"

"So? So you have to understand that what you've asked me to do...the question you have put to me, it's absurd. Yes?"

Alleroy read the quote again. "Emanuel, if you say no to one million dollars, don't you think that your answer of 'no' to my 'absurd' question is *also* absurd? Just as this quote posits."

"I can't believe—Craig, that's a purely specious argument." He took the book from Alleroy's hands. "Look...aside from that, let me ask you something; don't you feel some measure of disgust in asking me to commit murder?"

"Disgust? At offering you a million dollars?"

"To commit murder, Craig. Murder. There is something very wrong with you that you can think this is something that anyone would just...*do*."

At hearing this, Alleroy was seriously concerned that he was going to lose his customer. "Emanuel, I picked up the balance of monies that now make up a million dollars in cash last night. In a couple of hours you are going to go to work in the same foul smelling windowless bathroom you've been working in for more than twenty years. A place where men come to piss, shit, vomit...and you have to clean up their smelly bodily functions. Six days a week. That is your *life*. And it will continue to be your *life* six shitty days a week for the next twenty dreadful shit-filled years. You work in a job that I am sure you can't even tell people *about*. You and I both know that you're ashamed of what you do. And you don't even make a decent *living* from doing it. Emanuel, it will continue to be this way unless you do something about it. Think of it; you are going to spend the next twenty years doing what you've done for the past twenty years plus; work in a fucking toilet." He stared at Emanuel to stress the point. "A toilet. You spend almost every day of every month in a fucking shithouse. And, to add insult to injury, you make equally shitty money *for* it. Buddy, you have been royally used. I am giving you the opportunity to get out of there and, at the same time, rid the world of someone like me. A shark who preyed upon elderly pensioners."

The silence was deafening as Emanuel sat there thinking among other things; *I keep it clean, it's not foul smelling.* Craig was still staring at him. Emanuel's mind continued to churn. *A million dollars.* He *would* be in this job for another twenty years. He *was* ashamed to tell anyone what he did for a living. And, it *was* a living that made it impossible for him to live anywhere *but* The Delavan. *A million dollars.* He was angry with himself that he was still of two minds about this. He hated himself for letting the thought creep into his head that if he didn't have Estella he wouldn't think twice about running this piece of shit down. He was afraid that at this point no matter what he did, what he decided, he had let it get too far...that Estella would never understand. *When she learns that I even considered this...she... she'll leave me. That I had this secret. She left a man who kept secrets from her. What have I done?* He cradled his head in his hands. *I must be just as crazy as this motherfucker is.*

Alleroy leaned in close to Emanuel. "Emanuel. Buddy...listen to me." Alleroy's voice was a hoarse whisper. "You *have* to get yours. You are *owed*. You *fought* for this country and they turned around and fucked you royally. The Marines aren't supposed to leave anyone behind but they left you behind, didn't they? They caused you to waste over twenty years of your life. You *can't* let them win. You pass on this and the government that fucked you over wins. Again. Your life will have been wasted." He leaned in even closer. "Emanuel...the world's full of rich crooks like me. I've had every advantage in life. I grew up rich...and became even wealthier, and I still had to steal more because my greed told me it wasn't enough. And here you are, an honest man, a learned man, gave your body and your mind for your country...and you have *nothing! Less* than nothing. *You have to make this right!* Now...Now...*This* is the *only* chance you'll *ever* have to do this. To *do* something about it. *No* one is ever going to help you buddy. *You* have to help yourself."

He slowly moved back to the other end of the bench. Emanuel sat silent. His mind still churning. *Am I going to meet this guy tonight? A million dollars. I would love to see this smug motherfucker dead. Smelly bathroom?* He threw two nuts on the ground which were immediately snatched up by George and Gracie, watched them scamper off, and then scattered a healthy handful of birdseed down as well. He rose and began to walk away. Suddenly, he stopped and turned around to face Alleroy.

"If I'm here tonight, I'm here. If not, then we're done. Okay?" He continued on up the path leaving Alleroy in the midst of at least two dozen lucky pigeons. This was the first time in the twenty-two years that he had been coming to Mannahatta Park before going to work that he'd left early.

• • •

All through Emanuel's shift something about Craig that seemed off was gnawing at him. *He said he grew up rich.* And, on the train going home he kept turning over these same twosentences over in his mind; "*I was born with a silver spoon in my mouth. I grew up rich,*" and; "*My father was able to put me through college.*" As the train came up out of the tunnel and into the sunlight he realized what was bothering him. *That's it! That's what's bothering me.* He called Estella to tell her that as soon as they finished dinner he had to go down to his room and research a few things on his computer.

At dinner they looked with excitement at the pictures of the furnishings she'd purchased. They were like two kids on Christmas morning. Emanuel wrote her a check for half of everything she'd already laid out. She felt a bit awkward taking it, but she knew it was a matter of pride for him that he pay his fair share. Not only were they lovers, they were now partners - in everything. Emanuel kissed her and went down to his room, he couldn't wait to get to his computer. On the way down in the elevator he was sure he had figured this puzzle out. Now, he would see if what he suspected was true.

He booted up his laptop. *He was a rich kid. His father put him through college.* He searched; "how can I locate an army veteran?" Of the many answers he saw there was one called Vet Friends; Military Buddy Finder. He clicked on it. He had to register, create a user I.D. and password - which he did. He entered the "319th Military Intelligence Battalion." There it was. Among all the choices was "Search Veterans and Personnel." He clicked on it and it went to a page asking him for the name of the veteran he was searching for. First name, last name, and branch. *What did he say his last name was...why am I thinking of Tom Hanks?* He sat there searching his memory. *Tom Hanks...What movies was Tom Ha—Wilson! Wilson! His soccer ball "friend." Wilson. Junior, to be exact."* He entered the name; Craig Wilson, without the Jr. and waited. Almost immediately came the words; No results. He entered the name with Junior...and then with Jr. Nothing. *I knew it. What rich kid ups and enlists in the army? Especially when there's an action brewing. This guy is full of shit. I bet it's not even his real name. What was that Lieutenant's name? I remember thinking of an orange when he said it.* He sat there trying to remember the name of the officer who he said was his close buddy in the army that he was never in. Was there any information about the man he said he loved like a brother? Was he real? *What was his name? Why do I think it's like an oran—Valencia! That's it. First Lieutenant Robert Valencia.* He did a search of the name and there it was. A huge story titled; "The forgotten soldier whose death triggered an invasion." *Wow! Well, he sure didn't pick someone ordinary. I guess this is what came up right away when he searched Operation Just Cause, Panama. This scumbag sure made up a good story for himself.* He read the entire piece, and way down buried at the very bottom of this very long article was the information that Valencia was buried in a cemetery in Villavicencio, a town south of Bogota, Colombia. *Yeah, he cried over his grave...A few times no less. I bet he'll never remember this town.* He then searched for some information dealing with insurance claims in the state of New York. After reading what he found and making some notes, which he saved as a word doc, he sat back and thought about what he had just learned. The last thing he did was search "how much cash can fit in an attaché case?" It appeared Craig's case could hold up to a million dollars in cash. *Interesting.*

Still, he now suspected that the probability of there being a million dollars available to him in this insanity was the same as his odds of winning the lottery. That the *only* thing true about this whole deal was that this guy was a crook, got busted, couldn't collect on his life insurance, couldn't face his wife and children, and wanted to be killed so his family would get the money. But what was his real plan for getting killed? Emanuel didn't think it was being run over by a car because in order for that to happen, at his hands anyway, real money would have to be exchanged. And then he thought; what if there *was* a million dollars for doing this? What if he has five hundred thousand dollars with him tonight? What then? And, what if this "Craig's" army story's only purpose was so he would feel some kind of affinity for a fellow vet and, because of that, and the money involved, would agree to the hit-and-run? It was now a puzzle he *had* to have the answers to. He was going to meet this guy in Mannahatta Park at eleven. He closed his laptop and went upstairs to tell Estella that he'd soon be going out for a couple of hours. Of course he was aware she would think his going out at this late hour was strange. So, when he told her, he also reiterated that he would tell her everything about all of the events of the last two weeks very soon. And, for the hour they spent together before he left to go downtown, she resisted the fierce urge to ask him to tell her everything...now. The curiosity she had about this "business" he was occupied with for the last two weeks was very close to getting the better of her better judgment. He said he would explain everything to her shortly so she would keep her curiosity at bay until then. At ten o'clock, he left, and Estella went to bed. Where, until she fell asleep, she wondered what on earth her man was up to?

•   •   •

Over dinner Margaret noticed Rich still didn't seem to have much of an appetite. He had come home and said he had an idea for his treatment that he wanted to get down while it was still fresh in his mind. He then disappeared into his study for the better part of an hour while she prepped and cooked dinner. At eight she went to his study and told him that dinner was ready. He said he would be right in and after ten minutes he appeared in the dining room, sat down, and poured them both a glass of the Cabernet she had decanted.

"Is it that error?"

"The error?" He took a sip of wine. "Oh...No, no, it's the script treatment I'm writing. I'm pretty sure I've corrected the error."

"Oh. Well, that's a relief isn't it? It sounded quite serious."

"It was. It was. But, not to worry, I've straightened it out."

"Well, I hope you don't have another night like last night. You hardly slept sweetheart. The melatonin doesn't really help, does it?"

"Not really. I keep running this movie treatment over and over in my head and it just keeps me up."

He drank some more wine. "Actually...I didn't want to tell you this yet, but someone at Rack Focus Films is interested in the idea and wants to see it when it's ready. So...I'm going to work on it after dinner." He chuckled. "Not only does it keep me up all night, I'll probably go to bed late as well. I'll try not to wake you when I do."

"You won't."

Let's hope. He took a small bite of his food. "Meanwhile, this lamb is delicious, I wish I had more of an appetite and less of a nervous stomach."

He finished his wine, poured himself another glass and topped hers off. He was hoping that between his going to his study to "write," and the two glasses of wine she drank, she would want to go upstairs promptly at ten as usual. The last thing he wanted was for his wife to know that he was going out a short while after that - and that he would be taking her computer with him.

•   •   •

On the two train heading downtown to lower Manhattan Emanuel was still trying to figure the whole thing out. He was certain of one thing; that this guy, whatever his name was, wanted desperately to be killed. He believed the man's sentiment that if he could commit suicide he'd do it in a second. But, if the rest of it was, as he now suspected, just bullshit, and there wasn't any million dollars, or any five hundred thousand, or *any* amount of money - how did he fit in? *He kept showing me that attaché case filled with cash. Like Hitchcock's MacGuffin.* If everything *except* this guy's desire to be dead was a lie, then how was he going to accomplish his death - *if* he wasn't going to be run over? Was Emanuel supposed to choke him to death? Or something *like* that? Of course, *if* the offer of money was bogus there was no *way* that Emanuel was going to be involved in this guy's death. The train stopped at a station and he peeked out to see the LED clock. It read ten-forty.

Then, against his better judgment, he backtracked; what if by some strange chance, the money *was* real? You know, what if? He still hadn't decided what he was going to do in that unlikely event. And *then,* he arrived once again at what had now become the most distressing thought about all of it; whatever the outcome, he feared having to tell Estella any of it.

As the train approached more than one station on the journey downtown he told himself; "get off. Go home. Even if it's real, you can't do it." And the doors would open...and close...and the train would pull away from the station...and he would still be in the car. Each time he would say to himself; "what you're doing is crazy. Don't meet this guy. Fuck him. He's a cancer." And yet he continued on. Ten-fifty. He knew what he was doing was demented, but he was now in the grip of an unyielding compulsion to see how this thing ended.

THIRTY-THREE

Estella woke with a start. She looked at her alarm clock. Eleven. She had been tossing in her sleep less than an hour and had awakened out of this fitful sleep with a bad feeling. She told herself that she was worrying for nothing. Manny was an ex-marine, he could take care of himself. But what kind of business meeting, if *that's* what it *was*, necessitates that someone go out in the middle of the night? She slipped out of bed, got a glass, and padded over to the fridge to pour herself a glass of water. *Why am I so nervous for him?* Something was telling her that the man she loved was, at that very moment, dealing with something dangerous. What little hair she had on her forearms was standing up and she was feeling a tingling in the small of her back. *Oh, God, Manny, you'd better come home to me or...Please be careful.* She knew she wouldn't be able to sleep until he came through that door. She decided to make herself some chamomile tea in hopes of relieving the anxiety she was feeling. *If anything happens to you I will hate myself for not making you tell me what you're up to. And stopping you if it's something dumb.* She put some water on to boil and stood waiting until it did. *I should have pried...I had every right to know what you're up to. Come on...boil. We're partners. I had enough of this secrecy stuff before.* She placed a chamomile tea bag in her cup. *This can't be happening again.* Finally, the little bit of water came to a boil. She poured the water into the cup and dunked the teabag in it a few times. *What are you up to Manny? As soon as you come through that door you are telling me what is going on with you.* She blew on the tea and took a sip. She sat down on the edge of the bed, reached for the remote, and put the TV on. She switched the channel to the food network and sat sipping tea and trying to get take her mind off of the negative thoughts she was having. She got up and went to the window. *It's so dark tonight. It's a new moon. Oh, God...my middle name means moon. Please be alright.* She wanted to understand *why* she was having these thoughts. She sat back down on her bed. Was she feeling something he was actually experiencing? When they first met she felt an immediate link to him. It prompted her to research studies dealing with telepathic connections between lovers with a strong spiritual bond. It had nothing to do with how long people had been together. But there were case studies where two people had an attraction, an energy, which transcended physical limitations. It was electrical. Chemical. She was somewhat skeptical as she read about this "union theory" but, if there was such a thing, was this what she was experiencing? How else to explain this strong message she was receiving? And, if this message was real, then Emanuel was in trouble. Was it actual physical trouble, or trouble of another sort? Something that is causing him great difficulty? She sat there sipping her tea. *I know something is wrong. I am not imagining this. I can feel it.* After about three quarters of an hour she went back to bed, and a half hour later she finally fell asleep.

•   •   •

Richard Alleroy had driven as close to the Seventy-Ninth Street entrance to Riverside Park as he could. He got lucky and found a spot on Eightieth Street between West End Avenue and Riverside Drive. He parked the Mercedes and walked into the park. He had Margaret's computer with him and was heading to the boat basin. He reached the lit path running along the dock and looked around him to make sure there was no one else in the vicinity. Then, with a mighty heave he flung his wife's computer as far as he could into the Hudson River. He couldn't see it, but he heard it land and he was sure it sank. He turned, walked back to his car and drove downtown to meet Emanuel. It was twenty after ten.

It was ten to eleven when Emanuel clambered up the stairs of the Wall and William Street subway station and began walking the four blocks to Mannahatta Park. He was only certain of two things; this man was *not* what, or maybe even *who*, he said he was, *and* he was *not* going to run him over with a car he *would* have stolen. He'd decided that if this guy brought *any* money with him, *even* five hundred thousand dollars, which possibility he now seriously doubted, he was not taking it. His life was now rich enough because of Estella's presence in it. However, his nature, his love of puzzles, was compelling him, forcing him, to figure out for sure what this man's game was. Up ahead a streetlight was out. *This city is so broke we can't even get the streetlights fixed.* As he passed beneath the broken streetlight, he experienced walking in and out of darkness...and realized there was no moon in this night's sky.

At last he reached the park. It was deserted. He could see his bench, but where was "Craig?"

His bench was empty.

"Emanuel!" The voice came out of the darkness. "Over here!"

Alleroy stepped into the light and waved to him. He was down at the far end of the park where the benches were covered by the overhang. Seeing that Emanuel saw him he stepped back into the murky darkness. He had made sure he would arrive before Emanuel and would be waiting for him at a bench of his choosing in the covered area - which also happened to be beneath one of the park's streetlights which was also broken.

Okay, this guy is up to no good sitting here in the dark. Or...Does he want to make sure no one can see any of this because he really does have all that money with him? I guess I'm about to find out. He began walking towards the bench where Alleroy was sitting. A woman walking a dog passed him as he did. There didn't appear to be anyone else in the park. There was ambient light from Wall Street, the only street that ran alongside the park, and from the buildings around the park. But it was negligible and was blocked from leaking into this area by the large overhang. Emanuel's eyes were slowly becoming accustomed to the darkness that enveloped this small area in the park that Alleroy had chosen. *If he's got five hundred thousand with him I don't blame him for picking this—Manny, dude, get real. This guy has five hundred thousand dollars with him like you do.* Emanuel's eyes, now almost used to the dark, could make out that Alleroy had his attaché case with him. *And, a duffel bag. He's still wearing a suit? Whatever...But, this guy is up to no good sitting here in the dark. Or...Does he want to make sure no one can see any of this because...is it possible he actually has five hundred K with him?* He drew closer to the bench where Alleroy was sitting. It took a while, but Emanuel's eyes had now become fully accustomed to the darkness that enveloped this particularly dark spot in the park that "Craig" had chosen. *If he's got five hundred thousand with him I don't blame him for picking this—*

Manny, please stop. There's no five hundred thousand dollars. He reached the bench and sat.

"So...Craig...Buddy...What've you got there?"

"What I said I'd have. But I'm having second thoughts about giving it to someone like you."

Interesting...He opens with an insult. Why? Emanuel gave a fleeting thought to responding. He decided that for the time being he didn't care to go down this verbal path. There'd be time for that stuff later. What he *wanted* was to find out who this guy was. What was his game? For openers, was his name really Craig Wilson Jr.? He decided not to beat around the bush.

Emanuel took his cell phone out of his pocket and shone its light upward. Not directly at Alleroy but just so it lit the two of them a little. "So uh, *'Craig'*...what's your real name?"

Emanuel stared at Alleroy to see his reaction to this question. If he was surprised by the question, Alleroy didn't show it. Instead, he smiled and shook his head.

Emanuel returned the smile. "Why don't you show me your driver's license?"

"Why would I want to do that?"

"Because you know where *I* live, so I think it's only fair that I know where *you* live."

Alleroy looked at him. "I have no idea what you're—"

—"I saw you on the Wall and William platform. It was funny that you got shoved into that hot car. The only reason I didn't confront you then was that I was late for an important date."

All this time, this motherfucker knew..."I think you should put your phone away."

"And, if I had the time, I would've told you then *'Craig.'* But, since I'm in no hurry *now*, I'll tell you *now*." He leaned a little closer. "If you *ever* follow me again, I won't *kill* you *'Craig,'* I'll hurt you. *Bad.*" He stared at Alleroy and then leaned back. "Light bother you?"

Alleroy knew he had to ignore the last few seconds and plow straight ahead.

"Why would you want people to see what we're doing?"

"What *are* we doing?"

"You know, I have a lot of money here and...That's why I bought this with me." He unbuttoned his suit jacket and flashed Emanuel, revealing the holstered gun in his belt.

Emanuel's eyes narrowed. *And a silencer too.* After a couple of seconds, he decided, also for the time being, to let the presence of this gun slide.

"Yeah...I know. You have a lot of money with you. Where was your buddy's grave that you cried over again? Huh?"

Alleroy was surprised by this tack. *Why is he on about this?* He had looked this information up. But now, as he frantically plumbed his memory, he couldn't bring to the surface the unusual name of the small town in Colombia. "What are you talking about?" *He knows. Okay, it's on.* "So fucking what? Go fuck yourself asshole."

"Why all these insults, 'Craig'? Is this a nice way to talk to the guy who's going to help you out here? Anyway, that's two questions I've asked that you've just ignored."

"What, you didn't bust me that day I followed you because you had a hot date with your fat girlfriend?"

No sooner were those words out of Alleroy's mouth than did Emanuel grab him by his tie knot and pull him closer. "Don't say another word about her!"

"Why? Are you ashamed you have a fat girlfriend?" Alleroy sounded as if he was gargling.

With that, Emanuel half-smiled at him and patted Alleroy down with his free hand. He located Alleroy's billfold in his inside jacket pocket and extracted it. He shoved Alleroy back roughly, hastily looked through the billfold and immediately found Alleroy's driver's license. He shone his cellphone light directly on it.

"Nice address, 'Craig'...buddy. Richard Alleroy. Like the king, eh? Now, your royal fuck-up, just on principle, and because I'm curious as to what it's worth for a creep like you to want to be killed, you're going to tell me just how much insurance you have."

Now, it was Alleroy's turn to smile. "Fuck you. It's none of your fucking business toilet boy. And the more I think about it the more I think I'm crazy to give you this five hundred K before we do it. You'll say yeah, you'll take it, and then you'll be on a plane with your fat girlfriend... won't you?"

Emanuel's eyes narrowed again as he took in, and digested, what Alleroy was saying - and doing. He had all the information he needed, and was now working out the puzzle.

Alleroy wasn't finished; "Because you have no honor. None!"

Emanuel, who was in the process of putting all the pieces together, wasn't biting.

"Why the gun Rich?"

"Why?" Alleroy scoffed. "So I could shoot some dumb nobody like you who'd try to mug me for this five hundred K." He pulled the gun from its holster but fumbled it, and it dropped onto the pavement at Emanuel's feet. Immediately, Alleroy moved his attaché case behind him. "You know what... A toilet is the perfect place for a piece of shit like you to work in."

Now, the smile on Emanuel's face widened as he sat there looking at Alleroy. *What a cute move, I love it.* He picked up the gun, merely to get it out of play and ejected the clip. *And, this is the game! All these insults. This gun he "drops." This phony motherfucker wants me to shoot him. And to make it easier for me it's got a silencer on it. What a clever dick you are.* He began to unscrew the silencer. *This has been his play all along. He never planned to be hit by a car. He probably never even had forty or fifty thousand dollars in his case in the beginning, either. He gambled that I'd say no at that point. He knew I'd never take forty grand to commit murder - if it was forty grand. He just said that was what was in the case. It could have been half that, it was just bundles of cash. Pretty slick. Then, he comes to where I work. He knew I'd never stash two hundred and fifty thousand dollars at work either. If, it was two hundred and fifty thousand dollars. Which it probably wasn't. He actually thought he could anger me enough tonight that I'd lose my head, shoot him and grab the imaginary five hundred K that he keeps saying is in that case now.* The two men sat looking at each other. Then, Alleroy gave it another try.

"I'd love to fuck your, what's her name...Estella? I bet she's one—"

Emanuel snapped around and glared at Alleroy. He grabbed him again by his perfect four-in-hand tie knot, and slammed the gun butt into Alleroy's mouth. The blow knocked Alleroy backward off of the bench and onto the pavement. After a while, he turned over and struggled to his knees spitting teeth and blood. "Fuck you, you pieth of sssshhhit." Shit was a whistle.

Emanuel leaned down close to him. "Hey...'Buddy'...What on earth makes you think I would waste a bullet on you and put you out of your fucking misery? You *are* delusional. You wanna hear what's going to happen? What's going to happen is this; I'm going to kill you another way. A far *worse* way Rich. Are you listening?"

Alleroy was picking his two front teeth up from the now bloody pavement. "Go fuck yourself."

"You'll appreciate the elegance of this move, Rich. I'm going to report you and your attempted scheme to the National Association of Insurance Carriers. I looked them up when I looked up the members of the 319th - which you weren't. Forgive me, that's beside the point. Anyway, I'm going to contact both the central office of the NAIC in Kansas City, and also a lady named Linda D. Grady who's the current Superintendent of the New York State Department of Financial Services. They supervise the local insurance carriers. I'm going to give both of them your name and fancy address, and outline exactly how you planned to defraud your carrier, and why. I should think they'll notify the company that handles your life insurance and alert them to your little plan in the event you try this again. If they want a sworn affidavit from me, I'll gladly give them one. Look at the bright side Rich; you're going to live to enjoy flipping burgers in a McDonald's."

Alleroy managed a last feeble; "Fuck you, and your fat Estella too."

Emanuel dropped the gun to the pavement and kicked it, the silencer and the clip a few feet away from them. He rose from the bench and began to walk away leaving Alleroy on his knees groaning and wiping the blood from his mouth with his monogrammed white Irish linen pocket handkerchief in which he then carefully placed his newly bloodied and dislodged upper front teeth.

Emanuel had only taken three or four steps when he stopped abruptly, turned around and went back to the bench. Alleroy, just rising from his knees, watched as Emanuel, who *had* to know if he was right about if there was any money in Alleroy's attaché case - and wouldn't have taken any if there was - opened the case and saw that it was empty.

Alleroy sneered. "You stupid fuck...You think I'd ever give someone like *you* money? Fucking asshole!"

Emanuel unzipped the duffel bag. It contained what looked like curtain rods. He shook his head and smiled wearily.

He left Alleroy slumped on the bench. On the walk back to the subway, he was having second thoughts about his violence. *You overreacted Manny. You didn't have to knock his damn teeth out.*

All the way home, he couldn't think of anything other than how Estella would react to what he now had to tell her. He hoped with all his heart she would understand, but, his violence...He couldn't help being very afraid she wouldn't. She was asleep when he tip-toed in. He didn't want to wake her and he certainly wasn't ready to "talk." He left her a note saying he came home very late, all was good but it's all over, and she was sleeping so soundly he didn't want to wake her, he loved her, and he'd call her about dinner. He left quietly and went downstairs to his place.

He didn't see her that entire day since they woke up in separate beds for the only the second time since they'd become intimate. When her alarm clock woke her at seven, she looked over and she didn't see Emanuel in bed next to her. A bolt of fear shot through her body. *Oh, God no! No!* She shot straight up - and only then did she see the note. It was hanging off of her night table pinned down at one corner by her cellphone. She read it with relief surging through her body and immediately called him. She told him of the terrible feeling she'd had and how worried she was that he hadn't come home. He assured her he was okay, that he loved her and he would explain everything to her later. She told him how much she loved him. Relieved of her anxiety and fears for his safety she told him she had an idea she wanted to run by him. Something he might like, and they made a plan to go eat goat sancocho at Alebrescado that evening.

He got off the phone picturing the ways it could go when he told her what this whole thing was about. Actually, almost the second he woke up his thoughts were about Estella and having to tell her everything about his last few weeks. Barely seconds after he opened his eyes and had that thought he was overtaken by the same fear he felt in the hallway that night before he knocked on her door for the first time. He was scared to death at what her reaction to his "business" would be. He had considered committing murder for money. It didn't matter that it was for a million dollars or for one dollar. He had given a good deal of serious thought to cold bloodedly killing a stranger for money. He had spent nights talking with this stranger about this act. And then he violently smashed him in the face with the butt of a gun and left him on the ground bleeding and picking up his teeth. All he could hear in his head was Estella's voice; *"I once mistakenly married a man who had secrets. Many secrets. And he was violent. One of the reasons I love you is because you are not like that."*

As he showered and got ready to go to work, the thought of her aversion at hearing what he *thought* of doing, and what he *did* do, almost made him physically sick. He had the love of a woman who was, in his eyes, the most wonderful, most beautiful woman in the world, and the possibility existed that after tonight he might well lose her. The thought that he could again be alone after she had graced his life with the strength and purity of her being was weighing heavily on him.

Estella was relieved and happy that he volunteered to tell her what this mysterious business was that had so occupied him - rather than her having to ask. She stopped to read his note again. *At least whatever it is, it's over and done...and he loves me.*

That afternoon, Richard Alleroy, in his bespoke suit and polka dot tie and minus his two front teeth, who found out earlier that his dentist was on vacation for two weeks, sat stewing in his parked car for most of the day. For hours he had gone back and forth between staring straight ahead at nothing and then down at the gun in his lap while braising in a poisonous mixture of white-hot rage and purple self-pity. A mixture, which by five o'clock, metastasized into the rationalization that everything, *everything,* that had now befallen him was Emanuel's fault. This idiot Emanuel was the reason for the situation that he now found himself in. *Anyone* else would have done what he, Richard Alleroy, the master manipulator of Wall Street, had programmed him to do. *Anyone* else would have agreed to his brilliant scheme. Would have put him out of his misery as planned and by doing this *simple* act help him collect the twenty-five million dollars in insurance that he, Alleroy, was entitled to. *Anyone* but this unbelievably ignorant bathroom attendant. This moronic peon motherfucker who was too fucking stupid to take the damn fortune that would have changed his ugly miserable life. *You ruined my life, you nothing. You fucking piece of shit.* Finally, he shook his head violently in an effort to come back to the present, placed the gun on the passenger seat, started the Mercedes and headed north.

THIRTY-FOUR

They were holding hands as they rode down in the elevator to go to Alebrescado. From the second he knocked on her door she sensed he was somewhat nervous. When she asked if he was alright he said he was, that being with her and having a good meal was what he needed. She suspected it was a bit more than that but let it go. For the time being. She had something else on her mind and was excited by something she was going to propose to Emanuel. So, feeling in a celebratory mood, she insisted he let her call for an Uber to take them to the restaurant.

The Mercedes turned into Simpson and One Hundred and Sixty Third Streets at the very moment Manny and Stella walked out of The Delevan and got into the waiting Uber. Alleroy had no recourse but to follow them to wherever it was they were headed. *Ruin my life you motherfucker? No one does this to Richard Alleroy. No one! I'm going to fuck you up good. You and your fat girlfriend will regret you ever met Richard Alleroy.*

He looked at his reflection in the rear view mirror. *I look like a Goddamn hick. Keep your eyes on the road man, you can't lose them. My fucking dentist would be in Nantucket...probably on my fucking dime too. Cocksucker. He must have an emergency guy.* He grabbed his phone and punched up his dentist's office. After a few rings the secretary answered. "Doctor Greenberg's service, how can we help you?"

"The thervice?" *Stop lisping! You sound like a fucking idiot.* He made a concerted effort not to lisp.

"Isn't this the office?" It was difficult to say his esses without his front teeth, but he persisted.

"Look, this is Richard Alleroy, I'm a patient of Doctor Greenberg. I called before and thpoke—I...spoke...with the girl in the office. I need to speak with her now. This is an emergency. I need to see Doctor Greenberg's emergency contact tomorrow."

As agitated as he was, he nearly missed a turn that the Uber took a block ahead.

"Sir, I understand. Unfortunately, Doctor Ernst, his emergency dentist is also unavailable. I can— "

"What do you mean unavailable?"

"I believe Doctor Ernst had to have a serious procedure and—"

—"You're kidding!"

"He's in hospital. I *can* schedule an appointment for you with Doctor Greenberg two Mondays from n—"

—"THIS IS AN EMERGENCY!" He screamed into the phone. "DO YOU NOT UNDERSTAND THE WORD EMERGENCY?"

"Sir, I don't appreciate being yelled at. Doctor Greenberg will be ba—"

—"FUCK YOU, YOU FUCKING DUMB CUNT!"

He slammed his cell phone down onto the passenger seat next to the gun and, completely unaware he had reached a red light, hit his brakes just in time to avoid hitting an elderly man with a walker slowly moving across the crosswalk.

"MOVE, YOU OLD FART! FUCKING MOVE ALREADY!" *My fucking Jew dentist is in Nantucket. Great. Just great. So, get another fucking emergency contact, you moron.* "MOVE! You old..."

A block ahead the Uber was also stopped at a light. Settled comfortably in the back seat of the Uber, Estella snuggled up close to Emanuel.

"Manny...I've been thinking. And please tell me if this...if it's none of my business, and to forget it, I will. But...Manny, I know you are a great employee, and you do your job really well. So..." She decided not to beat around the bush. "How would you feel about working at the store I manage?"

The second Emanuel heard her idea he liked it. "I'd love it of course, thanks...But...I mean, doing what?"

She was pleased that he was open to what she was proposing. "I'm going to speak with management about an entry level position. And meanwhile, if you let me, I'll train you to be an assistant manager.

"*Let* you...Stella, I'd be lucky to have you do that. But...Babe..." He shook his head. "I don't have the qualifications for such a position."

"Manny, you're a high school graduate, you're intelligent, you're a quick learner...you're good with people, si? Si, Manny? Yes? Sabes que esto es cierto."

"Yeah...I mean, I'd love it but...Stella, I have no experience in the food business."

"Manny, you're smarter than anyone in management in that whole chain. And, I'll show you all the ropes. I know you're capable of learning the nuts and bolts of it pretty quick. And, don't forget, you have a twenty-two year spotless record of employment at The Coach and Crown. They'll surely give you an excellent reference, yes?"

As the Uber made its way slowly westward through traffic, the passengers within had no idea they were being followed by a black Mercedes. Why would they? They were happy, and very much in love.

There was no happiness within the Mercedes, however. Within the Mercedes the man at the wheel was now seething with a blind rage. *You knocked my fucking teeth out you piece of shit. I am going to fuck you up good. Where the hell are you two idiots going anyway? When I get through with you, you'll never be able to give her a good humping again, my friend.*

In the Uber, Emanuel was now enthusiastically warming to the idea of working alongside of Estella.

"They'll definitely give me a good reference." *Oh, Christ, she could be gone, along with any plan, in a matter of hours.*

"I could tutor you at night about the day-to-day duties of the position...you know, strategies to improve customer service and drive store sales. You could become my assistant manager as soon as the job becomes available."

The Uber arrived at Alebrescado. Emanuel and Estella thanked the driver, and got out. Arm in arm, they walked on air to the front door of the restaurant.

From a block away, Richard Alleroy saw the Uber stop and its rear curb-side door open. He sped to the restaurant, and parked directly across the street in an illegal space in front of a fire hydrant. He was almost three feet from the curb. He sat there and watched the couple slowly walk arm-in-arm into the restaurant. *What, you think you're going to have a nice dinner now? You broke my teeth, and you're going to eat? I've got news for you pal. And for your fat girlfriend also.*

As they walked, Estella held Emanuel close. "Manny, the odds are in our favor. You can definitely get an entry level job at my Key Foods, and I can definitely get you ready for promotion. I would also tell them that we're a couple. Actually, in this case I think this would be a plus."

He opened the door for them. They entered the restaurant and were greeted by the hostess. As they stood waiting for a table he said; "Stella, mi amor, mi vida, you know that by doing this you might be putting your own job up as collateral."

"What, by pushing you for a managerial position? Nonsense. I would trust you to do the job as much as I trust myself."

Now, as Alleroy watched them enter the restaurant, he reached over to the passenger seat and felt for the gun he'd put there. He picked it up, put it in his pocket, and opened the car door. He got out, and began crossing the street towards the restaurant. He ignored the traffic that had to stop for him as he made his way across the street, trance-like and muttering.

In the restaurant, the joy Emanuel felt as Estella explained her idea, was now supplanted by his fear of what might happen in an hour or so when he finally told her what he had been doing for the last two weeks. He so wanted to kiss her then and there. A corner table opened up and the hostess led them to it. She handed them menus.

"Would you like to order a cocktail?"

"Manny, let's."

Emanuel nodded. "Mojitos?"

She nodded "yes" enthusiastically. Emanuel held up two fingers and the hostess smiled.

"The server will bring you your drinks and take your order when you're ready. Buen apetito."

They thanked her and settled in to wait for their drinks. "I think we owe ourselves a celebration, Manny. We have a new apartment *and* we have a good possibility of working together."

"Ta nitido cariño." *I have to tell her. Oh God, I need a drink.*

Alleroy had now reached the restaurant's entrance. *I fucking swear, this'll be the last happy meal you two ever have.* He pulled open the door.

After their drinks came, and they had toasted their future, Emanuel found he could hardly swallow. A lump had suddenly formed in his throat. *I will ruin her dinner. But I have to. This cannot wait.* Somehow he got the drink down - and signaled to the server for two more.

"Manny...I still have this one."

"Stella...Stella..." He reached across the table for her hand. She saw how worried he was. She took his hand and squeezed it in an attempt to comfort him. Her brow was furrowed with concern.

Emanuel was searching for the right words. "My Stella, who I love more than life itself. I need more courage than I have for what I need to tell you about what I've done these last few weeks."

Done? What you've done? Dios mio. Has he murdered someone? "Manny, whatever it is I promise I will...I will try to understand."

"See? Stella, just that you say you will 'try' to understand. This, is only one of the reasons why I'm so crazy about you." He squeezed her hand tightly. "Your words are never empty. You don't promise you *will*. You promise you'll *'try.'* This...*This,* is priceless. It is all I can ask. Thank you."

Alleroy, having entered the restaurant, and scanned the room, had located the couple's corner table. The hostess, busy with another couple, now greeted him.

"Table for one?"

"I'm waiting for my friends. We'll be four. I'll have a drink while I wait." He went to the bar.

Alleroy watched as the server brought the two drinks that Emanuel ordered. He saw Emanuel immediately pick his drink up as they talked.

At their table, Emanuel was worried. "Stella, I hope you'll stay with me." And he downed the entire drink as she watched somewhat confused.

"Manny, what are you doing? You'll get sick. Stay with you?" Her confusion deepened.

"What are you talking about?" *What have you done?*

The server, who was standing and waiting, asked, "Do you folks know what you'd like?"

Estella, looking across the table straight at Emanuel, said; "Not yet. Please give us a few moments, yes?"

At the bar, Alleroy slugged down the double bourbon neat he had ordered. He turned again and stared daggers at the couple at the corner table. His hand curled around the gun in his jacket pocket. He ordered another double. *You ruined everything. You are not getting away with this.*

The server had understood Estella's request and left their table. Estella kept staring at Emanuel, a very worried look on her face. Emanuel, feeling the effect of the alcohol, wiped his mouth slowly. He put his napkin down. *Why was I so violent? She said she didn't know how any self-respecting woman can be with a man who can be violent...whatever the excuse. Oh God...Please, let her understand.*

She waited anxiously for whatever it was he had to tell her. A long moment of silence passed between them while she wondered what it was he had "done." *Oh, Dios...Por favor, no me digas algo terrible Manny. Please...*

He squeezed her hand. *Please, please understand.* "Stella...almost three weeks ago a man approached me and..."

Alleroy, now in a sweaty sheen, chugged down this second double bourbon as he watched them in the back bar mirror. He also saw his own toothless reflection in the mirror. *LOOK*

WHAT YOU DID TO ME! He almost screamed it out loud. *YOU'RE GOING TO PAY!* He was screaming in his mind. He wiped the sweat from his face and neck with a bar napkin. He was boiling over. *No one does what you did to me pal.* He balled up the sopping wet bar napkin and threw it on the bar. He pulled the gun from his pocket. *Kiss your fucking nuts goodbye, ace.*

At their table, Emanuel was thinking there was no way he could sugarcoat what it was he had to tell her. It had to be the brutal truth.

"He offered me money...a lot of money...to kill him."

And he also knew he had to tell her the worst of it.

"And I considered doing it."

Stella stared at him for what seemed to Emanuel to be an eternity. The look on her face was one of puzzled confusion.

"What?"

Her barely audible word hung in the air when the half-drunk crazed Richard Alleroy turned from the bar and rushed towards their table gun in hand. This would be his pay-back from the moron who had the fucking gall to outwit him *and* leave him disfigured. He was either going to kill her or shoot Emanuel in his groin. *This* would even the score. *Fuck him. He'll never be able to give this fat love of his life a good fucking.*

Even in his own semi-inebriated state, Emanuel managed to see Alleroy over Estella's shoulder the very second he came rushing towards them - *and* he saw the gun. Now, some of the restaurant's patrons saw a well-dressed seemingly deranged man with a gun in his hand rushing towards a table in the corner occupied by two people obviously in love. They saw the man at the table get up quickly and rush to stand between the woman and the oncoming lunatic with the gun. They probably couldn't see that, as he rose, the man snatched a knife from the table in order to protect both himself and his woman.

"FUCK YOU, SCUMBAG!" Alleroy, aiming for Emanuel's groin, pulled the trigger. The sound of the shot sent people ducking for cover as glasses and dishes clattered to the floor. Emanuel, a bullet lodged in his thigh, lunged at Alleroy before Alleroy could get off another round and stabbed him in his chest puncturing a lung. Alleroy dropped the gun and clutched at his chest as he fell to the ground screaming.

"YOU FUCKING BASTARD! YOU STABBED ME, YOU STUPID BASTARD!"

During this insanity a patron somehow had the wherewithal to call the police from under a table.

The patrons told the police what had taken place and Alleroy was arrested and taken away by ambulance. His wife was notified of his arrest and, handcuffed to his hospital bed, Alleroy finally had to tell her *almost* everything. As it was an inchoate crime in that it did not cause the death of another person, he received a sentence of twenty years in prison. The entire experience was difficult for Margaret, yet she remained in her husband's corner. She told their children that they had all been threatened by this man Emanuel over a business deal and their father made a mistake in seeking to protect them all. To get by, she sold some of their art and moved to a two-bedroom apartment in Astoria, Queens. Through her many connections she obtained a position at the Metropolitan Museum of Art. Though her children now had to leave their expensive schools, they enrolled in City College and continued on their career paths. They often visit their father in prison. His fraud has never been revealed to them - or anyone. Besides Emanuel and Estella, that is.

The bullet was removed from Emanuel's right thigh with only a scar left to constantly remind him of how stupid men can be – especially him. He explained everything to the still shaken Estella in the hospital where he was treated and where she finally calmed down. She was dismayed by the fact that he even considered doing such an "insane" thing, but forgave him.

Four months later, Emanuel decided to visit Alleroy in prison. He wanted to let him know that the whole thing made him understand that he didn't need a million dollars. That what he had was far more valuable. It made him feel good, sort of closed the circle, as it were. The visit was brief. Twenty seconds into it, Alleroy stood, summoned the guard to get him, and still, minus his front teeth, told Emanuel to drop dead.

Emanuel is now the assistant manager of Key Foods on Southern Boulevard and East One Hundred and Sixty-Seventh Street in the South Bronx. Emanuel William Graves and Estella Cendy Rosario now live in Pelham Parkway in the East Bronx. They have adopted an orphaned one-year old Dominican boy and are expecting their first child, a girl, in a matter of months.

The End

About the Author

Photo by Nancy Friedman

Tony Powers has acted in major movies (*Goodfellas, Catch Me If You Can*) and TV (*NYPD Blue, The King of Queens*). A hit songwriter (*98.6, Remember Then, Lazy Day*), his songs have been recorded by artists from Kiss to Louie Armstrong. His MusicFilm (*Don't Nobody Move (This is a Heist)*) won Silver at The International Film and Music Festival of New York, Gold at The International Music Video Festival of Saint Tropez, and was Details Magazine's "Video of the Year." His CD Who Could Imagine was called a 'masterpiece' by Joel Selvin, former rock critic of *The San Fransisco Chronicle*.

Note from the Author

Word-of-mouth is crucial for any author to succeed. If you enjoyed *The Attendant*, please leave a review online—anywhere you are able. Even if it's just a sentence or two. It would make all the difference and would be very much appreciated.

Thanks!
Tony Powers